The Sword: Xcian

by

Elle Arroyo

The Nine, Book 2

The Sword: Xcian

Cover Art by *Jennifer Greeff*

The Wild Rose Press, Inc.
PO Box 708
Adams Basin, NY 14410-0708
Visit us at www.thewildrosepress.com

Publishing History
First Edition, 2023
Trade Paperback ISBN 978-1-5092-5172-8
Digital ISBN 978-1-5092-5173-5

The Nine, Book 2
Published in the United States of America

The car jolted to a stop just out of view of the cameras. At least they weren't that stupid. Gun guy/bad teeth guy opened the door and shoved me out hard. My long legs got tangled under the front seat and I fell on all fours on the asphalt. The sting competed with the knot in my head and lost. If I survived this, Alejandro would never leave me out of his sight.

The guy yanked my hair, forcing me to my feet. "Move," he hissed.

I'd only managed a sob when he pressed a gun against my kidneys. I'd die tonight. A virgin. On my brother's birthday. Like some sort of sorry-ass pathetic—that was as far as my thoughts got when the gun was suddenly gone from my back. The guy yanked away from me. Without the hold, I fell to the ground. I heard the screech of tires as the sedan hightailed it out of there. My eyes caught a glimpse of a pale, glowing light under the shadows.

Xcian.

The name pressed against my brain as I passed out.

Prologue

1,993 years ago…

Death came for the trinity as darkness blanketed the land.

Genesis, the guardian of creation, stood overlooking the chaos below. Her fiery cloak billowing in the wind. Dark eyes filled with contempt for all she'd helped create. For the humans who knew no bounds. "Chaos will follow the death of the trinity." Her words rang true. "I say we end the humans and begin anew."

Michael, the guardian of light, stood beside her covered from head to toe in white silk, only pale eyes visible between the slit of his cowl. Eyes that belied the light. Eyes filled with pain and sorrow. Eyes that would drive even the purest of evil into repentance. "No." His voice cut through the sound of the human screams. "There is still hope for them."

Genesis rolled her eyes.

Death stepped out of the shadows, picking at a lint on the sleeve of his dark cloak. "It is done. The trinity is no more." Death's dark eyes looked upon the human destruction below. "I say we let them be. They have been given free will, after all. They can do whatever the hell they want." He smirked.

With the amount of eye-rolling Genesis did, she was at risk of losing her eyeballs inside her skull. "You *are* Death. You would say that."

"Lucifer Morningstar," Death corrected her. "I rather like that name better than Death. It has a fair ring to it, don't you think?" Lucifer smiled.

Michael glared at Death, who didn't meet the guardian's eyes. No one ever risked Michael's gaze. The guardian bit back his words. He had failed the trinity. They'd been slain in a public persecution, fueled by the chants and cries of the humans they'd been meant to protect.

"I don't care what you call yourself," Genesis sneered. "You are still you. Reeking with the stench of sulfur."

Lucifer sneered back. "You should be used to the smell of rotting flesh. What, with the abominations you've created who've learned nothing but how to better destroy themselves."

Lucifer wasn't wrong. The human realm knew no peace.

"Shut up. You're the abomination. Your demons are nothing compared to my creations and what I have yet to create." Her eyes slitted into a nefarious, calculating look.

"Takes one to know one," Lucifer spat back with a glint of humor in his dark eyes. Creation and Death have been repelling each other since the beginning of time.

"Okay, *children*," Michael admonished. "Let us get back to the topic at hand."

Erebus, the guardian of darkness, stood near Michael just beyond the reach of his light. "The veil has thinned. Others will come. We cannot just stand by and do nothing while they rip themselves apart."

Genesis snickered. "Free will." She flicked her thumb Lucifer's way. "The god of stink has a point. They *chose* this."

Lucifer opened his mouth, but Michael cut him off. "We will not let them fall. There is another way."

The silence that followed that statement was thick with tension. The thought of what they could unleash onto the human realm gave even the gods pause.

"It's a bad idea," Genesis whispered. As if the very mention of them would unleash their wrath. "They will not be so easily contained."

Lucifer shrugged. "I like it. Let them try where the trinity failed."

"We must bind them by rules in their design," Genesis said. She did like to dabble in experimenting with creation. "Give them limits."

Michael nodded his approval. "They will be born, not made. They will have no memory of their past lives and this will give them a deeper connection with the humans they'll be charged with protecting."

"They will ascend on their twenty-fourth year," Erebus added. "And will train with the gods."

"I take the heir," Genesis jumped in. "The power of his blood will be strongest."

Death sneered. "Then I'll have the second."

"So be it." Erebus looked toward the human realm in chaos. The acrid stench of smoke lifted into the air as their world burned. "I will release the Anunnaki. The Nine will protect this realm and may the gods help us all."

Chapter One

Sebastian

Stop fidgeting.

Inching closer to getting into one of the hottest nightclubs in the city, I couldn't stop thinking about my dad.

"Stop," Alejandro bristled.

Sometimes, I thought my brother had some deeper connection into my mind that included telepathy. "What?"

"You're thinking about Eric. Stop it. He doesn't need you."

"But Boomer—"

"Was always going to die."

My heart cracked a little bit. "You're such a jerk."

He shrugged his broad shoulders. Everything on Alejandro was big. He'd learned to project all his anger into his body by going to the gym every damn day.

My dad had found Boomer, a beautiful Labrador, at the pound. I'd met Boomer once when I visited moose country Maine, where Dad had gone to hide from the world. Knowing Boomer had cancer, he still adopted her. We all knew she was going to die. It didn't make it easier when it happened a few nights ago. Dad had called me really upset. My first instinct had been to get on a plane and go to him, but he put a stop to that right away.

"Stop," Alejandro repeated.

I glared at him. "How could you be so cold?"

"I'm practical. Sick dog. Dead dog. Eric knew it and so did we."

I wanted to poke him in the chest, but the line moved. Cammie clung to him like a monkey doll. She rolled her eyes at me as if saying, *duh. Who cares about your dad and a dead dog?*

"You don't have to be so cold about it," I mumbled.

He gave me a fist bump on my shoulder. His version of a hug. A painful one. "Just forget it for tonight. Okay?"

Guilt twisted my gut. Alejandro had been dying to get into Genero's for the past six months. We'd finally decided on trying to get in for his birthday celebration and had congregated super early to get inside. He'd refused to leave me at home, so he'd purchased a fake ID for me with the name of Harry Mann. Yes, he had gotten a kick out of that one at my expense. He had picked out my clothes, which had included skinny tight black jeans and a teal button-down shirt rolled at the sleeves. Apparently, teal lifted the color of my light brown eyes. "Yeah, okay."

With a beaming smile that competed with the sun, he turned back to Cammie, nuzzling into her neck.

"Your brother is something, huh." Jasper smiled, revealing his silver braces. Light blue eyes full of mirth behind his black-rimmed glasses, the guy was the embodiment of geek culture, and he wore it proudly. As a roommate, he wasn't too bad either. And he came complete with his own fake ID. Apparently, that was a rite of passage during senior year of high school that I had missed. "Do you think we'll get inside?"

Inside one of the hottest clubs in LA? Yeah, no. But I didn't want to ruin anyone's high.

"He always gets what he wants," Cammie said over her shoulder at us, making me squirm. My brother wrapped his arms around her waist, taking ownership as if saying he had wanted her, and look, I got her. The sneer on my face just happened. Thankfully, she had already looked away from us.

Alejandro's friends were all big jocks with girlfriends hanging off of them as if they were tree trunks. My overtired imagination made me out to be the outcast. Hard not to feel like one around my brother. While my brother was six feet two of solid muscle, I leaned on the thinner side of six feet. He had my mother's honey-blond hair with a touch of curls; mine fell straight in a deep black I usually tied in a low ponytail. His skin tanned. Mine burned. And his eyes were a shade of green while mine were brown. The differences didn't stop there. Alejandro protected me fiercely. Maybe a little too overbearing sometimes, but he'd taken up that position when our dad couldn't. And I loved him for it.

We reached the front of the line and Alejandro turned to me with a look I knew too well. The look that said, *you're going to take the blame for this one because you never really get in trouble.* Then he shoved me in front of the big stocky bouncer who apparently held our fates for the night.

The guy looked at me as if I were his next meal. My brother's plan fell quickly into place. The reason he dressed me like a twink. He must've known the bouncer was gay. It would've been nice had he warned me. Standing like an idiot with my mouth open couldn't be good, right?

Alejandro gave me a nudge at the small of my back, jolting me into action. "Hi," I said, totally sounding like an idiot. Unable to help myself, I drank him in. Thick dark hair short around the ears but long on top. Liquid blue eyes framed by thick black lashes. Then he smiled. And it fluttered my nerves. "Uh, I'm Sebastian."

"Hi," he returned. "I'm Chris." His voice matched his body, thick and husky. He reached out his hand and I shook it. The contact warm and cold between us.

"Good to meet you, Chris," I said. Still the idiot.

Pressing his lips together, mirth filled his eyes. "ID?"

Shit, right. No shaking hands. He wanted our IDs. Heat rose into my cheeks. Not because I felt attracted to the guy. Attraction or lust or even a hard-on had been something I'd never experienced before. Total embarrassment forced heat onto my cheeks. Yup, killing my brother and the giggling idiots behind me using me as bait seemed like a good idea right now. I gave Chris my ID. Using a small flashlight to look at the details, his brow furrowed. "Your ID says Harry." He lifted a brow.

Oh, oh. "Sebastian is a nickname." Oh God, kill me now. "Like, you know, Iron Man."

The guy smiled, revealing nice pearly whites. "You're cute." I wasn't sure if he meant it as a compliment. "You vouch for them?" he said, lifting his chin to the others behind me. I didn't even look back.

"Yeah, my brother's birthday." The guy arched a

7

brow, not believing me. "For real. Born on Valentine's Day, cursed by cupid with too many arrows." I gave my brother a sidelong look. "He's a man-whore."

The guy laughed. A nice sound that didn't match his hard body. "Is that a bad thing?"

"Oh, trust me. It's bad for him."

Chris gave us all one more look, keeping his eyes on Jasper a second longer than the rest of us, then sighed. He moved around the roped entryway and unhooked the barrier. The nine people in my party ambled through. I was last. The large man touched my arm. I stiffened, silently cursing my brother. At least Alejandro stopped to make sure the large bouncer didn't swallow me whole.

At nineteen, I'd yet to punch my V card, and Alejandro knew it. I just hadn't felt a connection with anyone. Girl or guy. Because of it, he assumed I was gay. I loved that he didn't care which way I played— either or, but I didn't have a playing field to begin with. It's not like talking about my low libido was a thing I could share with even my brother. The doctor said my problem wasn't physical. All my bits and pieces were working just fine.

Alejandro gave me a smile with a thumbs up. Apparently, he approved of the beautiful monstrosity, wanting to get to know me better, and maybe buy me a drink at the bar. At least that's what I took away from this awkward exchange. The flutter in my gut did not dissipate. More nerves than anything else. Chris seemed really sweet; someone I would like to get to know. But I knew the moment he realized he'd have to work harder to get a rise out of me (literally) than with anyone else, the interest would dissolve. It always did.

"Uh, would you like my number?" I couldn't get any redder by that point. That smile of his remained. Impenetrable. Knowing. It made my skin break out in bumps.

"Yes, I would."

I handed him my phone so he could see my number displayed on it. As he added it to his phone, I scowled at Alejandro, but a silver-haired god stood in his place. With neon lights at his backdrop, the guy looked surreal. Taller than any man I'd ever seen. His silver-white hair was tied at the nape of his neck and under the lights, his pale eyes were glowing. Contacts, for sure. He wore black cargo pants, shitkickers, and a black long-sleeved shirt that stretched across his wide chest. The sleeves were folded, revealing a dusting of pale hairs on his sculpted arms.

The guy walked toward us. A predatory gait that shouted for everyone to move out of the way lest be fodder. When he reached Chris, they greeted each other with a fist bump.

"Xcian," Chris said with enough ease in his voice to surmise that he considered Xcian a friend. "Didn't know you'd be here tonight."

Xcian. I even liked his name.

Xcian pulled back, still giving me no notice as I stared at him, apparently holding up the line. "I'm here every night."

The guy turned to me, giving me a once-over that suddenly made me scrutinize my appearance. I was born with androgynous features, though as my mother put it, keeping my hair long didn't help any. I rebelled. Even started to paint my nails. Tonight, they were black. As a kid, people often wondered about my gender. I'd gotten glares in the men's restrooms and called missus on more than one occasion. My delicate features had been something God himself had bestowed upon me, along with a dick. Not my fault.

"ID?" Xcian ordered.

I looked at Chris for backup, but the guy had already started to move the waiting line along. "I'm already *inside*," I noted.

"Yeah, well, I can throw you *outside*," he countered.

I didn't want a fist to the face, so I pulled out my wallet and handed the guy my Harry Mann ID while making sure my real ID remained tucked inside the sleeve of my wallet. He studied it in the dark, without a flashlight. I knew then he was dicking with me. And he probably had a really big dick tucked into those pants somewhere.

He handed me the ID. Just as our fingers touched, he pulled his hand away as if I'd infect him. The ID went skittering to the floor. We both bent down to get it at the same time and knocked heads. Though I'd have to say his head was harder than mine. "Ouch," I said, cupping my forehead.

"Shit." He dipped to get the ID before coming back to see to my injuries. Which weren't even a big deal considering the wound he left to my pride. I snatched the ID from his fingers without touching him this time. "Are you okay?" he asked. A mixture of concern and mirth in his voice.

"Peachy," I snapped. "Are we done here?" I wanted to get far away from this guy as much as I could. He didn't seem to like me dismissing him as his expression took a downturn.

"Yeah, we're done."

"Good." As I turned to head deeper into the club, I heard him mutter, "For now." That sent shivers up my spine.

The whole place vibrated with music. Bodies writhed on the dance floor lost in euphoric ecstasy. Alejandro belonged in places like this. Where the lights danced across his golden skin and girls threw their panties at him. I preferred the quiet shadows. Xcian's response to me made me hyperaware of our differences. That wasn't going to change anytime soon, despite my brother trying to break me from the prison in my head.

Like an observer at a zoo, I took a position at a corner, watching him consume more alcohol than any one person should. He danced his ass off, and even made nice with Jasper. I shook my head. Jasper had admitted to me the first day we met that he was gay. Did I have a problem with that? I didn't. And I also knew that Jasper had a crush on my brother, but he was barking up the wrong tree. Alejandro preferred curves and boobs, though I had caught him a few times watching gay porn. He had just shrugged it off, admitting that he'd been curious about the mechanics of it all.

My eyes strayed to the very talented bartender with sparkling blue eyes and a smile that broke the darkness. Okay, yeah, maybe I preferred watching the male form. Bear and twink alike. I still didn't know if that made me gay. My cock didn't react to the dude, but my pulse sprinted a little faster.

Alejandro came stumbling my way after a few hours. "Cammie is going to take me home," he slurred.

"I'm heading out too. You coming?" Jasper asked.

At that moment, I caught sight of Xcian near a pillar, arms folded in front of him, scanning the dance floor. Pale eyes glimmered whenever the strobe light hit them just right. He turned his head and latched on to me. I couldn't see his features under shadows, but those eyes stirred something in me. "Yeah, I'm just going to the bathroom first. Meet you outside?"

Jasper nodded and took off.

Alejandro poked my chest. "You are an asshole," he said. I rubbed the sore spot he poked. "You ignored him all night, and he has a crush on you."

I snorted. If Alex only knew.

Cammie turned to me. "You are cute." She ran her fingers down a loose strand of hair. "You can be a supermodel."

Yeah, that was me. Cute. Supermodel.

Alejandro smiled and gave me a ridiculous thumbs-up as if saying, see? There's a place for you somewhere. I didn't want to be a supermodel or otherwise. "Thanks," I mumbled. "Are you sure you both are going to be okay?"

She nodded. "Uber."

Alejandro drew me into a hug. He never hugged me, so I knew this was his drunk, sweet side. "I love you, bro."

"I love you, too," I whispered in his ear.

Then he shoved me away as if I'd been the one to hug him. "Don't forget I'll be in Bear Lake this weekend. You sure you don't want to come?"

"Nah, I'm good. Have fun. Let me know when you get home."

He nodded, squeezed my shoulder a little too hard, and let Cammie drag him out. I lost silver hair in the mass of bodies. What had I expected, anyway? The way he'd looked at me probably meant he didn't particularly like my type. Though, I didn't know what type I'd placed myself in yet. I giggled a bit. And swayed a little too. The result of having one drink too many. I beelined my way into the restroom.

My perverted thoughts led to Chris, the cute, burly bouncer, who hadn't looked for me to buy me a drink. I wanted to get to know him better. Start small, see where that road leads. That thought had me smiling when I stumbled out of the bathroom stall and into a porn movie. A real, live-action porn featuring Xcian with a blonde woman.

I hadn't heard them come in or the door lock, but apparently, both had happened while I used a stall because I needed privacy to piss.

Xcian had the woman folded over the sink, driving into her from behind, his back to me. He still had his shirt on, so his ass was the only part of him on display as he thrust into her. Ass muscles tight. And he had a nice ass. My eyes dragged over his body to land on the mirror in front of them. Her eyes were half-lidded, her lips parted with an expression of pure bliss. While his expression was stern, his brow furrowed, a sneer on his lips as if he were containing some deep-rooted anger inside of him. As if the very action had him pissed off. And were those fangs?

Then he lifted his eyes and caught me watching him in the mirror. He paused for a heartbeat, eyes wide, his expression blank before picking up the pace again. My whole world narrowed to his reflection in the mirror. The bathroom, the rushing blood to my head, even the woman fell out of my mind. Only Xcian and those eyes of his shooting straight into me. My body turned into one giant sensory vessel and my dick stirred. Stirred! The flutter of sensations coursing along the edge of my skin awakened every cell in my body, and it felt good. Observing wasn't my thing. I'd caught Alejandro's roommates in compromising positions before, and I'd never wanted to join them. I didn't even watch porn. No sensation ever before made me want to be touched, to be kissed, to be...I couldn't even think of what else. I'd never felt *this*.

"What the fuck?" the girl said. "Creep."

The world snapped back into place, beyond Xcian, to the girl sneering at me in the mirror. Horrified, I stumbled back, hitting one of the stall frames.

"Let him watch, baby," Xcian said. His voice was like smooth silk brushing over every part of my body. Husky, on the verge of release. "I want him to watch." He licked his lips, still watching me in the mirror.

I wanted to taste that tongue like I'd never wanted anything else in my life. The compulsion to step up to him and lick the column of his throat made my mouth dry. I wanted...I jerked back, realizing I'd been moving closer to him.

No way.

My stomach rolled. I spun to the door, needing to get out. Feeling trapped. Sweat beaded my brow. A sensory explosion had me jittery. My hands trembled. I finally got the lock open and pushed the door open hard, almost slamming into the awaiting line that had formed just outside. The curses that came out of Xcian made even me recoil. Imagining him tucking himself away after the intrusion, pissed as hell, forced me to move faster to the exit. I'd ruined his night. I needed to get out of this suffocating death box to breathe.

The people gyrating on the dance floor all turned to me with inhuman eyes. The intensity of it seared my skin, threatening to tear at my soul. Stumbling, my shoulder slammed into a post hard enough to sting. The jolt drew my mind back to my reality. The reality where people didn't have fangs or glowing eyes. My imagination working too wild, too fast.

Desperately, I scanned the crowd for Alejandro before remembering he'd already left with Cammie. The exit sign ahead gave me a solid direction. A few minutes later, I pushed myself outside, filling my lungs with the cool night air. My body slowly came down from whatever high it'd been on moments before. There was still a crowd of people waiting to get inside, but no Jasper.

My body moved without conscious effort with the need to get away from everyone. Walking briskly away, I pulled out my cell phone and texted my friend who had left me.

—*Where are you?*—

A few minutes later, he texted back. —*Couldn't wait. Shared ride with gigantor.*—

I snorted. All of Alex's friends fit that bill. —*Ok.*—

I shoved my phone into my pocket and looked up just in time to slam into outstretched arms, waiting for me. The guy wasn't as tall as me, but he was big. As in fat with glossy white skin, thinning hair, and bad teeth. As he shoved me into a dark alley, a second set of arms spun me to face bad teeth guy just as he slammed a fist to my face. Laughing, the taller guy holding me pushed me against the dumpster, headfirst. Pain had me seeing white as my legs gave out, but the second taller guy caught me. I ricocheted like a pinball between them and ended up in the arms of bad teeth guy. The second one was jittery as hell, hopping from foot to foot as if he were in a boxing ring. "Give me your wallet," he said, mere inches from my face.

I almost recoiled from the stench. Blood pooled over my eyelid. With shaking fingers, I wiped it away. Didn't help. Only stung my eye even worse. After two tries, I pulled out my wallet from the tight jeans. I only carried a simple sleeve wallet with my ID and credit cards. No cash. The jittery asshole tore the wallet from my fingers and searched it as if I could hide hundreds of dollars in it. "I don't have any cash." That realization seemed to piss off the guy, earning me a punch to my ribs. I doubled over but didn't drop to the floor again only because the jittery asshole held me from behind.

"Sucks to be you. Means we're going for a drive."

A third person pulled up in an old sedan. The first guy shoved me inside while the jittery man took shotgun. "Take us to the nearest ATM."

Clutching my ribs, I moved to the other side of the car, away from the jerk, when he showed me a small gun. "Don't try anything, asshole."

I nodded. The drive took me through the slums of the city. I'd grown up in Chicago. The slums were part of life, but I'd never adjusted to this city. I'd never been without Alejandro. What would he think of me now? An idiot who couldn't even navigate his surroundings. In pitiful need to be saved. The streets turned darker, dirtier, until we reached an ATM that should've probably been protected by a sentry unit with a thousand rounds of ammunition. Instead, it stood lonely in an abandoned strip mall. I wondered if they'd blame me if the thing didn't work and shoot me in the head.

The car jolted to a stop just out of view of the cameras. At least they weren't that stupid. Gun guy/bad teeth guy opened the door and shoved me out hard. My long legs got tangled under the front seat and I fell on all fours on the asphalt. The sting competed with the knot in my head and lost. If I survived this, Alejandro would never leave me out of his sight.

The guy yanked my hair, forcing me to my feet. "Move," he hissed.

I'd only managed a sob when he pressed the gun against my kidneys. I'd die tonight. A virgin. On my brother's birthday. Like some sort of sorry-ass pathetic—that was as far as my thoughts got when the gun was suddenly gone from my back. The guy yanked away from me. Without the hold, I fell to the ground. I heard the screech of tires as the sedan hightailed it out of there. My eyes caught a glimpse of a pale, glowing light under the shadows.

Xcian.

The name pressed against my brain as I passed out.

Chapter Two

Xcian

Taking the blonde should've dulled my interest in the kid, but fate, the twisted bitch, handed him to me on a plate. Despite my preference for soft curves, I had wanted him to join us. The want poured out of me in waves of endorphins that should've had him malleable. I'd never forced or drugged anyone against their will. My power simply pulled on what was already there. I lowered inhibitions so that humans could be themselves. And in my throes of passion, they usually wanted a fast fuck. I gave them what they wanted while dulling the demon energy surging inside of me in the process. Beneficial for both of us. For a split second, it had worked. He had started to approach me but then fought against it. The first human to deny me.

He'd freaked.

I saw it on his face.

The disgust of what he was about to do, about what he wanted just before he ran.

But he hadn't run far enough from me. The demons thrived for the chase, the hunt. I felt the pull instantly. Tracking the kid had been easy. Especially since his scent had overpowered all others in the bathroom. The scent of wildflowers in a field of green grass under a warm summer sky. I picked it up as soon as I reached the street, like a tether. Climbing into my car, I chased it. I would've preferred shifting into my true form and teleporting, but my gut told me I'd need the car. And my instincts were usually spot on. A gift passed down by my mother. Sometimes, a curse. I overshot him, parked the car, and backtracked just as a pair of guys shoved him into an alley.

People usually got what they deserved, especially humans. This kid had no business being in a club with a fake ID, no business getting drunk, and he had no business walking so late on this side of town. The kid needed to learn a lesson. And, okay, maybe his rejection stung more than I wanted to admit. As one of the Anunnaki, I was a judgmental fuck. Part of the job description. Saving humans from their own stupidity would only create more stupid humans. This realm was already filled with plenty of them.

Yeah, I tried convincing myself of that until he'd been shoved into a sedan. I caught sight of the gun in the attacker's hand. This robbery would not end with just a theft. My instincts warned me of that too. I either intervened or hear about the kid's death in the news later on. I knew that in my bones. The kid didn't deserve a bullet to the head for making a mistake.

I followed them in my car—the assholes too stupid to realize they had a tail. An Audi R8 stuck out in this neighborhood like a horned demon sitting in a church during mass. I parked far enough not to be noticed and shifted into my true form. Taking down the human piece of scum with the gun had been easy. The other two fled in the car. I'd meant to hightail out of there too until I saw the kid crumble to the ground.

I had no time for coddling an injured kid who

should've been home in bed in the first place.

And yet...I plucked his wallet from the ground and easily hauled him over my shoulder in a fireman's carry. Thankfully, in this neighborhood, no one cared enough to take notice. I gently lowered him to his feet and leaned him up against my car. With some finagling, I pressed my leg between his thighs to keep him upright. The position put him flush against my body and I couldn't help but take a deep inhale of his scent. Underlying the blood, wounds, and stench of the men who hurt him, wildflowers and sunny skies wafted out of him, sparking memories I'd buried a long time ago. Memories of a time when I'd been a human boy spending my days with Zane, just being kids. Before we had ascended and learned to use our soul as a vessel to trap the evil in this realm. A burning regret swelled inside of me, and I pushed that shit down behind the black pit of my heart. It did me no good anymore.

I hadn't really looked at the kid back at the club when I'd been an ass with him. But now, I took my fill of him. Black straight hair now loose around his face, pale smooth skin, and tall enough that I didn't have to break my back to lean into him. And I did. Lean into him, trailing the tip of my nose against his jaw, to his neck, just centimeters from grazing him with my lips instead.

My body vibrated with the need to kiss him properly, and my cock pulsed for him. A male. Although no one knew, because, well, I portrayed myself as a royal sex guru, I'd never been with a man. Zane preferred males. I did not judge. But for me, it'd never interested me. After I lost my heart to a female, I just wanted to stem the need. Nothing more.

Until now.

The consequences of being interrupted from completing my one-night fuck.

The kid's eyes blinked open. Two large brown spheres holding every emotion imaginable. Beautiful in their intensity. And currently, with his pupils blown. I quickly sensed a concussion, bruised ribs, along with lots of contusions. He'd live. A low groan pushed out of him and when he realized I had him pressed against the car, he started to fight me. The movement made me snap back to the present. Securing his hands, I pressed my body harder against his. "Relax. I'm helping you," I growled out. Couldn't help it. My voice didn't have another octave than growly.

He blinked the haze out of his eyes, breathing heavily. "Xcian?" My name on his lips made me shiver. Fucking shiver. "What happened?" he whispered and winced. His body going pliant against me. I released his hands, and he quickly lifted one to the wound bleeding on his forehead.

"Don't," I scolded, slapping his hand away. "Let it clot up."

Then he started to tumble forward, going nowhere with my body pressed against him. But his forehead dropped to my shoulder. I quickly held him up under his arms and guided him into the tight fit of the car. Once I strapped him in, I jumped into the driver's side. His head turned to me. I perused his features again. The blood and bruises made me want to find those fuckers in the car and kill them too. It had nothing to do with my need for justice and everything to do with the guy sitting beside me. I wanted to see his eyes open again. The slight tilt of his mouth when he'd been pissed at me

21

in the club. The hint of desire when he'd caught me in the bathroom. The feeling so strange.

I gave myself a mental slap and dug into his wallet. Behind the fake Harry Mann ID was an Illinois State ID that identified him as Sebastian Aiden Diaz and aged him at nineteen. Okay, so he had been younger than I thought. I also found a student ID and a credit card in his name. I probably could've found an emergency contact person on his phone and dropped him off. But I preferred to keep him by my side. Make sure he recovered from his wounds. Keep him safe.

Yeah, right. *Just* keep him safe.

Forty minutes later, we arrived at my place. At least one of the many I had throughout the country. The two-story farmhouse sat on three acres of land, complete with a couple of horses maintained by the groundskeeper. I parked the car in the attached garage and cut the engine. The kid hadn't moved. I probably should've taken him to the hospital, left him as a John Doe. Too late now.

Taking him out of the car knocked out didn't pose a problem. With so many head injuries between my nine brothers, getting an unconscious person out of a vehicle wasn't all that difficult. Especially one as thin as this kid.

Not a kid, I admonished myself. An adult. It didn't make it any better to know the man was unconscious and couldn't consent to my help.

Consent was the law.

I hauled him inside anyway.

Though the house had three bedrooms, I gently lowered him onto my king-size bed in the master bedroom. For a fraction of a second, his grip on me tightened as if he didn't want to let me go.

"I have to close that wound on your head," I explained as I left him sitting on the edge of the bed to find the first-aid kit. I always had one in case we needed to seam up the wounds we inflicted on our enemies if we wanted them to live a little longer. He silently watched me as I dragged the chair closer to my bed. His complexion pale, still in shock. I cleaned the wound with an antiseptic. "I'm going to put butterfly stitches with a waterproof bandage so you can shower."

Once done, he tried to stand. Pain marred his perfect features. "Let me help you." My fingers stopped at the buttons of his shirt, waiting for his consent.

"Okay," he said, still shaking.

I'd be an ass to take advantage of him in this state. A total fucking ass, but the spark that ignited as my fingers made contact with his bare skin went straight to my cock.

Those brown eyes latched onto me and he bit back a painful sound as I slid him out of the shirt. A sound that went straight to my cock again. Standing didn't help him, so I plopped him back down on the bed. I already anticipated what came next and quickly shoved a garbage can under him as he turned over and spewed.

Humans were utterly disgusting. I preferred the malice version of turning to ash in minutes than working with gooey fluids. It must've shown on my face because Sebastian chuckled. "You look about ready to pass out."

"This is gross," I admitted.

His laugh soothed my soul, like a cool breeze against my skin. "I think I'm done."

I carried the small can out as far away from me as

possible and dumped it outside in the trash. Sebastian was in the bathroom cleaning himself up in the sink when I returned with nothing but those damn tight jeans that made his ass look enticing. Dragging my eyes back to his face took more effort than it should've. He rinsed his mouth and lifted his eyes to me in the mirror.

"What happened?" he asked, turning to face me.

Without invitation, I stepped inside. "You were attacked."

"Yeah, but why didn't you just take me to the hospital or call the cops?"

I could've lied, but that would take too long, and I didn't really care what he thought about me bringing him here. He wasn't going anywhere. "I followed you out after you ruined my one-night fuck." This kid had me riled up while he gave me nothing in return. Not desire, lust, a bit of that youth horniness. Nothing.

"Shit," he said. And I did sense regret and embarrassment. "Sorry." His cheeks turned red up to his hairline. "I didn't mean to—"

"Like it?" I cut him off.

"I didn't—no. I..."

I could've let him keep digging himself into a liar's hole, but I had no patience. I shoved all common sense away and slowly cupped his neck. He took a deep inhalation of breath and let it out slowly. I didn't sense lust, my usual taste when this close to a human, just a slight increase in his pulse and the pungent scent of mistrust.

The kid didn't trust me. Smart.

His eyes slowly perused my face and held my eyes longer than the rest of me, but he still hadn't moved. I hated not knowing the outcome and pushed it along by leaning into him and gently brushing his lips with mine. So much for my preference for women. This guy shattered all my resolve, all my strength. I needed him. Now.

I chanced to give him a lick on his bottom lip. The kid stiffened slightly. But my lizard brain didn't care. "I want to kiss you," I said. For a heartbeat, I thought he'd consent, but then he pushed me away.

"No. You smell like you just had sex in a bathroom."

If I weren't so damn worked up already, I would've sworn the kid had a jealous lilt to his voice. Except shock overpowered my curiosity. To be denied. Never happened before. It took a monumental effort to restrain the need for my demons to hunt.

"Can I clean up?" He gestured to the shower. My large, walk-in shower. He gave it a look as if trying to figure out the mechanics of it.

"Yeah, go for it." I hated the choked sound of my voice. Denied something that should be mine. I needed to get out. "I'll bring you some clothes." I practically ran out of that bathroom and could only take a viable inhalation of breath when I reached the other end of the house. As a hunter by nature, the word no just made the demons rise to the surface and want things they shouldn't.

After a few long minutes of me contemplating my fucked-up existence and having finished half a bottle of bourbon while I did so, I returned to the room to find him sitting on the bed wearing the joggers and tee I'd left him. His eyes were clearer. "Do you always prowl the streets looking for someone to save, or was I just lucky tonight?"

Those damn eyes were on me again. "You shouldn't have been out there to begin with," I said, sounding more pissed than I probably should've. "Streets are dangerous at night, and you weren't even paying attention to where you were going."

He licked his lips and yeah, I wanted to suck the slickness from them. "You were watching me?"

That's why I should shut up. "Yes."

"Are you going to take me home?"

"No," I quickly said. The thought of leaving Sebastian right now felt like being stabbed, multiple times. "You should stay tonight. It's late, anyway."

"Where are you going to sleep?"

Right. Not with him, apparently. "I have a guest bedroom. I'll see you in the morning." With that, I walked out.

Chapter Three

Sebastian

The next morning, I woke up with sunbeams burning my eyes and my body on fire.

I groaned and turned away from the light. My brain slowly came back online, along with my memory of last night. All of them filled with the man-god with silver hair and pale eyes.

Xcian.

I should've been more freaked out that I'd ended up in some remote house in the middle of nowhere with someone I didn't even know. Xcian should've taken me to the police. Reported the attack. And his gentle treatment of me. The way he wanted me. *Me*. To kiss me and do other things to my body, replayed in my head. My dick had just twitched, as if reminding me that it's all it would ever do. The bathroom erection had been a one-time deal. That's all. Won't happen again. He'd laugh at me when he realized he'd have to work harder to get a rise out of me. I didn't think I could survive that.

And I had caught him inside someone else. Gross to think that I'd be sloppy seconds. Or he'd be sloppy seconds. Ugh. I turned to my side and punched the pillow in frustration. I didn't even know his full name, only that he worked at the club. Or at least bossed people around at the club. Every night.

A soft knock on the door startled me, but I kept my eyes shut like a kid trying to get out of mowing the lawn on a Sunday morning. "I know you're awake. I made breakfast. Come down so you can eat before I give you some pain killers."

Eat. And pain killers. I opened my eyes to a shirtless Xcian with his arms crossed over his chest, leaning on the doorframe. Long silver hair wet at the tips, and shimmering silver eyes on me. Taller than even Alejandro, and with a build to match, Xcian exuded testosterone. He smirked at me.

"Good morning," I croaked out, unable to think of anything else to say.

"Good morning. I'm sensing you are in pain?"

I nodded into my pillow.

"Scale."

"Twelve?"

He raised a brow.

"I have a low pain tolerance."

He approached the bed and for a moment I imagined him climbing in with me. He didn't. He dropped something on the bed. "It's been buzzing nonstop. I suggest you call your stalker."

Shit. Alex.

I sat up too quickly and instantly pain followed. I cupped my chest, which had turned a nasty shade of purple. Breathing hurt. "You have two bruised ribs," he said. "Not broken. It'll hurt like hell, but it'll heal if you take it easy for a few weeks. The concussion was minor, but your head probably feels like it's going to pop like a balloon. I can't give you pain meds without some food in you. So, get up." He arched a brow and walked out, leaving me to wonder who the hell had just walked into the room. The Xcian I remembered from the club had been an asshole. And this one an old maid.

I dropped back on the bed and lifted the phone. Ten missed calls. And one text from Jasper. I opened Jasper's text first.

—Sry. Came clean and told your bro that u didn't come home last nite. Hope you're still alive.—

Shit.

I called Alex. He answered on the first ring. "Where are you?" he growled out.

"Sorry. I kind of met someone." I turned on my side and bit back a wince. The silence on the other side made my stomach knot. "I stayed the night with him. I should've texted or called. Sorry. I just woke up. Long night." *Please don't ask. Please. Please.*

More silence followed, and I could just imagine what he thought of me. Being gay had been a theory until I actually acted on it. Was he disgusted? Did he hate me? Shit. "Be careful, Seba," he said so low I almost couldn't hear the words. "Use protection."

Oh, God. My face flushed hot. "Yes, *Dad*," I said.

"Don't call me that." The Alejandro I knew and loved surfaced with those words.

"We're just friends," I said because I couldn't currently label whatever the hell Xcian was to me. "And nothing *happened*."

A long pause followed as if he were trying to figure out what to say next. "Fine. Don't force me to stalk you again. Call or text me tonight too. Understand?"

Jesus, I needed a life. "Yeah. I will."

"Love you," he said.

29

We were always taught that we weren't guaranteed a tomorrow, and love yous today always mattered, so ending our calls with love yous had been imprinted on us. "I love you, too," I said and he hung up.

Moving like the little engine that couldn't, I dragged my ass down the stairs and to the kitchen, which smelled of bacon, eggs, maple syrup, and pancakes. All of it spread out as if Xcian were feeding a herd of elephants. His smile burned right through me. "Hey, I didn't know what you liked, so I made everything."

"Uh, okay."

At that moment, the screen of the front door opened and a tiny Latina woman walked inside. "I forgot the coffee," she said. "You cannot have breakfast for your *amor*, without *café*." She left the coffee pot on the counter and lifted onto her tiptoes and kissed him on the cheek. He still had to bend down to receive it.

"Thank you, Mrs. Soto," he said sheepishly

She gave him an over-the-shoulder wave as she walked out. His otherwise pale complexion turned pink as he shrugged. "Yeah, so I may have asked Mrs. Soto to help me make breakfast."

That he went the extra mile for me made me feel all warm inside and I laughed. The smile and blush remained on his face as he brought over everything. We ate in awkward silence until he finally caved.

"So who's Alex?"

"My brother. Went skiing. Found out I didn't make it home last night and was worried."

"The guy that was with you last night?" Xcian said.

"Yeah."

"He shouldn't have left you alone."

"He's not my guardian."

"Obviously, because he sucks at it."

Before I could think, I blurted, "As if you could do better."

Something in his expression flashed dangerously close to anger. As if I were goading him into something. Xcian had admitted to following me out of the club. It meant he'd seen them push me into the alley, and followed us to that mall. My stomach felt as if I'd swallowed a stone. "You waited." I didn't know how I knew. I just did. "You waited until they shoved me into the car to help me."

Anger cinched his face, and he plucked the plates off the table and tossed them out. I wanted to tell him he could wash them, not toss them, but I was too pissed. I got up too but winced at the sudden movement. He caught my pain and planted a vial of pills on the table. "Take one."

I didn't want to, but breathing hurt. And I had been honest. I hated pain. All kinds of pain. Especially the ones that hurt on the inside. I took the pill and swallowed it dry. "Answer me."

"I didn't hear a question."

I hadn't formed it as a question. "Why did you wait?"

"Because you needed to learn a lesson."

I stumbled a step back. "A lesson?"

"You shouldn't have been out there. I didn't lie to you about that. And lying about your age. Acting as if you're older? You really think you didn't deserve to be punished for that?"

I sucked in a gasp. The sting of tears too close. "So you let them beat me to punish me for using a fake ID to party with my brother on his birthday."

"Yes." His expression turned cold.

"Why did you stop it at all?"

"Because they were going to execute you the moment you gave them the money. That punishment didn't fit the crime."

"So you killed him."

"Yes." He took a step closer. "I killed him before he could kill you."

Ohmygod, this man was crazy.

"How is that wrong?"

The genuine way in which he asked threw me off balance. "Because you shouldn't kill people. It's wrong."

He narrowed the gap between us, standing close enough that I could see the ice blue rimming his eyes. "Even if he meant to kill you?"

"You can't know that he meant to kill me."

"So, I wait until he kills you. And then kill him?"

I opened my mouth, then closed it. "Yes."

"Why?"

"Because you can't know his intentions."

"I just told you. I do."

I shook my head. "No, you don't."

He lifted his finger and trailed his hand down my face and cupped my neck. I inhaled sharply at the energy behind that touch. "But *I* do. I've never lied to you, Sebastian. And I never will."

The way he touched me and said those words made me feel as if I already belonged to him. As if he were claiming me as his own. And it scared me because I liked it. "I think you should take me home."

He did.

Chapter Four

Xcian

Four months later...

Blood was a bitch to remove from my silver hair. I squeezed the excess water as best I could, sneering at my brother Hawke for precipitating the fight that left us both soaked and pissed. Hawke tossed me a beanie with a glare. My brother pricklier than usual since Zane returned from his trip to Maine. "If you can't handle the truth," I added salt to injury as I tucked my hair inside the beanie. "Then you shouldn't fucking be around."

Zane pointed a finger at me. "Stop provoking the shit."

I opened my mouth to argue, but snapped it shut. The shit in question being Hawke's feelings for Serena, who was engaged to our older brother, Zane. Sure, Zane *could* deny the engagement, but that would mean I would have to fill her with a baby. If not me, then Galen. Hawke was fourth in the line of succession. And although I didn't want a mini-me running around, Galen would, by his right. My brother's demon already made him batshit crazy. He needed a mate, and soon. We were the Anunnaki charged with keeping the human realm safe by using ourselves as vessels to contain the evil spreading in this world. Keeping the demons trapped inside of the ethereal realm required loads of power. True bonding mates eased the load so that we wouldn't either go mad or explode. Literally explode. The human shell the gods had given us could only withstand so much.

Zane, the eldest and most powerful of us, had already started to show cracks in his human shell. The guy smelled of need and demon. No one talked about it. And thus far, none of Zane's brides had lived to face the altar. That had all of us on high alert and edgy as fuck. I didn't want to lose my brother. I didn't want to ascend as eldest. Zane had to go through with mating Serena. To survive. "Fine," I said.

Hawke snorted, calling my bullshit.

The drive back home was unusually quiet. Zane refused to talk about what went down in Maine, but I knew it had to be about some mark he met a few years ago. A male. I had smelled the male scent on Zane for a long time afterward as if my brother had imprinted himself with the human's scent.

I knew all about the need to imprint on a scent. I still couldn't forget Sebastian. Something had shifted inside of me that I couldn't make sense of. I wanted to take in his scent straight to my soul. And I'd never had an interest in cock, but I wanted to experience his.

I shifted in my seat and Hawke gave me a hard sideways glance. "I'm pushing you out of the car if you make that sound again."

Sound? What sound?

"Have you fed?" Zane asked. "You're reeking pheromones."

Shit. I needed sex like I needed to pull my next breath. "I'll find something tonight. I'm good."

Hawke shook his head.

I wanted to tell him to fuck off. We each had our own vices. The demon power we contained oftentimes leaked into our own, giving us demon attributes. A side-effect of saving this world, and the humans didn't even know anything about it. They wrote our kind in romance novels and movies, as villains or lovers, without realizing the truth. Given a chance, we would rip this realm from their greedy, little dead fingers.

We reached the mansion and I hopped out first, sprinting up the steps. Wearing a long silver evening gown matching her long silver hair, Mother waited in the foyer for Zane. We both shared the hair and the silver eyes, though she hid hers with contacts. Her nostrils flared when she saw me. Something she always did.

"You stink," she said, rubbing her index finger under her nose.

"Good to see you too, *Mother*."

She waved her hand, dismissing me. *Great*. I sprinted up the stairs and headed to my room. According to the rule of the gods, the Anunnaki must be always numbered nine, though technically there were ten of us. A set of twins. Sage and Basil—a two-for-one deal that still had everyone questioning the gods' intent with *that* mistake. There had never been twins born as Anunnaki, but that was apparently above my pay grade. We lived long lives, healed fast, and could survive most anything, but we weren't immortal. Zane, Hawke, Galen and I had watched two of our brothers explode, never having mated. Another three went crazy enough to start wars that had almost ended the world. They had to be put down. Their souls found their way back into the cycle and reborn. The three youngest—Zack, Leander, and Aristotle had yet to ascend in their lineage, which meant their demons were roaming the realm. None of us remembered our previous lives. A small blessing.

I rushed through my shower, making sure I washed the blood completely out. I continued to my other basic necessities. My hard-on painful. We'd all been too worked up with this mating. Sex hadn't been on my mind.

Liar.

Okay, maybe it had been on my mind. Maybe I had followed Sebastian Diaz after I'd dropped him off at his dorm room the day I told him I'd murdered someone. Not surprising that he ran from me. I still couldn't stay away. He'd been my first male interest and the first to refuse me. That made him a walking, breathing contradiction I needed to settle. The reason I followed him back and forth from his classes. The reason I'd warned Chris not to interfere or I would rip his spine out of his body. Pure curiosity. Nothing more. *Yeah, right.*

Even after four months, the thought of touching him sent my body swelling with need. I was leaking even before I touched myself. And when I came, it hit me hard and long, but still not enough. It hadn't been enough since he told me never to contact him again.

Me.

He told *me* to fuck off.

I let out a long breath and let the water flow along my skin, washing away all evidence of my needs. The ache remained, just under the surface of my skin. Unsated. I had to learn to live with it. I would never trust my feelings. It had only ever led to pain and regret.

I shut the water, dried, and dressed.

Already forgetting my torment for a little while, I stopped by Leander's room and knocked.

"Come in," he said.

"Hey, Doof." I strutted inside and plopped on the bed next to him. He'd been drawing something in his notebook and had to wait for the bed to stop moving to continue. "Whatcha drawing?" I asked, picking up the remote and turning on the tube hanging on his wall.

He sighed, carefully put pad and pencil on his side table, and leaned back beside me, our backs against the headboard, legs crossed at the ankles on the bed. Shoes and all. "You stink like malice." Leander had a very sensitive nose. Had to do with his wolf-shifting abilities.

"We had some trouble."

Leander clasped his hands between his thighs. It made him look so small and vulnerable. At fourteen, a hive of malice had taken Leander. The events leading to his abduction had always been unclear. Zane had taken him somewhere, and Leander hadn't come back with him. That's all I knew. Zane, Hawke, Galen, Noah, the twins and I had scoured the earth looking for him. Like, we burned shit to the ground to get to him. He had spent eighteen months in a six-by-six cell. He'd been starved and tortured. We had obliterated the malice and humans involved and hid the whole shit with a massive forest fire. It'd taken Leander a year to talk again, and even now, he still preferred not to speak. Getting him out of the room without shifting was still a battle. Because of my ability to secrete endorphins and dopamine through my link with my demons, he'd started to seek *me* out. He'd slept most nights on the floor as his wolf form at the foot of my bed.

"How's Zane? Mom has the Sentinel coming in for tonight's celebration."

Zane and Serena would be celebrating their engagement tonight at the club. During the night of the Bloodmoon, seventy-two hours away, they would bond. It should've been a happy event, but...

"Zane doesn't love her," Leander said quietly into the room.

"It doesn't matter. He'll do what he must to secure our bloodline as heir."

"And if he doesn't?"

"He will."

"Ex, come on. You can't be that cruel."

"We aren't *human*. Love is not part of the equation. He'll bond with her and survive. Then, if he needs to plant a seed inside her, he will. And the cycle will begin all over again."

"Zane will never curse his sons with our fate."

I wanted to argue that point, but Leander was right. Zane's first act as heir had been rebellion and he had paid the price in Hell because of it. Because of *me*. Genesis, the goddess of creation, had expected the strongest and heir to train, instead, Zane had switched places with me and had gone with Lucifer because I'd been so fucking afraid. He'd never curse his sons with this shit. And I didn't blame him.

"It means that you'll have to do it. Galen can't be the patriarch," Leander added.

I sighed. No. Galen couldn't lead the Nine. I loved Galen, but the demons inside of him were too volatile. Galen himself, too destructive. "What do you want me to do?"

"Stay close to Zane. You have to protect him. Follow his lead."

I rolled my eyes. I didn't do well with following anyone's lead. Leander leaned into me and placed a gentle hand on top of mine. I suddenly felt as if I were somehow tainting him. "So...I've been meaning to ask you. Who's the female?" I gave him a look that didn't need to be followed by a *what the fuck?* "The female that you've been thinking about these past months. I can sense the desire in you. Wolf? Remember?" He tapped his nose.

I couldn't tell my brother that the female he thought had a hold over me was actually male, and I couldn't tell him how I couldn't get him out of my damn head. "You need to mind your own business."

He chuckled. "Where's the fun in that?"

I playfully shoved him with my shoulder. It didn't matter, either way. I couldn't do shit with any of the real needs I had. "Doesn't matter," I answered.

"Why not?"

"Why? Uh, didn't you just tell me I had to do what was right? Messing with a human is not right." I hated hitting him with a reality check, but the sooner he learned that we couldn't afford attachments, especially humans, the better.

Leander sighed and rested his head on my shoulder. "And that's why I know you'll do what's right, brother. Although it sucks that we can't be us."

"Hey, I'm still me. You're still you." I poked his nose. "At least I think you are."

He snorted. "Yeah, I'm me. But..." Leander shrugged and I knew what he meant. Living forever sucked when you didn't have anyone to share it with. I knew that deep in my bones. Every time I fed from those feelings in humans, I felt like a piece of shit. It hadn't taken long for all of us to realize why this realm held such importance. Humans were a delicate species. But when they loved, they could be majestic.

"I know, kiddo. But you don't have to worry about that, okay?" I lifted his chin, so he had to look at me. "Being us has perks."

He gave me a small smile that meant everything.

With the celebration at the club, it was going to be a long, dangerous night. I had to be clearheaded. I needed to feed properly. Sebastian Diaz, be damned. I slid out of bed before I did something stupid, like give Leander a wet willy. "Catch ya later, *Doofus,*" I said on the way out.

"You can't catch the wolf, *moron.*"

No. I didn't think I could ever catch the wolf.

Chapter Five

Sebastian

One stupid act shouldn't define us. One mistake shouldn't outline the rest of our lives. One show of weakness shouldn't change who we are.

People made mistakes all the time, so why did it feel as if my family had won gold in that department?

"We're going to have to separate!" I yelled over the music at my dad, ignoring the death grip he had on my arm. "It's the only way we have a chance at finding him." My dad looked ready to run, his eyes taking in all the writhing bodies on the dancefloor. "Trust me, Dad," I added.

Earlier, after Alex's graduation, we had gone out to eat a late lunch when Alex had told my dad I had dropped out of college. Pissed that he'd thrown me under the bus, I ratted him out. His girlfriend Cammie might be pregnant with his kid. Not my best moment. During his graduation party, Alex had gotten some news about it and took off without saying anything. Dad and I had looked everywhere for him until Chris, the bouncer at Genero's, answered my text to let me know Alex was at the club.

Dad finally released me, and I had to fight my own sense of panic at watching him disappear among the crowd, searching for my idiot brother. Alex was right when he told me I had to stop thinking my dad was going to do something stupid again. Like trying to kill himself. Dad had changed these last few years. Leaving Alex and me in college had made him better. That hurt too. I shoved the thought away. Alex needed me now.

The last time I'd been here had been for Alex's birthday. The night I met Xcian and caught him in the bathroom having sex with a woman. And he'd let me get beat up before saving me from a bullet because I deserved the beat-down but not the bullet. As if he had the right to judge me. He'd admitted to killing that guy. I'd had nightmares of it ever since.

I caught sight of Alex at the bar talking to a woman. Wearing a shirt and tie with black slacks, he'd have the woman eating out of the palm of his hand soon.

I let out a sigh and headed that way. The woman sat under shadow, and I couldn't make out her features except that she had long dark hair, and a shimmer in her eyes. Those eyes trailed the length of me, forcing me to shiver as if someone had walked over my grave. That's what grandma used to always tell me whenever I felt my skin rise. This whole place reeked of something I couldn't label, and I wanted to leave as fast as I could.

"Hey," I said, using my bossy voice, which I rarely ever used.

Alex smiled my way, but the smile didn't reach his eyes. He looked two seconds away from crying. "Hey, bro," he said. Wrapping his arm around my shoulder. "This is…I'm sorry, what's your name again?"

"Genie," she said.

"Genie," he slurred in my ear. "I think she wants me."

Genie sat on a stool no more than eighteen inches away from me and I still couldn't see her features, only an inkblot of shadows across her face. The hairs along my skin didn't let up. "Nice to meet you," I lied. "But I'm taking my brother home." Alex stiffened beside me, preparing to fight me. I turned to him. "Dad is here."

The mention of Dad wiped the smile from his face. Clarity returned for a few seconds, and he scowled. "You told him."

The accusation in his voice made me feel like a crappy brother. Though I wasn't sure if it was that I told Dad about the pregnancy or that he was *here*. I'd messed up big time.

Alex started for the exit, and I had to sprint to catch up with him. I'm not sure why I looked up at the loft, but I did. Behind a wall of darkness, I sensed the man that haunted my nightmares. Despite only seeing a silhouette, I knew it was him. Glowing pale eyes like two pinpricks in the dark. But he couldn't possibly see me among the shadows and thick crowd. And yet, I felt *watched,* and it only made me move faster to the exit. The more distance I put between us, the easier it became to breathe.

Inhaling a lungful of air once outside cleared my head. Alex hailed a cab and groaned next to me as we drove back to his place. Alex had a flight in the morning, and I told him I'd turn in the house key to the landlord since his roommates were already gone. He was heading to New York to start his adult life. At least that had been the plan this morning. I wasn't sure anymore. I texted Dad to give a status report, letting him know I'd found Alex and we were heading to his place.

"He loves you more," Alex slurred. "You know that, right?"

He meant Dad. "He loves you too."

"Nah, he sees too much of mom in me. You, on the other hand, well, you are him only with better opportunities you are shitting away."

Listening to the disappointment in his tone hurt. Because I knew it was true. This past year away from my dad had been hell. I had to call him at least once a day. Imagining him alone, secluded away from human contact and inside his mind doing something awful, gave me panic attacks that Alex had to ease me down from. Even now, my chest hurt.

"It's all his fault. I blame him for all of it," Alex said with derision. Then my brother softly whispered, "He should've died that day."

I swallowed the lump in my throat but said nothing. I'd grown up in a house where my dad hated his life, and my brother hated our dad. I fell in between trying to give my dad a reason to stay breathing while giving my brother a reason not to leave us. Leave *me*.

Thankfully, Alex didn't say anything else until we got to his house. I paid the driver while Alex managed to make it to the front lawn before he spewed. Then he crumbled on the stairs, looking so lost when he should've been excited to be starting his life in New York. I sat down on the steps next to him.

"It's not mine," he said. He sounded so sad it hurt my heart.

The baby. I almost let out a relieved breath but held it, sensing something off. "I thought that's what you wanted."

He raked his hand through his hair, his eyes latched

onto something in the distance. Maybe the house next door, maybe the lamp post. Something. "I can't—I can never have kids." His voice broke, and he wiped his mouth again with a trembling hand. "I tried giving, you know? For extra cash. The guys were doing it and I got a letter. A fucking letter. Can you believe that?" He still didn't look at me. His eyes distant. "Tear a guy up with a fucking letter. Sorry, but you're shooting blanks. No need for you to donate. I told her I'd help her raise it despite, whatever, but she doesn't want it. She just needed money, so I gave it to her. I gave her money for an abortion of another guy's baby. He'll never know either. Isn't that messed up?"

I wrapped one arm around his shoulder, and he leaned into me. Although he was a player, Alex always wanted to be a father. He wanted a family. He worked so hard for the perfect career, the perfect job. He would've worked hard for the perfect wife, house, kids, the whole works. All of it blown to shit. It all seemed so unfair. "It's her choice, Alex. You did good by being a friend she needed."

He wiped his face though I hadn't seen any tears. "She cheated on me," he snorted a laugh. "Sometimes, I think we're cursed. Nothing will ever turn out right for us."

I found it disturbing that I didn't have a counter to that feeling. Alex got to his feet and walked into the house.

The streetlights in front of the house snapped off, leaving a wall of darkness in front of me. The stillness seemed malevolent. The hairs at the nape of my neck stood on end as if I were being *watched*. Again. I followed Alex inside, locking the door behind me.

Grabbing a water bottle as I headed to his room, I reached him just as he dropped on the bed. On automatic nursemaid mode, I helped him undress. Alex ran hot and liked sleeping without covers so I didn't bother tucking him in.

"I love you, bro," he said. "You know that, right?"

I swallowed the lump in my throat. "I'll visit you in New York whether you invite me or not."

He nodded with a smile. "Yeah. That'll be nice." He rested his forearm across his eyes. His breathing even. I thought he'd fallen asleep when he said, "Just don't bring Eric."

I knew my brother had his reasons for hating our father, but it still stung. A lot. I left him asleep and closed the door. My phone pinged with a text as I entered one of the extra bedrooms near the bathroom.

—Chris: Everything okay?—

I let out a relieved breath, grateful that it had been Chris bouncing at the club tonight. He'd let me in, concerned for me and Alex. The Harry Mann cover had ended the first time Chris had called me and we went out for coffee. He admitted that he wasn't allowed to let me back into the club. House rules. I figured that was more Xcian rules, but whatever.

Me: —Yeah. Just family stuff. Thanks for letting me inside. —

Chris: —No problem. Glad you found your brother. —

Me: — Night. —

Chris: — Night—

After I showered, I dropped onto the bed, exhausted. This had been a day from hell. I closed my eyes and slipped into sleep.

I woke up to the sound of a loud crash.

Alex!

I jolted to a sitting position just as arms hauled me out of bed with surprising strength that would leave bruises. Pinned against a thick body, a hand over my mouth, I started to struggle just as the bedroom door swung open. I stopped fighting with the attacker behind me when four muffled shots destroyed the mattress I'd been sleeping on seconds before.

"He's not here!" a man's voice called out into the hallway.

Just then, a white wolf pounced on the man, throwing them both out of view. The arms holding me tossed me aside like a bag of rice back on the bed. I caught sight of silver hair rounding the door.

Growling and screams followed.

Alejandro!

I ran out of the bedroom and slid on blood leaking out of the dead guy sprawled on the floor just outside the door. His throat gone. Like *gone*. Then the eyes started to cave into his skull. His skin turned brittle and peeled away, revealing the bone underneath. Then even that crumbled and turned to ash along with the blood. All of it in the span of seconds measured by my raging heartbeat booming against my sternum.

The stench of rotten flesh and iron coated the back of my throat. This couldn't be real. I was having another nightmare. I forced myself to move. Dream or not. I needed to wake up.

I made it to the top of the landing just in time to be greeted by a macabre scene.

This wasn't real.

Wake up! Wake up!

A roar blasted inside the house. An inhuman sound on a level that threatened to make my ears bleed.

Run, Sebastian. This is real.

The bubble wrapped around my reality burst wide open. The monster with blue skin and horns ripped a man to shreds. The wolf tore at another. The blood. The smell. The ash. All of it was real.

Alex.

I ran to Alex's room and slammed into the door, swinging it open. Empty.

No. No.

Oh, God, please. I ran out of the bedroom. "Alex!"

A man, no, a thing with black eyes and no jaw, stood in front of me. A gun aimed at me.

Just then, Xcian crashed into me. The wolf jumped on the thing, and I shut my eyes as it tore into flesh. A wet sound of slurping followed. I screamed and fought against the body on me. Against Xcian. He lifted me off my feet in a bear hug. My blows meant nothing to him. Tears wet my cheeks. "Alex! Alex!"

"He's gone!"

"No! No!" I cried out, still trying to fight Xcian. He couldn't be dead. He couldn't. Xcian slammed me against the wall and secured my hands to my side.

"He left for the airport an hour ago! He's alive! Stop fighting!"

I stopped struggling. Alex. Gone to the airport on his way to New York. "What time—"

"Oh, for fucks sake," Xcian growled out, not letting me finish.

He grabbed my hand and dragged me down the stairs where the white wolf waited. Its maw tainted with blood and ash. Blood. Oh, God, I was trailing blood and ash with my bare feet. The residue between my toes. Under the ruins of the furniture, I saw...bodies. I struggled under Xcian's hard grip, pulling back and digging my feet in. "Oh, God! You killed them! You killed them! You psycho murdering monster!"

Xcian stopped and turned his body to me, letting his anger show. The guy was going to kill me. "If I wanted to kill you, I wouldn't be dragging you out of the house."

I reached for the handrail to the stairs with my free hand. "You killed them."

The wolf whimpered and wagged his tail, then walked outside and took a seat as if on guard duty. "Yes. They were here to kill *you* or did you miss the part where I saved your ass in the bedroom. Or should I have *waited* until they blew your brains out all over the bed?"

Bedroom. He'd been the one to pluck me out of the bed...I suddenly felt sick.

"Don't—" I heard Xcian say right before I spewed.

Not much for vomit, Xcian released me, and I took that opportunity to run. I sprinted over another decayed body near the back door. Thankfully, the door had been shot open, so it swung freely and fast. I was outside in the enclosed backyard. I just had to make it to the gate. A dozen or so paces left and—

Arms wrapped around my waist, forcing oxygen out of my lungs. Another burst of pain. I snapped my head back, hoping to connect with the soft cartilage of his nose, but got nothing but more curses. "Calm down. I'm not going to hurt you."

"Yeah, right," I cried out. Then I did something I hadn't done since I was ten. I screamed. A screeching, ear-splitting scream.

That seemed to have nailed my coffin shut. Xcian covered my mouth with his large hand, and I bit into his finger. Blood coated my lips. His blood. But he didn't move his hand away. Didn't flinch. His grip simply tightened. Then his lips glazed the shell of my ear. I heard soft, lulling music, a rumble in his chest, then it was lights out.

Chapter Six

Xcian

Sebastian lay on his side in the back seat of the Explorer, still blessedly knocked the fuck out. I smelled blood on him. The malice could've killed him, and it sent me into a blinding rage.

Zane had sent me to protect the sons of the man he'd been pining over for years. The guy had made an appearance at the club and Zane lost it. Knocked the guy out to protect him and took him like some fucking caveman. My brother, the eldest, heir, and idiot when it came to his damn heart. When Aris brought up the name and address of his sons, I had almost lost a lung.

Coincidence, my ass. No way both Zane and I could be attracted to the same bloodline. Was I attracted to the kid? I snatched a glance at him through the rearview mirror.

"This is so messed up," I said. Doofus grumbled beside me, and I glared at my brother-turned-wolf. "What are you doing here?"

He sneezed but didn't shift to his human version.

"Oh, you're going to explain yourself." I slammed an angry fist on the steering wheel. Then I called Zane to warn him. "The house has been compromised. I have the kid with me." On instinct, I snatched a glance at him through the rearview mirror again. Eyes still closed. Breathing. Alive.

"You're too fucking late, asshole," Zane growled out. "There was one waiting here for Eric. You are so fucking lucky he came out of this alive or I would've fucking ripped your fucking dick out of your fucking body. Tell me I'm lying. Just tell me."

I knew when to keep my mouth shut.

"Which one do you have?" Zane asked.

"Sebastian," I managed to say. "The other one took a flight out to New York early this morning."

"Good. Send a cleaning crew to wipe his house and take the boy to the mansion. They're involved now. We have to tell Father."

A pulsing pain started behind my eyelids. "I don't think that's a good idea, bro. You know what happens to humans when they venture into our world." *They die.*

There was a long pause, and I thought Zane had disconnected the call when he spoke. "He's my chosen, Xcian."

I bit back the growl that started slowly surging from my chest, and clutched the steering wheel hard, turning my knuckles white. If what Zane said was true, then Eric Diaz and his bloodline would always be at risk. That led me to glance back at Sebastian again, just to make sure he was okay. To ease my own soul. "He must agree in order for father not to harm his blood."

"Eric will agree when he learns what's at stake. Make sure the kid knows that he'll see his father so long as Eric agrees to my terms."

Because romance and dining the guy had been thrown over the cliff when Eric had learned of Zane's engagement to Serena. So now Zane intended on using Sebastian as leverage to get the man to do what he wanted, which at this point was *who the fuck knows*. "He'll hate you for it."

"So be it. Take the kid to one of our safehouses. I'll call you with instructions." Zane hung up.

I let out the growl I'd been holding inside. I owed Zane everything. My sanity. My life. I owed him my soul. And I had a feeling he was collecting payment.

After I calmed down, I called Chris to make arrangements with the cleaners and to have one of our assets in New York keep an eye out for Alejandro. I didn't tell him who the house belonged to. I knew Chris and Sebastian had been friends. Only friends. I'd made sure of that when I threatened Chris with torture if he ever laid a hand on the kid. Chris hadn't argued, though he did give me a look. The same look Leander gave me when he suspected that I'd been pining over a female. I never pined.

We reached the safehouse, a two-flat with a cellar deep in country farmland where no one would hear our prisoners' screams. On the outside, it looked like a normal two-story cottage. However, it had been reinforced with steel walls to limit the risk of our prisoners' escape. Every bedroom had a bed with iron chains infused with magical properties to tame even our own demons. And the cellar held items needed for interrogation. Not that anyone had ever survived our interrogation techniques. If Zane intended on using the kid as leverage, I had to lock him up in the cellar. Doofus whimpered as I took the stairs down to the containment area. Chains had been secured to steel beams and a small cot with a dirty, tattered mattress had been fastened to the far wall. I stopped in the center of the room, unable to move. This felt so damn *wrong*.

Sebastian was human, not malice. Innocent.

Leander shifted back to his human form. "You got to be kidding me, Ex. Is this what Zane wants?"

I remembered our options. Because we had one flaw—our *chosen*—if Eric refused Zane, Father would obliterate the human's bloodline. Sebastian included. That got me to move, and I carefully lowered Sebastian onto the bed. "For now. We have to keep him contained."

Leander shook his head. "This feels so wrong."

"Go get dressed and turn on the security camera. Zane's going to call with instructions." I looked at Sebastian's still form on the bed. Eyes closed, dark hair all over the place.

Leander gave one small shake of his head before he retreated up the stairs. As I clamped his ankle to the steel bed, I echoed Leander's feelings. Yeah, we weren't above reproach, and we had killed humans before, used them even to get to an enemy, but *this*, this felt so wrong on so many levels.

Sebastian shifted on the bed. My trance was wearing out. I didn't want to be here when he woke up. Couldn't bear to see whatever expression he reserved for me when he realized that he'd been right to run from me. I climbed the stairs two at a time and locked the door. The soundproof room meant no one would hear his screams.

"How is he?" Leander asked.

The thought that I had almost been too late to save him had messed with my head, and I had to restrain the compulsion to check on him again. Make sure he was okay. But he wasn't okay. He'd never be okay again. "Alive," I answered. "How did you end up at the house?"

He shrugged. "I heard Aris talking to you. Thought you might need help."

"This is the first time you've been out of the house in months, *months*, and you choose now? *Now*?" I clenched my hands into tight fists. Between Leander putting himself in danger to Sebastian being in danger, my patience waned.

"I'm supposed to be here. With you. With him." He lifted his chin to the door leading into the cellar. "You know it's true or you wouldn't have brought me here."

I shared my mother's gift of sight. Although, sight wasn't the correct term. It was more a feeling, an instinctual response that we couldn't ignore. And that instinct made me believe that I did need Leander with me.

"You are releasing pheromones, brother. My wolf senses it and I'm going to be humping your leg soon, so go feed."

Feed. I hadn't fed in days. "I can't yet. Zane is going to call, and we have to be ready for it." Just then, my phone buzzed. I looked at the caller ID, not that I hadn't already known who it'd be. "Here goes nothing." I answered the call.

"Let them talk," Zane said.

I wanted to tell my brother to go screw himself, but didn't. If we played this right, maybe Sebastian and his brother would survive this. "I hope you know what you're doing," I said as I headed back to the cellar.

Sebastian sat on the bed, head down, his hair covering his face as I approached him. He lifted his eyes to mine and his lips parted slightly, then he scowled, and I knew the bitch fest was going to start, so I cut him off with my cold words. "If your father does as he's told, then you'll see him again. Understand?"

The mention of his father seemed to temper him, and he snapped his mouth shut and nodded.

Our fingers brushed as I handed him the phone. His so damn cold. "Dad?" he said into the phone. His voice soft. I didn't even want to hear the conversation playing out on the other end of that call. If Zane expected Eric to accept and love him, this was not the way to do it. Even I knew that, and I knew shit about love. "Yeah, someone came to the house. I didn't know what to do." Sebastian lifted his eyes to mine, then quickly lowered them to his lap. "No. They said they're waiting for word from you so he can take me to you. Where's Alejandro? Is Alex okay? What about Mom? Dad, what's going on?" Whatever strength he had folded, and Sebastian started to cry.

I couldn't. I couldn't take this shit.

"I know you will, Dad," Sebastian said into the phone. "I love you."

I took the phone from his hand, needing to get away from the kid and his surging emotions thickening the air in the room. I hadn't fed, and feeding off his emotions was driving me insane. "Zane," I grumbled.

"If you hurt my son, I will fucking kill you. Do you hear me? I will find a way to *end* you." The human voice full of pain made me feel like shit.

Zane's voice came on. "Yeah."

"What's next?"

"Bring him to the ceremony."

"I'm not doing this. Fuck you and your tether. I'll ascend. I'll take the torch because you have lost your mind."

"Fuck you. I know what I'm doing. Just get him here." Zane hung up.

I squeezed the phone so damn tight, the screen cracked. I lifted my eyes to Sebastian watching me. "Why are you doing this?" he asked. "You don't have to do this."

I did have to do this because if Zane felt half the way I felt for this kid, he'd do anything to keep Eric safe. Even force him into a damn binding. I could imagine how losing Eric would drive my brother mad. How the demons must be feasting on his soul, waiting for Eric to deny him so that they could tear through my brother's body, killing him.

That was the fate we all had to look forward to when mating didn't work. When our *chosen* denied us. I'd kill Eric slowly if he hurt my brother.

Leander trotted inside in his wolf form and sat next to Sebastian on the bed. The blood and ash on his coat cleaned. The kid relaxed, and his long, thin fingers ran down the length of Leander's coat in long, languid strokes seemingly soothing the kid.

"You are beautiful," Sebastian said to the wolf on a hiccup. He didn't even bother to wipe his tears. Leander turned to Sebastian and licked his face. The kid let out a laugh that speared through my heart.

I approached the bed and Sebastian's smile faded; his expression turned fearful. Of me. I unclamped his ankle and dropped the chain on the floor with a loud clank. "Come on," I said. "You can shower and eat before resting in one of the upstairs bedrooms. Just leave the bathroom door open."

The kid didn't move. His reaction stung, or I was

just pissed and taking it out on him. I sneered at him. "Or do you prefer to stay here?"

Doofus whimpered. *Calm down.*

Before Sebastian could answer, I turned and climbed the stairs. I knew the human had to eat, so I busied myself in the small kitchen. Yeah, Mrs. Soto taught me how to cook after the last time I tried.

A few minutes later, I heard him climb the stairs. Doofus jumped on the sofa and glared at me as Sebastian slipped into the bathroom. The shower turned on shortly after. I pointed at my brother. "Don't. Just don't."

He groveled and lowered his head on his massive paws, blue eyes lifting to me. I rummaged through the drawers in the bedroom and found a pair of decent-sized sweatpants and a T-shirt. The kid stood a few inches shorter than me, but taller than Leander. The clothes should fit well enough. I entered the bathroom, which he had left open, and meant to leave the clothes on the toilet lid for him.

I did.

Until I glimpsed his lean body through the transparent shower curtain. Standing under the spray, eyes closed, head arched into the spout, he ran his hand down his long hair. I couldn't help but take him all in. He wasn't built like me. He looked softer. My eyes trailed along the light dusting of dark hair on his pelvis leading to his long, flaccid, uncut cock. My need for him surged dangerously close to the surface. I hadn't fed. The only explanation I had for my current want of him. Nothing else made sense.

He slowly ran his hand down his torso and his long length. Unable to look away from the slow swelling need of his member, my body responded to him, or shit, it was vice versa—he was responding to my pheromones. I didn't move, unable to look away like some sort of creeping asshole as he gave his cock a couple of long, smooth strokes. His eyes closed, his hips jerked slowly into his hand, and he moaned. Moaned! The sound of it had me moving closer, my body unable to fight the need to taste him. Just a small taste. His lips, his tongue, his cock. I wanted to lick him everywhere, explore his body. My erection pressed painfully behind my pants. I needed to touch him. The feeling so strange. I wasn't the cuddly type. I liked slamming into my catch from behind. I didn't do much licking or touching or even kissing, but with Sebastian, I wanted it all. Not a kid, but a man.

A whimper broke my trance, and I turned to find Leander at the door.

The sound made Sebastian realize he had an audience. "What are you doing in here?"

Heat blazed my cheeks. I never blushed. "I left you some clothes. Hurry up. Your dinner's getting cold," I said coolly, and gave Doofus a glare before walking out.

I ran my hand down the length of my cock through my pants. Leander was right. I had to hunt or risk letting my demon take over. And if that happened, I knew the kid wouldn't stand a chance.

Chapter Seven

Sebastian

I should've been angrier than I actually felt, knowing that Xcian had been watching me. Okay, so maybe I knew as soon as I got hard that he'd walked into the bathroom. His sheer closeness made me hornier than I'd ever been in my life. And being horny, made me feel normal. Like a man with a hard-on. The fact the doctors were right and that nothing was biologically wrong with me meant I had a chance to be normal. Except normal crashed the moment reality sank in. I'd been kidnapped by the only person who made me feel an erection. I only had to think of Xcian and how his hips moved as he drove his cock into that woman. To think about how it should've been me. Those thoughts had inflated my cock to a painful point, with no release.

It felt wrong. Xcian had kidnapped me, using me as leverage, and the boner overruled all of that. There was something wrong with me.

I scrubbed myself raw and made sure to clean the blood and ash between my toes.

Blood.

The image of those men torn to shreds and then decomposing as if on fast-forward, pulsed in my mind like fragments of someone else's reality. The gunshots, the screams, and then Xcian among it all. Ripping them open with his monster teeth and claws.

I placed my palm against the cool tiled wall and leaned my head forward, letting the water glide against my body. No. Xcian wasn't that type of monster. The white wolfdog hadn't been an accomplice to the carnage. I had made it up just like I made up the shadow that had been in the house the day I found my dad in the garage. I'd made up the whispers in my head, telling me to hurry and go save him. I imagined the explosion that had caused the beam my father's body had been hanging from to shatter, sending his lifeless body to the ground. That had been my thirteen-year-old self-projecting something else. An explanation for the inexplicable. That's what the therapist said. I'd imagined the voices, imagined the explosion that saved my dad's life because I needed to find reason in the event. Dad had been on the ground when I got there. Xcian wasn't a monster. And the white wolf was just a dog.

Oh, God. It didn't make it any better. Xcian and the dog had still killed those people and kidnapped me. Alejandro could be dead and Dad...Dad could be too. I couldn't lose them. The thought made me sick, and I couldn't stop my body from violently shaking until my legs gave up on me and I fell on my ass inside the tub. I hugged my knees tight into my body.

The water beating against me turned cold. I wasn't sure how long I sat under it, shivering, unable to move when Xcian appeared in the doorway. He watched me with no hint of compassion, with no expression at all. "Do you need help?" he asked, his voice cold.

"Fuck you," I snapped, and lowered my forehead to my knees, unsure if I could remain brave while still looking at him.

Words were all I had against him. I wasn't strong enough to fight him. And I wasn't sure if I even wanted to fight him. Shame felt like a toxic stone in my gut. My body's response to his voice, to being near him. Ashamed for wanting him.

He approached the bathtub and turned off the spray, then pulled the curtain aside. I still didn't want to look at him. I didn't want him to see the shame on my face for being a coward. For being mentally incapable of making sense without adding delusions to my reality. Warm hands under my chin guided me to look at him kneeling beside the tub. So close, I could see specks of ice blue within the silver rim of his eyes. They couldn't be real. No one had eye color like that.

"Everyone is fine." The sincerity in his voice grazed my skin. "Your brother, your mother, your father. They are all where they're supposed to be," he said. "No one. And I mean, *no one* will hurt you. I promise you that."

In my pathetic heart, I wanted to believe him. But it didn't change the fact that he still had me here against my will. "*You* will hurt me."

A shadow fell across his eyes for a heartbeat, then vanished. I wanted him to leave me alone.

He rose. "Get up," he said, a bit more stiffly than just a few moments ago. The true version of Xcian. The demanding, dangerous killer.

I got to my feet, trying not to feel dizzy but failing. I stumbled, and he held me in his arms, not caring that I was wet and naked. An electric charge coursed through me at the touch, and I hated my body's response to him. My dick in particular and the tingling that followed. For a second, I thought he was going to keep touching me, but he released me to grab a towel on the rack, then slung it over my shoulders. His eyes never met mine again as he gently dried my shivering body.

"If you're going to kill me, I'd prefer if you weren't nice to me. It's confusing." With that little bomb, he lifted his frost-colored eyes to mine, chilling me to the core. At least until he took a step away from me, leaving the towel over my shoulders.

"Get dressed. You have to eat something before we head out."

The command clear as day. *Do as I say or I will hurt you.*

Xcian nice to me? Yeah, right. At least he closed the door on his way out.

I dried and dressed in a pair of sweatpants that fit too big, and a shirt that made me look like a scrawny kid wearing his massive father's clothes. I wrung out my hair and dried it the best I could before straightening up the bathroom and hanging the towels to dry. I also took a quick scan of my escape options. The shower curtain pole was screwed into the wall. No weapon. Unable to bolt the door, I walked out of the bathroom, counted twenty paces to the open living room and kitchen area where Xcian was heating up some food. Real food. The scent of it made my stomach rumble.

That made Xcian scowl at me. His usual resting face.

"Sit," he ordered, gesturing to the small farm table in the kitchen.

I sat. A cold draft forced me to shiver. Nothing new. I tended to lean on the colder side temperature-wise. "I could use some shoes or socks." I wiggled my toes under the table, not that he could see.

"I'll make sure you have some before we leave."

"Where are we going?"

"To see your father."

Right. I poked my food while he ate without restraint. And he ate a lot. I managed to eat some of the eggs, but I gave the wolfdog my bacon. The orange juice made my head a little clearer. I started thinking about my plan of escape again and gave the place a good look. The front door didn't have a deadbolt. A good sign.

"What are you looking for?"

An escape route. "Wondering if Mrs. Soto is your accomplice."

"I've learned to cook so I could feed my victims without help."

Victims. The word made me shiver again. And not in any type of a good way. I needed to get out. My eyes wandered back to the door.

Xcian dropped his fork on his plate with a clang. "You think you could navigate the five hundred miles through woodlands on foot?"

"You have a vehicle."

"And the keys are on me," he said, leaning forward. "You think you can take me on?" He shoved back in his chair, making the thing scrape along the wood floor. The wolf whimpered and took a step back as Xcian stood and grabbed my wrist.

"Hey," I snapped, struggling, but he didn't let go until we were in the living room on the plush rug.

"Come on, badass, hit me." He lifted his hands in a boxing stance looking ridiculous. "Get it over with and try so we can get past that you are never leaving my sight."

I sneered at him. "You outweigh me by at least a hundred pounds." I may have exaggerated. "You think I'm actually going to fight you fairly?"

With a smirk, he invaded my space. Placing his leg behind mine, he shoved me, and I fell on the sofa behind me. I think I hurt my pride more than my butt. "You really like picking on people smaller than you, don't you? Make you feel all badass?"

He smiled, and that smile made me feel tingly inside. The first time I saw an actual expression of glee on his face instead of a scowl. I got up, acted as if I were going to dust my hands, then launched at him. My intent had been to echo the move he did on me. Leg behind his and a shove. I got the leg, but the guy was solid muscle. He simply slapped my hand away from his chest, spun me around so that my back hit his chest and he had both my wrists secured in his tight grip. Tight, but not painful. I felt his breath on my cheek as he leaned into me. I could've sworn he inhaled me. It sent shivers running down my spine. His erection brushed my ass before he shoved me away with a push that had me stumbling forward.

It was easier to be mad at him. "You're such an asshole."

He approached, but I stood my ground. "I saved your life."

"You kidnapped me." Every cell in my body told me to take a step away from him as he narrowed the gap between us. I didn't. Standing close enough that I could practically take in all his perfect, unblemished features.

"I'm keeping you safe."

"From whom?"

He licked his full lips, his tongue darting out slowly and slipping back into his mouth. He was messing with me. I knew it. Like the way he looked at me in the bathroom. Like the way he had practically invited me for a threesome when he'd been humping that woman. This was all some sick joke for him. Shame slid through me. I still wanted to feel his lips against mine. But I didn't move. I couldn't move.

"Fuck it," he grumbled, and fisted my shirt, pulling me into his body. My mouth crashed against his and we were kissing. Kissing! Or rather, he was kissing me. Tugging my lips, repositioning his mouth, and plunging his tongue into me, his hand in my hair, securing me at the back of the head. Pressing me. And I let him. I followed his movements, explored his mouth, tasted him. So soft and hard all at once. It made me dizzy. I shouldn't want this. I should've stopped him. I didn't.

A moan escaped my mouth as his hands slipped under my shirt and touched my skin. The sound seemed to charge him because he pressed his body harder against mine, his leg between mine. I rutted against him, seeking the delicious friction that jolted me out of any sanity I had left. The explosion of senses from his mouth owning mine, his tongue sucking and nipping my lips, his hands on my skin, too painful without a form of release.

I opened my eyes to his beautiful face as he fisted my hair and pulled me back. He licked my throat, sucking my earlobe. Then his lips were brushing the shell of my ear. "What do you want from me, Sebastian?" His voice had somehow gone deeper. The heat of his breath against my neck forced me to shiver. I couldn't think.

Think.

Thought went out the window. My body belonged to him.

"I want more," I whispered. I just didn't know what more meant. And he wasn't about to explain it to me. Instead, he slowly lowered his hands and cupped me over my sweats. I arched into the touch. My cock painfully sensitive. But hard. For him. "Make me come, Xcian," I managed to croak out. "Please." I wanted it so badly.

He didn't deny me this. Instead, he took my hand in his and led me up the stairs to one of the bedrooms. My eyes didn't have a chance to adjust to the dark surroundings inside the room when he kissed me again.

And I let him.

Chapter Eight

Xcian

I should've gone slow and careful. Not my style. I hungered and needed, commanded and took. And I took all he offered me, explored his mouth in ways that I'd never opted to do before. Kisses were too intimate. The soul too easy to capture with a kiss. My death would one day be sealed with a kiss, just not now. Or if it were to be this kiss, it'd be worth it. Despite the kid's innocence, I'd lit a fire under him, and he matched me step by step. Sucking, nipping, moving back in deeper, absorbing me all in.

I led him to the bedroom my brothers used whenever they needed to control the demons inside of me. This one hadn't been tainted with the blood of our prisoners. This one had been stained with my sweat and carried my scent. The scent I wanted on him.

I shut the bedroom door on Doofus, ignoring his whimpering. A warning for me to stop whatever I was doing with this kid. This human male. A male I wanted to devour. I wanted to explore every inch of his skin, every heated breath. I wanted to hear my name on his lips as he came. I couldn't get enough of his mouth, and explored every inch, digging my hand into his thick hair. The male, soft and cool to my heat. He had no facial hair and his skin felt as soft as I had imagined. He had features that were soft and yet sharp. Light brown eyes that seemed to cut into the soul, and soft, full lips. Lips meant to be sucked and devoured. I'd waited too long to feed. The only damn reason I could come up with for this undeniable need I had for him.

This whole reasoning threw me off my game and I bit him hard. He whimpered into my mouth, pliant, needy.

The back of his knees hit the bed, but I didn't let him fall onto it. Not yet. I pulled his shirt over his head and yanked his sweats down, freeing his cock. He quickly stepped out of them as I grazed my fingers through the hairs just under his navel, down his long shaft to his balls. His erection was like soft velvet along my palm. No question that Sebastian was all male. And I wanted him still. He held onto my shoulders, legs shaking, his cock weeping with precum. I ran my finger along the soft cleft, spreading the liquid around his head, my mouth watering for a damn taste.

He wasn't going to last. "Sit down," I ordered.

He sat on the bed. His hand covered his erection, and a hint of blush peppered his gorgeous cheeks. I ignored my own painful needs and cupped his chin. "Don't cover yourself from me. Ever."

I wasn't sure how he'd respond to my order. I couldn't help it. I was a dominant ass. Better the kid knew that now.

I pulled off my shirt as I kicked out of my boots, then lowered my jeans as he watched. His eyes widened as my cock bobbed in front of him. I palmed my shaft close to his face. He licked his lips and lifted his eyes to mine. "One day, I'll let you suck it. Would you like that?"

He nodded. A brief, barely there movement. My fingers dug into his hair. "I love how your hair feels," I said, unsure why I said that. I kept talking like an idiot. "It feels soft." He cocked his head into my touch and my demon purred. What the fuck? I had to get this over with. Whatever I meant to do.

"Lay back on the bed," I ordered.

He did. Spread out before me to taste. I climbed on the bed, guiding his thighs open, and gave his cock a slow lick from base to tip. I paid extra attention to the tip, giving it a circled lick, and sucked it into my mouth. The familiar scent of wildflowers in a field of green grass under a warm summer sky glazed his skin and flooded my senses. A clean scent. All him. He tasted of musk with an underlying sweetness I'd never sensed before.

I lifted my eyes and caught the hunger in his expression. Lids half-opened, pupils blown, lips swollen and parted as he inhaled sharply. The sight of him breathtaking. He dug one hand into my hair, releasing the tie and letting the strands fall around my face, brushing his thighs. He petted me as if I were the most valuable thing in this world, a soft touch. Gentle in its sincerity. I almost whimpered, but pressed my lips together and concentrated on what I was doing to his cock. Not that I had any clue. I'd never sucked a cock before, but I went with it. Taking him to the back of my throat, listening to his moans edging me along. My own erection hard and stiff, needing attention. But not yet. Too enthralled with the male under me with every moan he released.

"Xcian," he breathed out.

My name falling in ecstasy from his lips made me

purr. The soft rumbling pulled the last of his resolve and he exploded into my mouth. Semen filled the back of my throat and I swallowed it all, licking the tip as he turned boneless under me.

Damn, the kid looked delicious. I wanted more of him, needed more of him. My erection painful. He planted his heels on the edge of the mattress, dropping his knees open, splayed for me to take. And I wanted that more than I had ever wanted anything in my life. I kneaded his thighs, spreading his ass cheeks, wanting to see the pucker of his hole. I wanted to taste it too. I wasn't done with him. Not by a long shot. I was just about to move when a soft shiver ran through him, and I looked up to see his forearm across his eyes. The taste of shame coated my tongue. A subtle acrid taste. Although he had submitted to me, he regretted it too.

"Sebastian," I whispered. My voice unusually soft and full of an emotion I didn't want to examine closer. I lowered myself on his body, using my elbows to keep myself from crushing him fully. He still had his hands on his face. "Please, baby, talk to me." *Baby? WTF?*

"I can't. I'm sorry. I want to. I just…I've never…I, uh."

The truth slammed into me harder than a ton of bricks. "You're a virgin?"

I said the wrong thing because the regret and shame soured my tongue as he covered his face. Yeah, human emotions sucked. I didn't even want to label the pinch of pain just under my sternum. "It's okay," I soothed, and slid to his side, cradling him in my arms. Once tucked into me, his head under my chin, he lowered his hands away from his face and hugged me back.

"I'm sorry." His voice cracked. "I've never...I mean, I've never."

"It's okay, Sebastian." I ran my fingertips up and down his arm, hoping to soothe him, while a host of emotions rattled through me. I'd been his first. Me. A strong sense of pride surged through me that he'd given me this. "It was perfect." As perfect as anything I'd ever experienced. Although my erection hadn't been tended to, my demons remained silent. I kissed the top of his head and closed my eyes, letting my mind slip away as I listened to his breathing even out. For a fleeting moment, the world slipped away in darkness. Not an evil darkness, just a floating darkness. A soul without pain. A soul content to just let go. And I did. I let go. For the first time, I felt a silent peace within me. Something I'd never felt before. Being with Sebastian, having him safe in my arms, felt right. I hadn't realized this was what Zane must've experienced with Eric. The reason he would burn the world to keep Eric safe. For a moment, I envied my brother. I almost dropped into a deeper sleep when I heard a soft click echo in the room. The bed shifted as Sebastian rolled away from my arms.

I blinked open my eyes and blinked again. Sebastian stood pressed against the closed door, watching me with an expression of sheer panic. I started to move, breaking through the calm sagginess of sleep, when I felt a tug at my wrist and cool metal against my skin.

It took a heartbeat to realize what he'd done, and I lunged for him. I didn't get far when the chain reached its limit and pulled me back into the bed. No way. I yanked hard at the chain, using my free hand to wrench it free, even though these chains were magical. They were made specifically to tame *me* in case I became rabid. Something that had happened a handful of times in the centuries I'd lived on this realm. My energy began to deplete just for exerting myself.

"What the fuck are you doing?" I snarled. Betrayal raged through me in its purest form. Then panic set in, and I started testing the limits of the chain. And its integrity. I wanted to roar. To shift. To release my demon and tear Sebastian Diaz piece by piece.

"Stop it!" he cried out as I continued to tear at the chains. "You're going to hurt yourself."

"I am going to get out and peel your flesh from your fucking bones!"

Sebastian paled. I was an idiot to trust him. To let my guard down. To fall for this level of betrayal again.

He seemed to get his wits and started to gather his clothes. He pulled on his sweats, *my* boots, and his shirt, then he picked up my jeans and pulled out the truck's keys. He dropped the jeans and lifted the keys so that I could see the results of my idiocy. "You think you can get far from me? I will hunt you down and end you!" I roared, but the more I tugged, the more the magical brace drained me of my power. Had I been completely bound, I wouldn't have had the strength to even move.

Then Doofus started to howl somewhere in the house. That made Sebastian pause, and fear replaced resolve. I used it. "That's right, fucker. Doofus is going to tear you apart. You remember what he did to those fuckers at your brother's place?"

Sebastian shook his head as if warding away the image. "That wasn't real." He took a step away from me until his back slammed against the door again. More afraid of me than of Doofus.

"Oh, yes it was real."

"But you turned into a monster too."

All the blood drained from my body, and I didn't move. Humans couldn't see our real form. Only those species linked to the ethereal could see the true form of the Nine, including our bonded mates.

Sebastian shook his head again as if trying to clear the visual from memory.

Zane had messed up big time with Eric's bloodline. If Eric's bloodline was something more…if Eric had a bloodline into the ethereal, then they were at risk of everything gunning for us. I had to stop Sebastian from running. He wouldn't last out in the world without protection. Without me. But I couldn't do shit to him. My influence didn't work on him. I should've realized that night at the club when he'd broken away from my allure, when he pulled away from his desire for me in the bathroom.

Unable to influence him with my power, I played with his fear. "Let me go, Sebastian." I put as much force into my words as my weakening magic allowed. Any other human would've adhered to my command. Sebastian didn't move. "Release me."

"No!"

Before I could growl and demand it like a petulant child, he turned and threw the door open. I caught a glimpse of Doofus for a fleeting moment before the door slammed shut.

Fuck! I couldn't do anything but roar, so I did.

Chapter Nine

Sebastian

I slammed the door shut just as Xcian roared. An inhuman sound that popped my eardrums. My legs gave out and I slid to the floor with the door at my back. Where I'd trapped my lover. My lover! After we had sex. My first sexual experience and I had manacled the man to the bed. My kidnapper! And I wanted to do as he ordered. I wanted to release him, to apologize for what I did to him. I wanted him to hold me like he'd held me when I lost it. A stupid virgin who cried at the loss of my sexual innocence, though I still technically hadn't lost my virginity. Xcian had been kind. Hadn't pushed me for more. He'd hugged me.

Hugs were a thing after sex, right? Not murder. Xcian was going to murder me, and I still smelled him on me, felt his mouth on my cock, tasted his tongue on my lips. I groaned and dropped my face in my hands. Oh, God, what had I done?

The roar stopped. Now he just fought the chains and cursed.

I wiped my tears, and Doofus, who'd been sitting curiously watching me, got up, tail wagging, and licked my face. I hugged the large, soft animal. "I'm so sorry," I cried into his neck. "I had no choice. I didn't." After I found the chains, I was afraid Xcian meant to use them on me. I had no choice.

I leaned back and tapped the door with my head. I had to think. *Think, Sebastian.* What's next? I had to get out of this house. I lifted my fist, the keys digging into my palm. "Time to go," I said, and got to my feet.

Doofus whimpered but he followed me down the stairs and out of the house. Patches of gray clouds thickened overhead. A hint of static energy in the air. It'd rain soon. I had to be far away when that happened.

Far. Far. Away.

I opened the door for Doofus, who climbed in with no trouble, and I got into the driver's side. "Okay," I breathed out. "I could do this."

No. I couldn't do this. I failed my driver's exam in high school. Decided it was something I didn't need to survive. Wrong. So wrong.

I knew the basics. Everyone knew the basics. I had the key, now I pushed the start button. Nothing happened. Doofus sneezed beside me. "Give me a break, okay? I've never driven before."

Even the dog looked shocked. Whatever. I pushed the brakes, then pushed the start button and the thing just made a clicking noise. I got nothing. As if it'd rather die than let me drive it.

"No, way."

I didn't know much about cars, but I knew a click was bad. It got worse when I popped the hood open and found an empty space where the battery should be. No battery. "Where would he have put the battery?" And how did he know I'd try to escape? Doofus woofed and I let him out. "You wouldn't by chance know where he'd put the battery?"

Doofus lowered his head, ass in the air, and

wagged his tail. Sometimes I wondered if the dog I'd seen rip throats was this tamed animal at my feet.

Think, Sebastian. The battery.

I ran back into the house, tearing it up, looking for the thing and maybe a phone. I found keys to the garage and shed, but no battery and no phone. All I found were more chains, more pointy instruments of torture, a motorcycle I couldn't drive, and a gun. Doofus made a low, growly noise at the back of his throat as I picked it up. "Just in case. Just…" The thing was heavy in my hand. Violent. "Just in case. I won't use it." I kept it and entered the house again just as something crashed on the floor overhead.

Xcian had turned into a rabid animal in the bedroom. Doofus remained at my side, but even the dog gave me a reproachful look. As if I'd made a mistake. "He kidnapped me. They have my father. What do you expect me to do?" I tried to reason. With a *dog*. "I need a phone."

The dog grumbled and dropped onto his belly.

"You are no help," I scolded.

Xcian had a cell phone. He'd let me use it to talk to my dad. I looked up at the ceiling as if I could see him through the layers that separated us. I listened instead. The cursing stopped, and the silence became eerier.

Doofus jumped to his feet as if he were ready to move. "Stay here," I ordered the dog. The last thing I needed was for the dog to get a clue and listen to his owner tell him to sic me.

Doofus had been at the house with Xcian. I had seen him attack the men too. Whimpering, softness aside, Doofus was also a killer. "Stay," I reiterated again. The dog sat down, and I could've sworn he gave me a dirty look before following me up the stairs. No one ever took me seriously. Not my brother, not my dad, not even the *dog*.

I reached the bedroom but refused to enter. I didn't want to see. But I needed my brother more than I needed to be afraid. And to get to my brother, I needed the phone. Alex would tell me what to do. He'd know. I trusted him with everything. Well, mostly everything.

With my ear to the door, I listened for anything on the other side that could give me a clue as to the man's state of mind. Xcian could've gotten a projectile weapon and he'd use it as soon as I opened the door.

You have a gun, moron.

Stepping away from the door, I aimed the gun at it as if I could see him on the other side. Would I be able to shoot him? No. I wouldn't.

Then Doofus barked and I jerked. The gun fired and the bullet sailed through the door. Doofus quickly scampered away, and I threw my body against the wall beside the door. My heart thudded against my ears.

Ohmygod. I killed him. I killed him. The silence stretched on forever. I killed him. "Xcian?" The last time I said his name was in the throes of passion. Now I sounded like a scared little boy. I got no response. *Please be alive. Please.* Tears prickled the back of my eyes. "Xcian, are you okay?" I thumped the back of my head against the wall. Stupid question if he was dead.

"Why don't you come in here and find out," came a gravelly, pissed-off, deep voice.

I let out a relieved breath. Better pissed-off than dead. "Do you need medical attention?" More silence. I hadn't expected him to answer. I waited until I couldn't anymore. The apology stuck in my throat. "Listen. I just need to use your phone. I'll call whoever you want to come get you. Okay?" That was reasonable. "Dammit, you kidnapped me. My father could be in danger, and you are helping whoever has him." The thought of that made me sick to my stomach. "I can leave. Walk out of here. I don't need the truck. I can find someone. Find a phone somewhere else." I should. But it meant leaving him like this and I wasn't sure if anyone would find him in time to save him. Why I cared was for idiot me to consider later.

"Come in, then," came the deep voice. The vibration of it against my skin.

Make a choice, Seba. I heard my brother's voice say.

I took a deep breath and let it out, then I opened the door and entered the room. Xcian laid spread out on the bed, naked. His back against the headboard. The bullet hole had landed a few inches to the left of his head. My stomach rolled. I could've killed him. He could've been dead because of me.

"Little boys shouldn't play with guns."

The space between us vibrated with something toxic, fueled by his anger.

The gun was still in my hand. I unclamped my fingers around it, and it fell at my feet with a thud. "I didn't mean...I mean, it was..." I tried to find words that wouldn't come because, at that moment, Xcian's free hand had started to slowly move down his ripped abs, and he sifted his fingers into his pubes. His cock fully hard, with angry veins bulging on the underside. A liquid pearl-colored drop slowly traveled down his shaft, and I followed it with my eyes. He slowly folded one leg and spread his knees. Exposing himself. All of him. And Xcian was perfect. I swallowed the thick wad in my throat, my heart drumming a senseless beat inside my chest.

I slid my gaze from his strong legs, up to his throbbing member, his hard abs, chest, and finally his cold eyes. His long silver hair draped over his shoulders. Sweat gleamed on his forehead. Had to be from the exertion of trying to tear away from the chain because no one in their right mind would find being held hostage a good time to masturbate. Right? And yet, Xcian gripped his long, thick cock as if it were something he needed to control and started to stroke himself all the while his glare tore through me. Those eyes. The intensity of them held me, and threatened to weaken my resolve. To tear down whatever will I had that kept me from licking the wet trail that pearl had left behind. From smothering him with my body, from letting him do whatever he wanted to me.

I wanted, no, I *needed* something only he could provide. I didn't care to label the need, to define it, so long as he sated me. Only him.

His lips parted, his lids lowered to half-mast, long lashes fanned his cheeks as he dipped his head back, exposing his throat. A moan escaped his mouth. A tangible thing that went straight to my own dick now tenting my sweats. The room turned hazy. Heat bloomed inside of me. Something warm and good. Something that melted all my troubles away.

Xcian arched his hips, his hand stroking faster. The pearl of liquid desire thickened at his tip, and I wanted to taste it. To taste him. "Come to me," he said. His voice all sex and promises. My legs moved by no will of my own. Closer. I needed Xcian like I needed to breathe. The tether between us strong, but so good.

Then I bumped my knee into the bed's frame, sending a shot of pain through me, and I blinked away the haze. Xcian hadn't stopped masturbating. His lips parted, looking so damn glorious. But...no. He was the enemy.

He gave one final jerk and came hard. Liquid spurted in a jet stream onto his stomach and the force of it knocked me back, away from the bed and the need to lick him.

His chest rose and fell as he breathed deeply, coming down from the high, then he opened his eyes. Two glowing pins in the fading light. "I could use a wet towel, if you don't mind."

Before I could think, I rushed to the bathroom. I let out the breath I'd been holding and used the sink to support myself. Being around Xcian was toxic. His insatiable lust was thick and tangible, and something I wanted. So damn bad, it hurt. I shoved my pants down and took hold of my own painful erection. It took nothing but three strokes for me to find my release. I bit my lip hard to keep from moaning. And when I finished, I wiped myself, washed my hands, and walked out with a wet towel for him.

Xcian smirked at me from the bed. "I could've helped you with that," he said.

I tossed him the towel. "The cell phone," I said, my voice shaking.

With no hurry in the world, he wiped his mess from his body. Then he lowered his eyes to the foot of the bed. "My jeans. You missed it in your haste."

I kept from sneering at my stupidity and picked up the jeans. Sure enough, I pulled the small device from his back pocket. Of course, it was password protected. I lifted my eyes to him. "Password."

"Say please."

I sighed. I should leave. Just run. Take my chances in the woods. Go anywhere. Not here. Instead, I gritted out the word. "Please." I entered the password he gave me.

"You shouldn't get your brother involved in this. If you care about him."

I glared at him. "Of course I care about him. I have to warn him."

"I told you. Your family is safe. If he comes back here, then that may change."

I hesitated. What he said made sense. Alex would come back for me and to do what? Be a target too. "What, then?" My voice cracked again. "What can I do to get my dad back?" His expression remained neutral, with no sign of any emotion. He didn't care. He didn't care about anything.

Xcian slowly got to his feet. His movement was limited to only stand flush against the bed. Dark storm clouds moved like smoke inside his pale-colored eyes, focused intently on the door. The room darkened, shadows moved across the floor, and the ground began to shake.

"Unlock me." It wasn't an order or a threat. It sounded like a plea drawn out by fear. Which made me afraid.

"I don't have a key."

The bedroom door swung violently open and crashed against the wall. A whirlwind at the threshold sent a gust of wind inside the room. The dark tendrils solidified, and a woman stepped out of its enclosure. A woman with hair like a dark void and eyes like midnight. Skin as pale as Xcian's eyes and lips as red as blood. I knew her. From somewhere I couldn't place. The memory surging but still just out of reach.

Her eyes bore into Xcian. *My* Xcian who stood naked watching the woman. The need to protect him had me moving between them, cutting off her line of sight to him. It put me close enough for him to snap my neck and run with this creepy woman. But he didn't kill me. Instead, he cupped my waist and tried to move me aside. But I didn't budge. "Who the hell are you?" I blurted.

Wrong thing to say.

Pain followed. And I screamed.

Chapter Ten

Xcian

Sebastian had taken a protective stance in front of me. Protecting me from Genesis. A threat. It didn't matter that he didn't even have a weapon. It mattered that he used his body to shield me. *Me*. As if I were his to protect.

"Who the hell are you?" Sebastian asked.

Genesis was the bitch imprinted on one side of Charon's *obol*. Lucifer etched on the other side. Payment for the ride into the afterlife. And Sebastian gave her no respect. Something lurched forward and slammed into my sternum. A feeling I didn't even want to label. Not now. But Genesis turned her eyes to me, a head taller than Sebastian, I could still lock eyes with her. And she knew. The slight curve of those bloodred lips indicated as much.

Then magic shot out of her hands and Sebastian slammed into the wall, hanging like a fly caught in a snare, his eyes open but unseeing, drifting into another world. Terrified, he started to scream.

Genesis locked eyes with me. "This is the pet you chose to replace *me*?"

She was killing him. I felt his life draining away a mere distance from me, and the damn shackles continued to drain my power. But not my raw anger. Not my hate. And not my need to protect what was *mine.*

I shifted.

Fangs pushed out of my gums, muscles expanded, flesh tore and reframed itself to fit my massive frame. My skin turned a pale blue and two horns pushed out of my forehead, curling about six inches long. I pushed into my ethereal power, where the bend in reality was strongest. The space between here and there. The area where evil resonated deepest.

And I opened the connection.

The world unfolded in front of me. A burning chaos of destruction led by the malice but orchestrated by something bigger. A spreading darkness pulsed. My vision faded and returned with an image of my mother. Pale silver hair dipped in blood. Her silver eyes haunted as she lifted her bloodied hands, a body at her feet. The image faded back to fire and I felt Genesis all around me. The beginning of all things.

"Isn't it arresting?" she said. Her lips brushed the shell of my ear. The familiar feeling of finding home enclosed me with a sense of purpose. Though it was all an illusion. Genesis had showed me kindness, opened my heart, and then she bled me to make her army.

I fought against her hold over me. A powerful switch in my headspace. I wasn't the kid she'd trained, abused, and left for dead. I wasn't the vulnerable teenager starved for her affection. No longer the vessel she required. I'd been tainted by the demons I'd collected over the centuries, and I opened their cages. Power jettisoned into my body. I vibrated with it.

"Everything you touch will be destroyed, Sword of

the Anunnaki. You will never be free."

The power of Nine rushed through me and I pushed her out of my headspace. The darkness swirled around me, and the cuff snapped. Demons were creatures of visceral needs. They all wanted to wreak havoc and destruction. They thrived on it. Lived off the energy it exuded. And they were loyal if you gave them what they craved. I did that now as I released Moloch. The demon pounding away at my temples knew hate on an intimate level. The beast hated Genesis as much as I did, and the demon surged inside of me. The power coursing through my veins felt euphoric. My body sparked with the intensity of it and my demon of lust clung to it like a sap on a tree. Filling me with its power as well.

I lunged for her. The bitch had nowhere to run.

I clamped my claws around her throat, lifted her off the floor, and body slammed her back down. The hardwood flooring exploded under her now solid weight because the bitch couldn't turn to smoke while in my grip. My body felt too stretched, my senses muted everything but the power coursing through me. A mixture of pleasure and pain. Genesis's dark eyes contained swirls of light, my light, the light I pulled from her source. Because at the end of the day, Genesis was just a demon, and I was Anunnaki, made by the gods to protect humanity from evil like her and now she was mine.

I lifted her by the throat, her feet dangling, feeling the delicate bones on her neck give. Her pale skin turned ashen, eyes caved to the back of her skull, and my body pulsed, consumed by the energy of her. Eating it up.

The world around me shook with a loud blast. Windows exploded inward, and pain traveled down my leg. A wound already healing. Then another on my shoulder. Burned through flesh healed. The human stood at my flank, a weapon in his hand, and my heart melted.

Fucking melted.

I stumbled and released Genesis, who immediately vanished.

The world around me burst into shards of light as I came back into myself, pushing all the demons back into their cages with the last of my energy. I crumbled into his arms, struggling to breathe. His lips moved above me, and I heard his soft voice like a warm blanket.

"It's okay." Tears slid down his face. "I got you. You're safe."

He had me. I knew his name. I knew him. "Sebastian." His name ghosted my lips. The only good thing I had. The world tilted and I with it.

****

I woke up in another bedroom staring at familiar dark eyes. My body hurt, my tongue felt as if I'd swallowed sand, and my eyes were sensitive to even the dim light in the room. I groaned as I sat up.

"Dude, you almost exploded," Basil, my brother, said, doing the whole hand gesture, sound effect thing as if I didn't know the mechanics of an explosion. Though flesh and tissue would've been more like a popped balloon than an explosion.

My body was one giant vessel of pain as he handed me a cup of water, which I drank greedily. "What happened?" My mind still fuzzy, it took a moment to figure out what century I'd landed on.

"You did something stupid, like always."

The memory of it slowly came back to focus. Demons. Power. Genesis and… "Sebastian?"

Basil lifted his chin to the other body I'd missed on the bed. Sebastian slept curled on his side, facing me. "Leander blew the whistle on whatever this—" He motioned between me and Sebastian. "—is."

The hairs on the back of my neck stood on end. "You were both trashed when we got here. The room shredded. Had I not seen what really happened, I would've been jealous. I'm still jealous. That boy is hot."

The pulsing in my head returned, and it had nothing to do with my demons. "What are you talking about?"

Basil chuckled. "Your greatest hits, bro. You do know the rooms have video surveillance. Though no audio. Too bad."

I wanted to strangle him as heat rose to my cheeks at the thought of being seen giving Sebastian a blowjob. I'd always been on the receiving end of that, not *giving* it. And I usually didn't care who saw me in what naked condition, but I wanted to protect Sebastian's privacy. "Delete the shit."

"But—"

"Now," I growled.

"Fine. I'll have Aris—"

"Aris?" I felt sick to think that my fifteen-year-old brother saw too.

"Yeah," Basil said. "Duh, he handles this stuff. Tech stuff. Nothing ever works around me."

Because he was still living the 16th-century greatest

hits. "How much time do we have before the mating?"

"If we leave now, we'll make it just in time. Zane's pissed, by the way. But we're all here. Jolly and ready to test fate."

"Can you give us a moment?"

Basil's expression softened. He nodded and walked out, closing the door behind him. I placed the glass of water on the end table and slid beside Sebastian on the bed. Close enough that his breath brushed my face. As my mind cleared, I remembered him dying. The terrible feeling of loss that followed and doing something apocalyptically stupid. Letting my demons free. Giving them power over me. Demon and vessel had a symbiotic relationship. We fueled each other but one always had control. If the vessel lost control, too much power would rip right through the vessel. I'd seen my brothers pop because of a miscalculated attempt to use more than what their body allowed. The reason we were stronger with a bonded mate. To share the power between us.

I slid a strand of hair away from Sebastian's forehead. So why was I still alive? I should've popped.

Sebastian had seen me. I wondered what he thought of me now. The monster. The brutal killer. The kidnapper. For the first time in my long life, I wanted to be human. Someone he could share his life with. But unlike Zane, I had no delusions about what happened to people we cared about. They died, violently. Or they betrayed us. I didn't believe in happily ever afters.

I remembered the sharp pain that had eventually pulled me away from Genesis. The gun. Sebastian had shot me and saved my life.

It was his fault in the first place, moron.

He had shackled me to the bed after we had sex. After I held him and wanted to protect him. The betrayal sank in like everything else. Sebastian wasn't my savior. He was my penance. My sin. And I would burn because of him.

Chapter Eleven

Sebastian

The darkness didn't last. It pulsed. Faded in and out. Dreamlike visions swam in front of me, but they didn't feel like dreams. This felt real. Like a video call with someone in real time. Somewhere. I couldn't think. I could only see.

And like a switch had been turned on, I saw Alejandro.

Crucified in the center of a dark hall, raised above a dais. His head lolled forward, arms stretched out to the max, skin blistered, oozing with blood. Naked. The smell of sulfur hung in the air along with the iron smell of blood and the putrefaction stench of human decay.

I started to move forward, only to be stuck in place. "Alex!" I screamed. My voice was raw. Then shadows peeled off the wall beside me, solidified into a dark presence with no face. Only evil.

"Are you strong enough to save him this time?" The words pierced through my heart.

Alex slowly lifted his head, eyes bloodshot. Wet tracks down his cheeks. "Run, Seba. Run!"

I jolted awake. My eyes flung open, and I let out a little whimper I bit back before it turned into more. After a moment, the room came into focus. A bed. Dark walls. The sound of a shower running. The scent of

Xcian around me. The warmth of him still an echo on my skin. I let out a sigh. Just a nightmare. Until I remembered the woman. My screams. And Xcian. His pain became mine. His screams in my head had drowned out everything else. The sense of him clawing his own skin as if a prisoner in his own body right before I shot him. The bullets had jolted him back into his human form.

Xcian wasn't human.

I quickly cupped my neck, searching for bite marks. Vampire? I felt nothing and almost giggled from a sort of crazed hilarity that wasn't really funny at all. Then someone knocked on the door and my heart lunged into my throat. If Xcian was showering who the hell—

The door opened and a dark-haired god of all manly creations walked inside, backlit by radiant light. Black eyes, thick brows and lashes. Broad shoulders and ripped, but still able to blend in with the shadows. His dark eyes landed on me, and I never wanted to fall asleep again. Those eyes, chased by nightmares. I shivered and was grateful when those eyes slowly turned to Xcian now at the bathroom door.

"It's time." That voice brought images of claws on a chalkboard.

"We'll be right down," Xcian said.

The man's eyes languidly met mine again before he turned back out. He left the door open, and I half expected the shadows to follow him out. "Who's that?" I asked.

"Noah. My brother."

Apart from their creepiness, they looked nothing alike. "Is he also a demon?" I snapped. My voice sounded braver than I felt.

Xcian didn't even flinch. No emotion crossed his features. Nothing. "You have no idea what we are, so I suggest you follow my fucking orders."

The rumble in his voice made me shiver. "Where are we going?"

"To see your father. Make sure he does what he needs to do to keep breathing."

I swallowed the lump in my throat. The fact that he had taken me in his arms, his mouth, his touch, when I meant nothing to him, when he could blatantly threaten my father's life, twisted all my insides. A monster in an alluring shell. And I hated myself for wanting more of him.

When I didn't move, he sighed and started opening and closing drawers until he found clothes he could wear. Without hesitating, he pulled off the towel he'd wrapped around his hips, remaining completely naked in front of me as he dressed. Then he gave a slow look at his boots on my feet, said nothing, and walked out of the room barefoot.

I followed. The lump in my throat wouldn't let me say what I wanted to say, and I was all out of ideas.

I counted six guys waiting for us. A pair of identical twins were in the kitchen rummaging for food, bickering back and forth about the lack of edible, unexpired groceries. "This is a—"

"Safehouse. I know but—"

"—they still should have something—"

"—sweet. I know—"

"—right."

They moved as one and finished each other's sentences as if it were not creepy at all.

"That's Basil and Sage," Xcian said over his shoulder. The twins looked at me and I almost hid behind Xcian.

"Oh, look at him—"

"—all dressed."

My cheeks heated up, wondering what the hell they were talking about, and I turned to Xcian who just glared at them. They quickly closed what they opened. "We'll just wait—"

"—outside."

Xcian took my elbow and led me to the others in the room. A kid on a laptop with a ruffle of dark curls and bright, dark eyes smiled at me. He had to be about fifteen. "That's Aristotle, the youngest."

"And smartest," he added.

Then Xcian introduced me to another tall, gangly guy that could compete with Jasper for long limbed version of weebs. He had earbuds on, but still lifted his chin in a nod my way. "That's Zack. And you saw Noah." He pointed at the scary, nightmare guy, and then finally the last kid with a silver streak in his dark hair, pale skin, and bright blue eyes that were hauntingly sad. "Leander."

Leander turned away without acknowledging me.

"You have six brothers?"

"Nine, actually," Aris said. "There's ten of us, but we sometimes forget the twins are separate entities and count them as one." He winked at me. It was hard not to like the kid. He seemed normal. As if he wouldn't grow horns on his head like his older brother.

"Let's go. We're losing time," Noah said and walked out.

Leander and Aristotle rode with Xcian and me in

Xcian's truck. Someone had found the battery. And the others went with Noah.

I kept my eyes out the window and watched the scenery turn from farmland to more urban areas. We hadn't been that far from civilization. I should've taken my chances and hiked it away from Xcian and his creepy normal family.

While Leander hadn't said two words, Aristotle talked all the way. He talked about soccer camp, about entering tenth grade in the fall. He talked about tech stuff. Normal teenager random thoughts. I had wanted him to talk about something relevant. Like who the hell they were. Why did they need my father? Things that seemed important at the moment. The normalcy freaked me out.

Xcian wasn't normal. I knew what I saw. What happened had not been my imagination, although the memory of it was slipping away like a bad movie.

Xcian, the monster. Not human. And I had kissed him. I had allowed him to touch me.

Leander stiffened beside me. The kid looked tense as high beams blinded us inside, a truck traveling too close behind us. Aris stopped talking. The lights behind us started to flash blue, followed by sirens.

The police.

"Don't stop," Leander said so low I almost missed the words.

"Where is Noah?" Aris asked, fumbling with his phone.

I felt the truck accelerate. The lights behind us didn't lose step, on our ass.

"Xcian," I gritted out. "Maybe you should stop. It's the police."

"They're not human," Leander said.

Not human?

A flicker of lightning zigzagged in the night sky. The lights of the city came up close in front of us. City meant people. People meant more cops. Cops meant I'd probably never see my dad again.

"Noah is three minutes behind us," Aris said. Surprisingly, the kid sounded calm.

Just then, a second car clipped the side of the SUV, forcing us into a spin. The sound of crushing metal exploded inside the car as my ass lifted off the seat, secured by the seatbelt digging into my shoulder. Our bodies upside down as the SUV rolled over, landing on the roof and scraping along the asphalt. Even before the vehicle stopped moving, Xcian jumped out. Then Leander followed. Gunshots pinged around us. Aris and I were still inside, trapped.

Run, Seba!

The two words that seemed to jolt me into movement. Unclipping my seat belt, I landed on my arm and a jolt of pain followed. "Aris!"

"Yeah," he responded. "I'm okay. I think I'm okay."

I let out a relieved breath. "Let's get out of here!"

I kicked out the window and crawled out. Ignoring the gun pops and growls echoing under the deluge of rain. I grabbed Aris under his arm and started to slide him out of the car when strong arms grabbed the back of my shirt. I had no choice but to let Aris go. I couldn't even scream. Aris did that for me when he called out to Xcian. A short second later, the man holding me fell to his knees with no face.

Scrambling back from the dead thing that started to

disintegrate under the rain, I fell on my ass when a second cop-thing grabbed me in a bear hug, dragging me over to his truck. He slammed me against the quarter panel hard. Black inhuman eyes glared back at me for a second before blood splattered on my face and the guy fell.

The rain washed the blood away.

The cold turned into a thick wall, crushing me. Breathing became a chore. Flashes of lights danced in front of my eyes as Xcian ripped through the men like paper.

I had two options. Pass out or run.

I ran.

Pumping my legs as fast as I could, I didn't look back to see if anyone gave chase. I kept moving forward, leaving the chaos behind. The fast rhythmic beat of my heart the only indicator of time. Moments. Movement. Still dizzy, I kept my focus on one goal: to keep *moving*.

The trees had to thin out at some point. I had no clue where I was going, only that I needed to get to somewhere public. Somewhere Xcian wouldn't bother with me. Too much of a risk. Tears blurred my vision, turning the lights into washed-out shapes in front of me. Twenty yards and I broke into the outskirts of a neighborhood.

Warehouses lined one side of the street, while tenements lined the other side. And that's as far as my plan went. An SUV swerved in front of me, and I made a sharp left. I ran into a narrow gangway between buildings, blading my body to fit. I jumped over a fence. Running deeper into the abandoned buildings. Adrenaline masked whatever pain my body would feel later. Among the wall of boarded-up businesses and vagrants, stood a massive church like a beacon.

A church!

I gave the area a glance, looking for Xcian, the SUV, the cops, something. Saw nothing and sprinted to the side of the church, praying that one of the doors would open for me. I wasn't sure of the time, close to dawn maybe. Too early for mass, for sure. I tugged on door number one, got nothing. I tugged again on a second door, and it opened.

I slipped inside. Leaning against the door, I waited until the drumming of my pulse settled. When I heard nothing chasing me, I slowly started deeper inside. My footfalls sounded loud in my ears, the echoes ringing off the thick walls. Drenched, I left a trail of water behind me.

The low light threw shadows everywhere. Candles flickered at the corners, throwing dancing shadows there too. The place was eerily empty. I quietly took a spot somewhere in the middle and let out the breath I'd been keeping shallow. My hands shook as adrenaline ebbed. I gently pressed the knot where my head connected with glass. My arm bruised, but mobile. My shoulder hurt where the seatbelt had dug into my skin. My body would heal. It was my mind that I had to mend. The images seared into my brain. Xcian, the monster. Afraid and waiting for him to burst through the door and drag me out.

When that didn't happen, I chanced a look up at the large cross hanging above the altar. Just a cross. No image of Christ. No image of Alejandro. Whatever that thing showed me hadn't been real.

Are you sure about that?

The lingering thoughts made me doubt.

I wiped a tear, hating myself at the moment. I needed Alex. My brother. My dad. I felt so alone.

"Are you okay?"

I lifted my head to a priest. Wearing a cassock, his hands clasped in front of him standing in the aisle, backwashed with flickering shadows. The man had dark hair and dark eyes. Sharp features and pale skin. He looked like a ceramic doll almost. I was sure if I touched his skin, he'd be cold.

"Not really," I said.

He took that moment to sit on the pew in front of me and turn his body to face me. I watched him inhale deeply, as if calming whatever the night had brought him. "Would you like to talk about it?"

"I need help. There's someone after me and I could really use a phone."

"You'd like to call the police?"

No. "My brother. He's in New York, but my dad, he's in trouble."

The man arched a thick brow. "What kind of trouble?"

At that moment, a loud thump made us both turn to the double entrance doors. Xcian stood there, pissed off and looking like some sort of demon. Blood stained the front of his chin. Silver hair peppered with bloodred stains. Wet from the rain pouring outside. Breathing heavily.

The priest got to his feet and the smile that followed sent chills up my spine. At first glance, his features looked human but wrong somehow. Like looking through cracked glass, the guy's pieces didn't quite fit together. The closer I looked, the more his features blanched as if becoming everyone and no one. Not human.

"Xcian," he said. "I may have found your *pet*."

Yup, not human.

Noah remained in the shadows like a nightmare. And Xcian glared. I just couldn't tell if he was glaring at me or at the man standing behind me, one arm wrapped around my waist, his cheek pressed against mine. His body so cold. He smelled of Sunday mass and funerals.

When had I moved?

I licked my dry lips, and the priest dipped his head into the crook of my neck. I took in a sharp breath, waiting to feel his cold tongue against my skin.

"Don't you fucking dare, Paris." Xcian's words were deep, but low. A rumble that vibrated the air with an electric charge that promised violence. I'd felt that before when I had chained him on the bed. He hadn't gotten around to acting on what he promised. To shed my flesh from my bones or something like that.

"So he's *your* pet."

"No," I said, at the same exact moment Xcian said yes.

Paris seemed more amused by this than anything else. He squeezed me into his body harder. Possessively. Xcian saw that too and the air around his body shimmered.

And I giggled.

Giggled.

Xcian didn't find that amusing. His face hardened all the more while Paris chuckled. "I think he wants to stay here," he said. "*Pet*."

No. I didn't want to stay with Paris. And the word

pet from his lips made me bristle. But before I could say anything, Xcian took one solid step forward with violent intent. The wall of something evil preceded him and touched my skin in warning. Paris felt it too. He released me and took a step back.

Xcian grabbed my hand and pulled me toward him, pinning me at his side. "Touch him again and I will end you."

I shuddered at the threat, and it wasn't out of fear.

Laughing as if this had been the best part of his day, Paris padded down his cassock as if needing to do something with his hands. "I hear Zane's bond is being forced. Even I know the consequences of that."

"Your source is full of shit."

I opened my mouth to ask what Paris meant, but a tight squeeze of my hand had me snapping it back shut. My mouth too dry to speak, anyway. Sweat broke out at my hairline. The church sweltering.

"I guess we'll see what tonight brings then."

Xcian didn't answer, but his look said it all. Then he was hauling me to the exit. Once outside, the rain washed out the haziness and my brain cleared. Xcian had the car door opened for me while Noah had already climbed into the driver's spot. "Get in," Xcian ordered.

I pulled out of his grasp sharply but couldn't go anywhere. Xcian's body pinned me. Glowing ice-cold eyes landed on me as if I were a thing. I hated him at that moment more than anything.

"You're a *monster.*" Because I needed to get it out. I needed for him to know I knew. His eyes dimmed and darkened. My chest hurt. A lot. His expression remained stone cold. "Why did you kiss me?" Because I couldn't say anything else.

"Because you are a means to an end. A fucking hole to stick my dick in. Nothing else," he growled out, breaking something inside of me. My heart, my trust, or something deeper. "Now get in the car."

"No." Fuck him. "You have nothing if you kill me. My father won't do whatever you're forcing him to do. Everything ends."

"You'll sacrifice yourself so easily? You have no idea what I can do to you." There wasn't any space between us. His erection pressed against my hip, and mine complied too. I almost, *almost* rutted against him just to feel the friction again. "Get in."

I wanted to get in. I wanted his touch. All of it felt so wrong. "Don't do this." My last chance to stop this. Somewhere in the back of my heart, I hoped Xcian cared enough to free me. Instead, he slammed his mouth against mine, shoved his tongue inside. I wanted to push him away. To bite him hard. To take back control, but I didn't. I kissed him back. I kissed him until nothing but him mattered and then nothing else.

Chapter Twelve

Xcian

I carefully put Sebastian into the SUV with Noah's help. "Do you mind explaining what is going on?"

I didn't want to explain shit. It wasn't my mess. This was all Zane. After we got Sebastian safe in the back, Noah drove, and I took shotgun as we headed to the airport. "Zane believes Eric Diaz is his chosen."

Noah took that bit of information in. Out of my brothers, Noah thought things through, came up with different ideas. Even out of the box ones. He never reacted. But his projections often led him to dark places he wasn't afraid to suggest, or act on.

"You mean a male? Zane believes a male to be his *chosen*?"

I didn't answer.

"Impossible. We're limited to our biology, and he will not be able to carry an heir with a male."

"He can still have sex with Serena." Though I knew Zane wouldn't if it risked losing Eric.

"He could put his seed in whoever he wants. But if it's not his bonded mate, it won't matter. It's not the seed that carries the trait. It's the act that bonds him to the child." Noah glanced at me as if I were a bug he wanted to crush. "You know this. He knows this. Serena knows this."

Yeah. I did.

"And what does the kid have to do with this?"

"He's Eric's son. Zane's using him as leverage so that Eric goes through with the ceremony."

Noah cursed. "Our brother has gone insane. And you let him?"

"As if I had a choice!"

"You're second. You could have restrained him."

The thought of restraining Zane until he drained of power the way Sebastian had restrained me put a bad taste in my mouth. "It wouldn't matter if Zane's bonded with the male."

Noah let out a breath. "True. This sucks."

"There's something else." I shut my eyes and pressed my fingers to them. Still feeling Genesis in my thoughts. "I think our mother is planning something. Something bad."

"What?"

I couldn't tell my brother what I'd seen in my vision. I knew the body at her feet was one of my brothers. And I knew it'd happen. I just didn't know when. "That's what I intend to ask her."

"Be careful, Xcian. Mother doesn't favor you."

Ouch. Though true. "I know."

"Maybe you should tell Zane."

"No. This stays between us. He has enough to worry about right now. Let's see if he's right and he bonds with Eric. It still might not work. If it doesn't, everything is as is, if it does, then I'll tell him."

Noah nodded.

Sebastian woke up with a jolt while we were three hours into the trip. His breathing fast as he scanned the private jet, eyes glazed. A nightmare. I turned to Noah who gave nightmares, but he shrugged. *Not me.*

"Where are we?"

"Over the Pacific," I answered.

Leander's eyes met mine. I knew he was angry at what I'd allowed to happen with Sebastian, and Genesis's presence had freaked him out. We hadn't talked about it. I had too much on my mind right now to go there with him. He turned back to look through the small cabin window.

"Where are we going?"

"I'm taking you to your father. We have a few more hours. Rest."

He snorted and snatched the bottle of bourbon in front of him. Visibly shaking, he struggled to uncork it and when he finally did, he proceeded to suck from the bottle. My brothers watched wide-eyed. They already got their fill of what Sebastian was to me. A pet. Plain and simple. Nothing more. Only Noah knew the truth about Zane using Sebastian to force Eric into the ceremony. Angry, I grabbed the bottle and pulled it sharply away from him. Some of it spilled down his chin onto his T-shirt as a result.

Angry, he leaned into me and slapped the bottle away from my hand. It went skittering to the floor, leaking on its way. "Fuck you," he hissed out and jumped to his feet. "I'm not your pet."

Denying me only made me lash out and I grabbed his wrist as he tried to pass me to go for the bottle. I pulled him onto my lap and instead of straddling me, like I had wanted him to, he twisted his body to land on my lap with his back to me. I clamped my arms around him and anchored my legs around his. He fought and growled for a few minutes until he finally went pliant against me. Leaning his head back on my shoulder. The fight had made me hard, and I knew he felt my erection against his ass. I grabbed his hair, pulling his head back. The scent of him filled with arousal. I forced his head to turn to me and kissed him. Couldn't help it. I needed the damn kiss. And he gave it willingly. Hesitantly exploring my mouth with his tongue until someone coughed.

We weren't alone. Oops.

"You are my *pet*. Get that through your head."

I thought he'd push away from me. Go back to where he'd been sitting next to me. He didn't. "Where's Doofus?"

Leander turned to look at us. Pain marred his eyes. I'd known Leander had been too close to the human. Not many people could get close to Leander the way Sebastian had. They mostly feared the wolf. And Leander's hypersensitive senses usually caught a foul stench on everyone, so he stayed away. Not the case with Sebastian.

I eased my hold on him and liked that he hadn't moved. "Doofus is fine. Doesn't like to fly."

He made a small noise of understanding. I knew he wanted to ask more questions. I had questions of my own. Like how the hell had Paris found out about Eric, and what the hell did the malice want with Sebastian? They were there tonight for him, not any of us.

After a while, Sebastian took his own seat, and we landed just after dawn, exhausted.

On the tarmac, Sebastian gave me a look I didn't want to try to interpret as Bennett, Zane's bodyguard, led him into a separate car. We weren't too far from the airport. After giving Chris orders to take Sebastian back to LA after his visit with his father, I found my mother with Zane in the living room. Zane was pacing as always, while my mother drank a glass of wine trying to calm him down. They both looked up at me. Zane looked like I expected. A hot mess.

"It's about time," he said. "What the hell took you so long?"

I lowered my eyes at my mother, who sipped from her drink, watching me with eerily familiar eyes. My eyes. I had often wondered what she saw in me that made her hate me so much. Did she see herself reflected back? Or something worse. I paid attention to my brother, already almost bowling me over. "Did you bring the kid? Is he here? Is he okay? Don't tell me you hurt him."

I restrained myself from slamming a fist into my brother's throat. "He's fine. In the guest bedroom."

"Good. I'll tell Bennett to take Eric to see him. We can start then." He turned to our mother as if asking for permission.

She nodded. "I'll be there shortly."

Zane walked out, and I fixed myself a hefty portion of bourbon.

"I'm not surprised you almost managed to ruin your brother's ceremony."

Thankfully, my back was turned to her, and I inhaled the booze, letting it settle like a stone in my gut before I turned to face her. "And you would know, having sent Genesis for me."

She snickered. "I sent her to make sure you didn't ruin everything." She got to her feet, pristine and perfect. "How is your new little toy? Rather young and male to be of flavor."

I clenched my teeth, keeping from telling her what I really wanted to tell her. I'd learned throughout the centuries to navigate carefully around my mother. Despite my father's short temper, Mother had a crueler streak. At least to me. "You should ask Genesis. *If* she still lives."

"It takes more than your incestuous demons to kill her."

I wasn't so sure about that. I almost had killed her. Her life force draining away under my hands. I'm sure Lucifer would get a kick out of having the god of creation at his backdoor. Those two belonged together. "Why Eric?" I asked. "You've known that Zane preferred males since he was five. So, why are you allowing this now with Eric Diaz?"

She gave a curt shrug. "Mr. Diaz is an important piece to secure our place in this realm."

"Our place, or yours?"

She smirked. "I am nothing more than a vessel for offspring. I've delivered my part. Fifteen births, to be exact. I've had my joys and disappointments."

Yeah, I was one of her disappointments. "Serena will take your place now," I said, just to add lime to the wound. "Your services will no longer be needed." Her nose flared, lips thinned, and her demeanor turned cold. Mother disagreed with being put aside. With no longer being a valuable commodity. More than just breeding because she led more than my father ever could. "Drop the bullshit, *Mother*. You don't want Serena to take over as matriarch."

She approached me and served herself two fingers of bourbon and swirled it in her glass all the while piercing me with her stare. I couldn't read her the same way I could my dad or my brothers. I'm sure she couldn't read me either. "Unfortunately, your father is sterile. He can no longer plant seeds."

I almost choked on my spit and cleared my throat without letting it seem as if I wanted to cough up a lung and give her this round. No more Anunnaki births. Never being reborn. The thought spun a thread of excitement through me. We weren't immortal. We healed from almost anything. We lived long lives, but we weren't immune to death. Our extinction would weigh heavily in this realm. But for the first time since my existence, I saw an end. The thought had never occurred to me. Death, just time. But not to be reborn made me human. Except, I knew my mother must have other plans. She'd never give up her power without a fight. "And I bet you'd fuck one of your sons to produce an offspring if you could. To be relevant. All of them except me."

That earned me a slap.

"You will not be patriarch. You will not father sons with Serena. You will do what you always do—fuck up. A travesty of a soul. Galen will lead the Nine. He will put this toxic human realm back to its original setting."

"You're insane."

She licked her rosy lips. "Aren't we all?"

Chapter Thirteen

Sebastian

I met Chris Wilson the same night I'd met Xcian.
Though at the time, I had no clue Chris was also part of
them. Not until he'd been the one to escort me back to
the plane after I'd spoken to my father for all of three
minutes.

Chris had said nothing during the long six-hour
flight and the hour drive to yet another cabin in the
woods, giving me nothing but time to think about the
conversation with my father, which had been diluted
with lies.

My dad had drawn up a ridiculous story about
mobsters trying to keep us safe as his reason for having
me kidnapped and marrying Zane. A man. I didn't care
that my father found his gay roots old, but that he lied
to me.

Doofus had magically appeared the next day,
followed by the man now talking to Chris on the porch.

"It's done. Eric Diaz is now the bonded mate of
Zane Crawford," the man said, lifting his drink in
salute.

Doofus whimpered at the sight of the man and
slipped under the table while I peeked out the front
window to see them on the porch. Dressed in all black,
the guy blended with the night sky. Even his hands

were gloved. The mention of my dad had me walking outside. Framed by thick dark eyebrows, his eyes met mine and I suddenly felt pins and needles swarming just under my skin. The pupil adjusted to the smallest fractal of light.

The rest of him was beautiful. Ridiculously thick lips, pink. Features that were neither round nor sharp, but somewhere in between. His nose ended in a small cleft. All of him perfectly symmetrical, as if designed not birthed. He smiled, revealing perfect teeth, though his incisors were curiously longer. I couldn't determine his body frame with the layers he wore and his hair was covered with a cowl. He lifted a bottle of beer in a salute. "Welcome to the family, kid," he said. His voice deep, and husky.

I cut my gaze from him to Chris, who shoved a chair out with his foot. "You might as well sit." And then to the other guy, he said. "Be nice."

The guy made an innocent gesture as if he couldn't be anything but nice. I sat.

"Sebastian Diaz, this is Finnegan."

Finnegan smirked, but there was a hint of madness in that smirk. Hatred, pure and simple. "The bonding took. Means, your father belongs to them now, and you and your brother by extension."

The mention of Alex made me sit up and my heart gallop. "My brother. Is he okay?"

"Not sure. I don't keep death's logs on me."

Chris kicked him under the table. "I said be nice."

Finnegan rolled his eyes, a human expression on a not-human person made the gesture look creepy. He drank the beer, and I couldn't help but stare at his full lips and his tongue on the small round neck as he swallowed. With an elegant air, he lowered the beer on the table and inspected me. "He doesn't look like a guardian. More like a pet."

"Screw you. I'm nobody's pet."

"Hmmm... perhaps a distraction?"

"I'm right here."

Finn shook his head. "Too young. Wrong gender. Not Xcian's type. Maybe for the shifter?"

Ouch. "And who's the shifter?" I asked.

Finn gave me a pathetic look I wanted to slap off his face. "You are probably better off clueless. Don't get involved. Live your life. For however long you have left."

"So it's really done?" Chris asked, ignoring the guy's words and leading the conversation back to the real topic.

Finn took another beer from a small cooler I'd missed next to his chair and popped it open using his teeth, then handed it to me before taking another. "Yeah. It's done. Zane has bonded and Eric has accepted. Forever intertwined until death do us part."

"You mean my father?"

"Yes. I mean your father has bonded with Zane, the heir and eldest of the Nine, and will now live forever with the gods. Does that compute? Or do you need an illustration?"

"This is all wrong," Chris said. Still ignoring how I wanted to punch this Finn's lights out. "What's Xcian going to do?"

"He's going to do what his brother couldn't. He's going to mate Serena, bond with her, punch out baby nines. Be father patriarch."

I took a long swallow of beer feeling it sink into

my gut like a stone. "Who's Serena?"

Finn smirked. "This one is like his father. Not very smart."

Before I could say something, he got to his feet, pulling up the cowl to hide everything but his eyes. "I gotta go. Duty calls."

Chris lifted a drink to him. "Be safe, brother."

"Be safe," Finn said, and disappeared. It wasn't a subtle disappearance either. The air rippled around him, and he was sucked into a vortex. The power of it forced me to bite my tongue, and I tasted blood in my mouth.

"What did he mean?"

"You're father's no longer human, Sebastian. He's accepted the bonding. Means that he shares Zane's life force. They share each other's soul, strength. Your father will help Zane carry the burden of the demons he's trapped."

The no longer human part made me a little dizzy. "Because of me. Because Zane forced him."

"A bonding can't be forced. Your father *chose* Zane."

Over me.

Chris didn't have to spell it out for me. I already knew.

We both got to our feet just as headlights broke through the darkness. "They're here," Chris mumbled. "I'm out. Good luck, Sebastian. Remember to call if you ever need me."

I hugged the big man a little tighter than I probably should've, then he took off around the back. I walked around the house with Doofus beside me.

Despite the blinding light, I knew who it was, and when Xcian climbed out of the car looking as always—

pissed to be near my vicinity—I couldn't help but watch Doofus go to him as they disappeared around the back. His words echoed back at me. *"Because you are a means to an end. A fucking hole to stick my dick in. Nothing else."*

I dragged my gaze back to the car.

Although I already knew the lies and that my dad had chosen Zane, my heart still tore a little bit inside watching him get out of that car. His face pale, his eyes bloodshot. My dad wasn't this happy newlywed I had thought he'd be. Maybe he hadn't lied totally. Maybe Chris was wrong, and this bonding thing had been forced on him.

I felt like that little boy seeing him home after the three weeks he'd spent in the psych ward after his suicide attempt. I needed my dad back. I couldn't stop the smile that made me feel as if everything was right with the world. That he'd make everything better. "Dad!" I sprinted toward him and fell into his arms. Tears spilled between us.

"Are you really okay?" he whispered.

Xcian slipped inside the cabin. "Yeah. He's, um, been protecting me this whole time. What about you?" Just then, a giant of a man came up behind Dad. Blond hair, blue eyes, perfect in every way, and not human. He placed a hand on Dad, and I would've told him something, except my dad seemed to melt at his touch. His body went pliant, leaning into the man even while still holding me. That small telltale sign slapped me with the truth.

Dad had chosen. And it wasn't me.

"Uh, Sebastian, this is Zane."

"Nice to meet you, Sebastian," Zane said with no

sense that it'd actually been nice to meet me. "I hope your accommodations have been adequate. We should go inside."

He didn't even let me answer. Cold as a Chicago winter storm. I looked at the car they'd driven in. "We should—"

"I know," my dad said, cutting me off. "We will."

I let out a relieved breath. Maybe my dad was still my dad. We'd escape this mess, find Alex. Call the cops, or something. My plans usually started and ended with escape. Except when Zane announced that Dad would be sharing a room with him, my dad had looked content. Relieved almost. In love.

A bonding can't be forced. Your father chose Zane.

The faster I got that through my brain, the easier it would be. I wanted to send Zane to Hell, but then I caught sight of Xcian watching me, waiting to see my reaction to this whole mess. I wanted to cry and burrow myself under my bed like I had when the ambulance took Dad away that night. But Alejandro had been under the bed with me. He'd been the one to tell me everything would be okay even if it had been a lie. "Go get comfortable, Dad," I said instead. "You look like you slept in cat litter."

"Wow, thanks."

I hugged him because I was a hugger. "We're going to be okay," I whispered in his ear. I wanted to believe that. I did. I dropped on the sofa and Doofus must've sensed my distress because he jumped on my lap.

"Doofus," Xcian ordered. Doofus snarled. "Off the sofa. Now."

Doofus shook his head, and I laughed. The dog—the only thing that made sense in my world. I nuzzled into his nose. "He's a mean man, I know."

Doofus purred in agreement.

"It's okay, Ex," I said, unsure where the nickname came from. It just came out of my mouth. "He's good."

I tried to ignore my dad and Zane disappearing upstairs. The thought that my dad had chosen Zane over me, over us, made me hurt all over. And when I heard the moans of their obvious union, I couldn't stand to remain there.

I walked out.

Chapter Fourteen

Xcian

"It's okay, Ex. He's good."

My heart slammed against my ribcage at the sound of my nickname on Sebastian's lips as if it were the most normal thing in the world to say. But then Eric and Zane were gone, obviously consummating their union, and Sebastian walked out. Even the television couldn't mask their moans. Doofus gave me a reproachful look as if it were all my fault.

"Shut up," I mumbled as I followed Sebastian. Knowing the kid, he'd probably try to run from me. Again.

Instead, he slipped into the garage. A crash followed, and I sprinted inside just as he threw a hammer at the wall. With no anger in his eyes, only tears.

He spun too quickly for me to stop him and threw a screwdriver at my head. His aim didn't suck this time, and the handle plonked off my forehead. Pain followed, and I leaned forward, cupping my forehead, and cursing, feeling like an idiot to have been caught off guard.

"Ohmygod, Ex. I'm so sorry. I didn't know you were there."

There it was again. Ex. The term of endearment

stirred something under my sternum that made the pain worthwhile. Even if it was a lie.

"Are you okay?"

I rubbed the knot, already healing. "Yeah," I growled out. "That's twice you almost killed me."

The kid blanched. I wanted to ask why he cared about me at all. After everything I did to him. After the lie about him being nothing but a hole for me. Guilt festered like everything else until it tainted the very core of my soul. If I still had a soul, that is.

He dropped his hands to his side and took a step back, crossing his arms across his chest defensively. "You already got what you wanted. My father brainwashed into your little freak family."

The gears in my head switched from guilt to needing to set this kid straight in two seconds flat. "Your father *chose* Zane. They are bonded, mated, married, whatever the hell you want to call it, so get used to it. This," —I pointed between us— "is permanent."

"And what exactly is this?" he asked, mimicking my gesture between us.

Technically, it made me his uncle. Fuck that. I narrowed the gap between us and he took a step back, tripped on something on the floor, and started to fall. My instincts hyperaware, I caught him around his waist and pulled him into my body where he belonged.

Our bodies flushed. The drumming beat of his heart against my own. They say when we find our bonded mate, our hearts beat in sync with theirs. I suddenly wondered what that would feel like with Sebastian.

He opened his mouth and closed it as I cupped his

face with a desperate need to finish what I started in my bedroom before he chained me up. He'd *chained* me up to escape. Used my desire for him to get me off guard. Idiot.

I was an idiot.

The kid's eyes scanned my face and fear lifted out of me like a breathing, living thing. I feared that he'd find something wrong with me. Something lacking. Something my mother had seen in me a long time ago that made her hate me. And I cared. I cared what he thought. I took a step away from him. "This is a lie," I spat out in answer to his question. The lie coated with venom. A lie within the lie. The mother of all bullshit. I wouldn't give up my soul to another like Zane just did. Sebastian would ram a bullet through my heart and leave me bleeding. It's what I deserved.

I had to give it to the kid—he was learning to school his emotions quickly. "Are you going to let me go now?"

No.

"Didn't you learn anything? Everything seeking to hurt us will be gunning for you."

"And these things seeking to hurt me, they aren't human, because you're not human."

"You already know I'm not. You've *seen*."

He lowered his eyes away from mine, and I wanted them back on me. That innocence he'd had when we first met slowly dissipated. "When I was a kid..." he started, his voice far away now. Not even here, in this moment. "...my father, he tried to kill himself."

I knew this already. Eric had spilled the shit in the car on the way over here. I kept my mouth shut.

"I thought I imagined seeing her. A woman in

shadow. She was there, and she had been the one to shatter the beam that he used. She looked right at me and I felt—death." He lifted his eyes to mine. "I felt the same thing with that woman who came for you. Who is she?"

"Genesis, the goddess of creation. My ex," I added. My petty self wanted to get a rise out of him. It took a heartbeat before I caught the sweet taste of jealousy pouring off of him.

"Does she want you back?"

"No, she wants me dead."

"Do you want her back?"

And there it was. Jealousy. "No. I thought I made what I feel for her clear when she hurt you." The reminder of Sebastian screaming, hurting, because of her sent my demon rising to the surface and I had to bite it all back down as he watched.

"Why would she save him?"

"You're not stupid, Sebastian. You know why."

He swallowed. "To lead us to this moment."

"Yes."

"Why? Why my dad?"

"I don't know."

"Who's Serena?" The question came out of nowhere, and I stumbled. "You said you'd never lie to me. Do you remember that?" he added. "You also said I deserved to be punished, do you remember that?"

I did.

"Serena was Zane's betrothed until your father fucked it all up. Now she's mine." He inhaled sharply and his eyes turned away from mine. "You think you're ready to hear the truth about all this bullshit?"

"Have you had sex with her?"

Grinding my teeth, I answered. "No."

"Have you ever been with a man?"

I took a step closer, and he didn't back away. "Questions go both ways, Sebastian. Do you want me again?"

"No," he quickly said.

"Liar." I brushed my fingers across his cheek, and he sucked in a sharp breath. "No lies, remember?"

"Am I just a hole for you?" His voice shook.

The thread of my reality was fraying and I couldn't risk Sebastian. I couldn't risk my own sanity. Not again. I waited too long to answer, and he shoved me back hard.

"That's what I thought."

Swallowing back everything left unsaid, I followed him back inside. We sat on the sofa watching nothing and trying to ignore what my brother and his new husband were doing upstairs. Sebastian finally succumbed to exhaustion and rested his head on my lap, falling asleep almost instantly. Yeah, I couldn't stop the rattling inside of me where I was broken.

I loved the feel of his hair under my fingers. That's how Eric found us when he finally came down from his sex high. He said nothing about Sebastian on my lap. I almost dared him to, so I could've snapped at him. He'd said enough in the car when he admitted to the suicide attempt. I hated the fucker, and the feeling was mutual.

Shit didn't start to get real until Zane came down and Sebastian woke up to listen to the explanation Zane gave them about the Anunnaki. Sebastian kept snatching glances my way. He already knew all of this, having seen it firsthand. We weren't human. We protected the human realm. And we carried our demons inside of us. That particular truth seemed to interest Sebastian more than anything else. Watching his clear disapproval of Zane made me wonder how far he'd go to protect his father. To sum it up, Zane told them that their lives were no longer their own. They would be hunted because they were involved in our lives now. For all eternity. Sebastian took that information in silence. Eric, on the other hand, couldn't get it through his damn head that they belonged to the Anunnaki now.

"Zane," Eric said, "you know we can't just stay prisoners here."

A glimmer of hope passed through Sebastian's eyes that he'd escape me. Hell no. He was never leaving my sight. "Haven't you heard anything?" I shot out. My demons rising to the surface. "You leave our protection, you die. How long do you think it'll take a malice to peel the flesh from your bones?"

"Xcian," Zane scolded.

I ignored my brother. Fuck him. "Or do worse to your sons?"

Eric got to his feet. "This is a lot to take in. I'd like to speak with my son. Alone."

I stepped forward, sensing the ignorant human who would see his sons die for his pride. I hated humans. Zane got to his feet, Sebastian and Doofus followed. I couldn't stop the shitshow that followed. "You are the reason we are all in this mess!" The reason I would never be able to be with Sebastian. The thought had me seeing red.

My body started to shift. Muscles expanding, contracting, shifting into my god form. The horns pushing through along with my fangs. The need to protect Sebastian too damn strong. Even from his father. Then I charged and met Zane. I needed to expel this surge of dark energy coursing through me, and Zane could handle it. Ignoring the father-son duo escaping along with Doofus, I slammed into Zane as if the world depended on it. The cabin wouldn't survive the onslaught as we fought.

Zane, stronger than me, managed to secure me into a headlock. "Calm down!" he roared.

I couldn't. I didn't want to. The anger freed me of everything else. But my brother wouldn't relent until my knees buckled, and I dropped in a heap to the ruined floor among the debris as my mind cleared of the rage.

"You piece of shit," Zane snapped, shifting into his human form. I heard him search through the kitchen cupboards and walk back. He handed me a bottle of bourbon. I snatched it from him and took a generous drink before handing it back. He did the same and plopped on the floor among the debris. The shattered sofa, coffee table, and torn area rug. Not to mention the splintered floor, the smashed television, and indents on the walls. "He left," Zane said, shaking his head and taking another drink of the liquor. His hand shook. I'd never seen my brother such a mess. "I'm sorry, Ex," he said, using my nickname he had only used when we were kids. "I never meant for any of this to happen. I didn't want this for you."

Through it all, I knew Zane was telling the truth. Not like we had any say who we fell in love with, or who became our bonded mates. Forcing it would be catastrophic. I should be happy for him. Not wishing him to be a miserable asshole so I wouldn't be in his place. "I know," I managed to say. "Sorry about almost killing your husband."

Zane rolled his eyes and took another slug. "My husband hates me."

"I doubt it. He's a father first. Despite what he did, I think he might be a good father."

"A better father than ours," Zane said.

I leaned in and took the bottle from his hand. I was going to need the liquid courage for this. "Maybe now's a good time to tell you that our mother is working with Genesis to ensure that Galen leads the Nine."

The look on Zane's face was priceless. I'd take that to my grave with me and hopefully to the next life. Oh, right... "And Dad is sterile." I let that sink in for a little bit. He took it pretty well. He bolted to his feet, and I heard him spewing in the toilet. No sense in fighting the inevitable. We had to find Eric and Sebastian before something worse found them. I texted Aris for a location on Leander. Aris sent me the coordinates with the face of the devil emoji. He didn't agree to my keeping tabs on Leander without consent.

Zane returned wiping his lips. "So what do we do?"

I shrugged. "Fuck if I know. You lead, I follow."

He gave me a look and an *oh shit* sputtered out of my mind. "And what's up with you and my stepson?"

Stepson? That sounded wrong on so many levels. "Nothing," I lied, deciding to nip that convo in the bud. I walked away from him and headed to the garage.

Zane followed behind me and glared at my baby. "No fucking way."

"Aris has eyes on him. I think I know where they're going. We beat them there, or you wait until it's all over and I get them back."

Zane cursed. "I'm taller than you."

"My bike."

I smiled as my big-ass brother sat on the bitch seat.

Chapter Fifteen

Sebastian

Alejandro opened the door of the suite, and a surge of relief slammed into me like a brick wall. Warm blonde locks like Mom, hazel green eyes, and breathing. Alive! My savior. We'd driven all night to get to Mom's hotel, not having any other choice. With no money or IDs, the plan had been to get some money from Mom and bus it to New York to get Alejandro. We hadn't been expecting him here, and I hadn't realized how much I needed my brother until that moment. He didn't even recoil when I launched myself at him, wrapping my arms tight around his neck, drawing him into a hug. "You're okay. You're okay."

Alejandro usually shunned my hugs, but he never pushed me away when I really needed him. Like now. My body shook like a leaf against him, tears stung my eyes.

"Me?" he whispered in my ear. "I was so worried about *you*."

I wanted to tell him about the attack at his sorority house, about Xcian saving me and kidnapping me, about the monsters, about Dad marrying Zane who wasn't human. But my words wouldn't come out. It felt so much more than three days since I'd dragged Alejandro out of that stupid club after Cammie's news.

The day he had left for New York. The day everything changed. It felt like a lifetime ago.

"Can we, uh, come inside," my dad said. I'd forgotten about him.

Alejandro led us inside, ignoring Dad. He gave the large wolfdog at my side a glare. "I'm allergic. You know that, right?"

I did know that, but I hadn't been able to leave Doofus at that cabin while Zane and Xcian fought. Dad had assured me they were brothers, brothers fought all the time. Except these brothers had turned into monsters. Demons.

Sensing my distress, Doofus whimpered. I dropped to my knees and nuzzled into him, earning a glare from Alejandro.

"Uh, do you need a private bedroom with your dog?"

Doofus barked.

I laughed.

"I think that's a yes," Alejandro said, laughing too.

Things felt so damn normal. At least until Alejandro lifted his eyes to Dad hugging Mom. His expression darkened as if he blamed Dad.

"We were worried," Alejandro said to me. "What happened? Why couldn't you call? Where were you?"

"It's a long story."

Alejandro snorted, as if not believing me, and started for the balcony where they'd been eating breakfast.

"No, really," I said, rushing to catch up to him. "It's a really long story. And we should go before they come."

"Before who comes?"

Just as we reached the balcony, Doofus started to growl at Pedro. A low rumble full of teeth. The last time I'd seen Doofus violent had been against the men that tried to kill me. Doofus had torn out their throats with his muzzle of sharp teeth and Xcian, Xcian had—

"Sebastian," Mom scolded, breaking me from my thoughts. "That thing shouldn't be here."

Alejandro quickly took Mom's hand and led her away from Pedro as if he sensed something too. Something dangerous. I couldn't move.

Hackles raised, Doofus started to approach Pedro, teeth bared.

"Put your wolf away, son," Pedro said, nervously.

Wolf. Not dog. As if Pedro knew. Stark fear crossed the man's eyes as they swirled with black shadows, inhuman eyes.

Doofus lunged at him.

The scream wouldn't even tear out of my throat. Someone screamed. Mom or Dad. Or it could've been the door exploding behind us.

Doofus made contact just as Pedro shoved Alejandro in front of him. Slamming into Alejandro, the wolf forced all three of them over the railing.

I could've moved to save them. I could've tackled Doofus to stop him. I hadn't. Everything else happened in my peripherals. Dad trying to go over the railing to follow them, but Zane had moved too fast and saved him. Dad's cry for Alejandro. Xcian near enough to feel the heat emanating from his body as he leaned to look over the railing. My eyes dragged from the clear blue sky, over the twenty-story drop, and saw nothing. No splattered bodies. No people screaming. Nothing but sidewalk.

"It's not real."

A hand landed on my shoulder. Despite the fabric between us, the touch scorched my skin. Xcian's pale eyes glimmered, his expression tight. My brother's name caught in my throat. "I don't understand." Doofus had belonged to Xcian, but I had trusted the dog. Warmed up to him.

Xcian cupped my face. His warm hand on my cool cheek drew a soft whimper from me. A sound that sounded equally pathetic and needy. The feeling of safety, of Xcian's protection swept through me in a moment of weakness. Not real. The safety he offered, the soft touches, the warmth, was all a lie. I shoved him away. "Don't touch me."

He looked hurt. Really hurt.

"He's alive," I heard Zane tell my father.

Alive.

I had to believe Alex was alive.

"What about Leander?" a man I'd never seen before said. "We can't just leave him."

Wolf-Shifter-Leander.

Finn's words played in my head. He'd mentioned a shifter. The wolf. The damn wolf was Leander. The kid with the striped hair. The one that wouldn't look at me. One of Xcian's brothers. The betrayal sank deep as I tried to process everything. The conversations played in the background meant nothing. I couldn't trust anyone here, but I had to believe my dad when he promised to bring them back.

And I had to believe that we were safe after being dropped off at a penthouse somewhere in the city.

The guy pacing in front of me stood taller than my six feet height. He had a shock of dark unruly hair jutting out of his head, blue eyes, a square chin, and a thick neck that seemed to define the rest of him. Thick muscled arms, broad chest forcing him to leave his bomber jacket open, thick thighs, and he wore shitkickers that trampled more than walked. His eyes and perpetual snarl made me believe that scars went deep. Way, way deep. The guy hated the world. I was a speck in the world. Gum on his perfect, shining boots. He'd blend in perfectly in Gears of War as a COG soldier. Not an exaggeration. Jasper would get a boner over creating this guy in digital format.

Hawke, my new uncle.

"The penthouse is paid for. You will have a stipend for food and other," —he arched a brow at me— "amenities you feel you may need. If you need more, you can call the number on the refrigerator."

Hawke leaned into me, one brow arched. "You and your mother are not high-value assets. That means if you try the shit you tried with my brother—"

Escaping.

"—I will not hesitate to send you all to the streets to fend for yourselves. Got it?"

I cleared my throat, feeling my mother's nails dig into my arm to shut me up. I nodded.

"You are free to roam as you please, though I suggest not going out after dark as that's when the nightside are at their most potent. If you need to contact us, just call the number on the fridge. You also have new cell phones that have some emergency numbers saved on it, in case you find yourself in the middle of a hive hellbent on eating your face off. Though that may be a bit late to call. Do not make me have to clean up your excrements if you chose not to heed my warning."

With that, he made an about-face and stomped out of the apartment.

Mom finally released my arm. I'd have bruises for sure.

She rubbed her belly. Five months pregnant and having to suffer this mess had to be a strain on her and the baby.

"You should rest," I whispered to her. "I'll wake you up when Dad calls." Because he would call. He'd call as soon as he had Alejandro. He hadn't totally bailed on us.

Yeah, keep lying to yourself.

She tapped my hand without a word and disappeared down the hall. A door snickered shut shortly after. Leaning back on the sofa, I closed my eyes. The replay in my head didn't help calm my mind. Alejandro gone. Doofus's fault. And Pedro's eyes had shadowed over. It couldn't be real.

Yeah, dude, but you saw Xcian turn into a monster. And let's not forget the malice who turned to ash after Xcian tore them apart.

My world had unfolded another layer of insanity. I would've prayed, but I was afraid of which god would answer my call. Inadvertently selling my soul would suck.

Shit.

Too tired to think, I didn't fight the swirls of shadows behind my closed lids. A slight tug at my core dropped me into a dark space. A void where the dark pulsed like a living breathing thing. The cackling sound of fire drew my attention to the center of the room where a lone body hung in chains above a fire pit. Naked. The surface of his skin was ashen. The color of his eyes like green fire under a wall of knotted hair.

"Seba! Run!"

The sound of my brother's cry tore me from the nightmare, following me to consciousness. A cry stuck in my throat. Jumping to my feet, I stumbled, caught myself with the back of a chair, and scanned my strange surroundings. It took me a few long, desperate minutes to remember everything.

Darkness had fallen outside and the view from the penthouse window reminded me that the world hadn't imploded. Not for anyone else. Just me. Then the phone rang. I ran to it, plucking it off its cradle before the third ring. "Hello?"

"Sebastian, it's your dad."

"Alex?" My voice broke.

"He's alive. We have him and Leander."

My heart cracked a little bit at the thought that the wolfdog had been playing with my affections too. Just like Xcian. But I was relieved he was okay too. "Can I speak with Alex?"

There was a long pause. "Seba, he's in a coma right now. Asleep."

I took in a sharp breath. "What hospital? I should be there with him, Dad."

"He's not at a hospital. He's at Zane's place. My place," he corrected. "He'll be safe."

"Safe from whom?"

"From things. I can't explain right now."

This felt so wrong. "Dad, I want to be with him."

I heard him cup the phone and ask someone, probably Zane, about me staying with them. The firm *no* came across clear as day. Dad hadn't argued that either. "Sebastian, it's safer if you stay where you are with your mother. I'll call with any news."

"What about Pedro? Did you find him?"

Dad sighed. "No. Sebastian, Pedro isn't human. He's a malice." I felt a wedge in my throat as my dad just kept talking, stumbling over his words. "We'll come to you soon. Just stay put, okay?"

The sting of rejection forced a wedge into my throat. "Mom needs to see a doctor to make sure the baby is okay. Would that be okay?"

More asking before he came back to the phone. "Zane will make the appointment and send someone for you both to take you."

"What about you?"

"I want to stay with Alex."

Right. Be a father when he's dying! "Okay," I managed to say through the wedge in my throat. Not that I had a choice. "I'll see you later, then." I hung up the phone before he could say anything else. Like, I love you.

After a moment, I followed the sounds of soft sobs to my mother's room. I'd never heard my mom cry before. She'd never had a family growing up. Mom had talked about being raised in the system. She'd always wanted a family and had fallen head over heels for Dad. They'd been on the edge of friendship since high school. It should've been a happily ever after life for them. I don't know what happened that led her to leave us. But she'd been happy again with Pedro and the new baby on the way. The baby had been a surprise, but a blessing.

I knocked and waited until she called the okay to come inside. The dark room was spacious like the rest of the apartment. She sat up quickly and wiped her face.

"What is it? Is it Alex?"

"He's alive. Dad has him."

She got up. "Oh, thank God. Is your father coming for us?"

I shook my head. "Alex is in some kind of coma. They're keeping him at Zane's. Keeping him safe."

"Safe? Safe from who?"

I shrugged, unable to voice the answer stuck in my throat. The only threat against us were the people who had him. My father included. She plopped back down. "What about Pedro?"

I shook my head. "Not yet. I'm sure we'll find him too. Zane is going to make an appointment with a doctor to have you and the baby checked out."

"*Aye, Dios mío,*" she said, pressing her palm to her eyes. "None of this makes sense. How could they just disappear like that?"

"Mom, how about we leave explanations for after you rest."

She gave me a look. She wasn't letting it slide. That Mom glare she'd perfected had me spilling everything, starting with the attack at Alex's house and ending with Dad marrying Zane, who wasn't human. Surprisingly, she seemed to believe it all. I didn't tell her about Pedro or Dad forced into the marriage. It didn't matter. Dad had fallen in love with Zane. In the end, Dad had chosen *them*.

She tapped my hand. "Thank you," she said. "For being honest with me."

"You should sleep. I'll wake you if we get more news."

"Okay. I will."

She fell asleep even before I closed the door behind me.

Chapter Sixteen

Xcian

Five days of silence was hell.

Noah had security on high alert. Aris grumbled to anyone who listened that he wanted to go to some camp with humans. Zane looked like a lost puppy unable to wag his tail. And Leander hadn't shifted back into his human form since Eric had pulled him out of the aether with Alejandro. A monumental step backward for my brother that I couldn't help him with. He spent most of his time in Alejandro's room. Sometimes on the bed with the male or at the foot of the bed. Other times, he spent it near me. I wasn't an animal whisperer by far, but I could sense some of Leander's emotions under the animal's instinct. And it wasn't good. Ever since Genesis made an appearance, Leander had been off. I should've locked him in his room. I should've locked Zane in shackles. I shouldn't have kissed Sebastian. The list of my fuck-ups kept getting longer and longer, and I felt as if I'd been shoved into a ticking time bomb that was going to explode in my face any second now.

We couldn't afford to become unfocused. The malice had scored a big win taking Leander again. It showed our weakness. Pedro had slipped through our defenses. How long he'd been a malice was a big fat question mark. The malice could slip into any human body after death, but only milliseconds after the human soul leaves the body could they tether themselves enough to hide from us. Pedro must've died without anyone's knowledge. It could've been something as unassuming as a heart attack. A stroke. But unless the fuckers had access to death's playbook, how could they know where to send the malice?

Unless Genesis had a part in it. The goddess of creation could get her nasty hands into the book of death. It wasn't a physical book, more like a web database that could be hacked and accessed as read-only. A far reach, I knew that, but too many variables existed not to try to fit the pieces together, and Alejandro in a coma had something to do with it.

I dropped the weight bar I'd been lifting, and it pinged across the floor. Aris had the unlucky timing to walk in as I snarled. I had to remember that the youngest was still living his first life. I quickly used the towel to hide my rage and wipe the sweat off my face, breathing deeply to calm my already unsettled nerves.

"Uh, um," he started, taking a step back. It reminded me of Sebastian. Afraid of me. "I found something about Mr. Ortega that you might want to take a look at. It might give us a timeframe of when the malice took him over."

"When?" I asked.

"You don't want to look?"

"I trust you, Aris. When?"

"He had an unfounded cardiac episode in the emergency room, but according to his employment incident, he had passed out. Unresponsive when they called the ambulance. But when he got to the hospital, he was cleared. It happened a little over five years ago.

Uh, just before he met Mrs. Ortega, who was Mrs. Diaz at the time."

I cringed right along with him. The malice were sterile. Was the baby Layla carried Pedro's or Eric's? I raked my fingers through my hair, my brain charred at this point. "What do you think that means?" I asked him. I needed a fresh pair of eyes on this shit.

"I think that they used Mr. Ortega to get to Mrs. Diaz so that she'd break up with Mr. Diaz and then…the future is history. And here we are."

Right. "They played us using Eric." I threw the towel in the dirty bin and growled.

"I don't think we should tell Zane or Eric."

"Why?"

Aris turned a deep red. "They're in love. Why ruin it?"

Fucking love. I'd never bond with anyone. I'd rather have them killed before I latch onto someone like that. "They're in love and Zane is lying to Eric about his son's mental state. Because we all know Alex is still in some kind of hell."

Aris flinched. I decided to give the kid a break. "Fine." Aris spun to get out of dodge. "Aris." He turned around. "You know I'll never hurt you, right?"

He let out a breath he didn't realize hurt me straight to my soul. "Yeah, it's just, sometimes, I forget."

I nodded. "Thanks for the info. And I'll talk to Dad about sending you to camp."

That got him to smile. "Thanks." He paused at the door. "Oh, and there's something else. Alejandro has been getting a visitor that disturbs the surveillance in his room. I'm thinking, Finnegan. Just a heads up." He scrambled out the door.

Finnegan. Zane's bitch demon. What the hell did he want with Alejandro? One way to find out. I showered, changed, and slipped into Leander's room to check on him. Empty. I found him in Alejandro's room at the foot of the bed as if protecting the male. He whimpered and lowered his head back onto the floor.

"It's not your fault," I said, knowing that guilt and blame carried the heaviest weight. He closed his eyes. End of story. I glanced at Alejandro before heading out in search of the wraith.

A wraith by design, Finnegan had been cursed by Lucifer after he bonded with Zane, who hadn't accepted the bond. A one-way trip to torture. I would've felt sorry for the guy had he not put Zane through hell for centuries. Love sucked. I found him in the sunroom basking with a six-pack.

"Hate to break it to you," I said. "You should wear less clothes if you expect to tan." Except for his face under the cowl, I'd never seen the guy's skin. Finn looked like the knock-off version of death. Even his hands were gloved.

"I'm tanning through my eyeballs," he said, eyes still closed.

Finnegan wasn't considered an ally. Not by a long shot. The guy would tear us a new one if he could find a way to free himself from Zane. Dead do us part didn't work for the bonded. And that Zane reincarnated over and over didn't make things easier for Finnegan. We all considered Finnegan an extra appendage. Like a human's appendix. Rupture it and it could kill you, leave it alone and you'd forget about it. I took a seat next to him and planted my feet on the ottoman.

"I take it that the chocolate I left the brat didn't work as a bribe. Perhaps I should leave him a female next time."

Finnegan was easy to hate too. "Why the stalking?"

"I don't stalk." He sounded like a petulant, spoiled child.

"What's so special about Eric?"

Finnegan snarled. "Nothing. Absolutely. Fucking. Nothing. I'd tear his head off his shoulders if I could."

I remembered the suicide attempt and what Sebastian had admitted about Genesis being there. Things seemed to click. "Let me guess. You whispered sweet nothings to get him to try to off himself."

Eyes still closed, face stoic, he shrugged. "I can't do it myself. The whole kill-a-human-for-no-good-reason sends ripples throughout the cosmos, or whatever. But humans can be of use and do it themselves, if you know which buttons to push."

"You are a piece of shit, you know that."

"Demon. Hello?"

"So, he was protected."

"*Is* protected."

"By?"

"The gods. Strife. Chaos. Butter. Who knows which one."

"Why?"

Finnegan dropped his feet on the ground and leaned forward, eyes squinting into the sun. The guy was beautiful in a fluid way. Hard to explain. As if he could mold to whatever you wanted him to be. Full lips, large, beautiful eyes, and nose that fit his face symmetrically. No human was symmetrical. Not even the Nine. Finn looked the part of a direct descendent of a god. Too bad it had to have been Lucifer. A wannabe god who got thrown out of the party. "What do you know of the trinity?"

"They were the original guardians of this realm."

Finn licked his lips. "The trinity became irrelevant after they fell. Replaced by the Nine—the Anunnaki. And they faded away into legend."

"I heard the stories. They had their chance and blew it. Started manipulating things to their advantage. Became corrupt."

Finn wiped his chin. "They were set on a high pedestal. Unrealistic to achieve. Thankfully, the gods learned and made you and your brothers lacking. Fuck-ups. No expectations. Anyway, yes. Their bloodline still exists. Bred together with a Nephilim, they can transcend. Eric carries this trait. Layla's origin is unknown, but I'm sure if I'm able to examine her, she is of my brood. Sebastian is still up in the air. But Alejandro is in a state of transition. I'm pretty sure he will rise as guardian, but we won't know until he wakes up. *If* he wakes up."

"Why are you so interested in him? If he does wake up as a guardian, we can deal with it."

Finn snorted. "You guys are on the verge of extinction, if you haven't noticed. Alejandro might be a new breed to replace you fuckers. If I were you, I'd concentrate on your boy toy. Because if Alejandro wakes up as powerful as I assume he will, everyone will be gunning for that kid to control the brother. Sebastian is the only thing Alejandro cares about." Finn rubbed his hands together, his expression turning into something nefarious. Usually a bad plan. He got to his feet. "And my interest? I believe he'll be strong enough to break my bond with your brother."

I snorted. "Impossible. Only the gods could do that."

"Or death. If I'm right, then your nephew will be the harbinger of death and he'll be able to wipe us clean. I think I'm ready to leave this place and give my father a good finger up the wazoo. You?"

A god killer. Well, that turned sour fast. "Does anyone know this? Does Genesis, my mother?"

"I haven't told anyone."

"You need to protect him, Finn."

Finn gave me a look and nodded.

"And one more thing? Is it possible for malice to breed naturally?"

Finn's expression took a downturn. "Nothing good ever comes out of that unnatural union," he said dryly. "But yes."

I didn't even have time to process all this shit when Noah interrupted us. "There you are. Fuck. We have a problem."

"That's my cue to leave," Finn said and disappeared.

"What is it?"

"Gideon called. It's Sebastian."

Chapter Seventeen

Sebastian

I woke up with the scream wedged in my throat and soaking with sweat. I sat up and swung my legs to the side of the bed, just breathing. Alejandro was in pain. Like with Xcian, I felt it under my own skin, like nails scratching underneath the surface. I heard him scream. Not to save him but to run away from him. It'd been five days since Alejandro came back. Dad hadn't allowed us to see him. Mom had gone silent after her doctor's appointment, not even talking to Grandma. Nothing from Xcian. We'd been discarded and forgotten.

I took a quick shower and changed into joggers and a T-shirt.

I found my mom in the kitchen as always. She slammed the fridge and huffed. "There are no onions in this place. Can you believe it?" She shook her head at the blasphemy of it all. Who dares not have onions for a pregnant woman with onion cravings?

I perked up just for having something to do. "Do you want me to go to the store and get some onions?" I asked as she settled for a bottle of water and proceeded to chug it as if it were the last water bottle on the planet and she had to have it all so that she could complain five minutes later why her bladder was so full. She waved her hand as if irritated by a pesky fly.

"No," she gasped on an inhalation. "That's okay."

I knew my mother well enough to know she would not be able to sleep until she got what she needed.

Onions.

"I'll get it. Stores only a few blocks down and I need to get out of here. *Please. Please. Please.*" I repeated the please a few more times until she consented. That always worked. I kissed the top of her head and rushed back to my bedroom.

"At least wear some jeans!" she called after me.

Mom always had to make sure we looked our best in public. Even clean underwear just in case you got shot and the doctor needed to strip you. Being cooped up for five days with only baby doctor appointments, where my poor mother got violated by instruments of death, was revolting. Mothers were a necessity in life, yeah, they deserved to be praised to the Heavens, but the vagina was a disgusting place to be. Not that I'd seen my mother's va-jay-jay, but she had me watch birthing videos with her as if she could forget having two kids.

I shuddered.

I wore some expensive jeans that fit me snug and perfect, a teal-colored shirt, and some nice boots all paid for by Zane. I added a thin dark jacket just because it matched with the black Doc Martens. I picked up the folding pocket knife Alex had given me for my eighteenth birthday as a form of rite of passage.

"Like a condom, better to have it and not need it, then need it and not have it." That had been Alex's favorite saying.

I shoved the knife into my jacket pocket. Alex

would be proud.

I ran my fingers through my wet hair and pulled it in a messy bun on top of my head and then looked at myself in the mirror. "You are only going for onions, asshole. Onions." I walked out to the scrutiny of my mother.

I plucked the keycard for the entryway off the credenza and shoved it into my back pocket.

"Store and back, mister," Mom ordered.

I gave her a thumbs up and once outside, I breathed in the cool night air. The twenty-four-hour mart wasn't that far, and I got there in two minutes. I purchased the onions and took the long way around the busy night streets back. I didn't know the area well. Alex always said I had no sense of direction. I didn't particularly care tonight. I just let my legs move. It'd been five days and no word from Dad or Xcian. Nothing. Our security detail lasted two days and then left us alone. Mom had been going stir-crazy. If she hadn't brought her laptop to work from home, she would've hopped on the first flight back to Chicago and I would've gone with her. No one had bothered to tell her the truth about Pedro. Not even me. I didn't want to put her through more stress than necessary, especially with the baby. Besides, Zane had promised to take care of things. Once Alex woke up, we could all go home. Except I had no home. I had intended on moving in with Dad. Not an option now that he belonged to Zane. Alex would let me stay with him when he woke up. If he woke up.

I stopped at the curb and caught sight of someone moving fast. Honey-colored hair hunched down, wide frame. *Alex.* I sprinted after him. It made no sense. It couldn't be. While my brain warned me to stop, my heart kept me moving forward. Hoping. The compulsion too strong to ignore. The guy walked a few blocks down the alley and slipped into a building.

As I stood looking up at the massive gothic design structure that could've passed as Dracula's castle, I had the slight thought that the gods, whichever ones, had sent me to die. I probably should've gone straight home after buying my mom a couple of onions, which I shoved into my jacket pocket to hide them and the smell before paying the ten-dollar cover and walking into the goth scene. Okay, so vampires would never get old. Hell, romance novels are writhing with horny, blood-sucking, handsome devils. I mean, the allure is real. Something about the gritty seduction of dark liner, black lipstick, and a basic sneer that said either fuck me or leave me the fuck alone had a certain appeal. Real vampires were dicks. Goth vampires were kinda cool. The sensory output of the place wreaked truth. It said that the world sucked. Don't try to deny the shit. Protect yourself from it. Know what you want and grab it or tell it to get off the crazy train and let you ride it with insanity as your wingman.

Ever since Dad had tried to kill himself, I felt this darkness inside my soul. Something carnal, trapped, and I'd always been afraid to let it out. In this place, no one gave a shit about my past. No conversation about where you go to school, or what type of job you want when you grow up. A pulse of energy touched my skin. It made me feel everything I couldn't feel around my family.

This was truth incarnate.

Sweat, sex, and booze gave the place a heady scent. It made me lightheaded. Ever since my mom left my dad, things hadn't been the same. I had always been hypersensitive like my dad. Mom called me a sensitive boy, Alex called me a cry baby, and Dad just gave me tons of hugs. I liked hugs. I liked Xcian's hugs. I didn't want to think about Xcian here either. That had been all lies.

I caught sight of the guy I followed inside move behind the bar and his eyes met mine. Not Alex. What the hell would Alex be doing here? He was in a coma, screaming for me to save him. "What'll you have?" the non-Alex look-a-like asked. He blended in with all the goth around him. Silver studs piercings on his lip, brow, tongue. He stood shorter than me, thinner too. His clavicle bones protruding from his T-shirt. He looked nothing like Alex.

"Uh, whatever you have on tap. Please," I added with a smile that stretched my face. Alex always said on tap was the safe bet whenever he had no clue what to order. The guy didn't look like he'd agree with Alex. He rolled his eyes.

"It's your funeral." He poured me a tall glass of a thick, red, viscous liquid substance with similar properties as tar.

"Maybe if the glass wasn't transparent, I'd drink this." His very dark-painted lips quirked up in a half smile. "Did I just say that out loud?"

"Hmm, hmmm," he said. "Drink up, honey. This is where the fun starts."

Although the place bulged at the seams, it was only me and this goth, thin not-Alex guy at the bar. That should've been a deal breaker.

I usually didn't succumb to peer pressure unless instigated by my brother, but I found myself lifting the tall glass anyway. The liquid moved like nothing edible should ever move. It undulated and glimmered. The heat around my body pressed against me like a living, breathing thing. Then I felt it—a cold breath against the back of my neck sending a flood of goosebumps along my skin.

"Gideon," a husky voice belonging to a man who blended with the shadows said beside me. Inky black hair, black eyes and black leather duster with shitkickers made this guy look like danger. Every exposed skin on this guy was paperwhite. Yeah, like paper, unblemished and smooth. I wondered if he'd crinkle like paper when he smiled. The guy didn't look like the smiling type. "What are you doing to this beautiful creature?"

His dark eyes met mine, and a silent scream rushed through me. I recognized him but the image was distorted. My brain couldn't place it. Then he smiled, and a sharp warning unsettled me. His teeth were as white and as sharp as the awareness in his eyes. He knew me.

"Paris," Gideon said coolly.

Paris kept his eyes on me. "I'm sorry, I don't believe we've met properly last time." He oozed seduction. Last time. The church. Paris from the church.

I cleared my throat. "I'm Sebastian," I said. Stranger danger be damned.

"Sebastian," he repeated. My name on his lips sounded sexy as hell. He pushed the foul drink away from me and back to Gideon. "Toss that. I'll take young, tall, and handsome on a private VIP tour."

My mind suddenly pulled free from the visceral reaction to him. To this place. The allure binding me to him. I'm pretty sure if I were normal, I would be sporting a boner right about now. "I, uh, should go."

He possessively wrapped his arm around mine. "Please, I insist."

I wasn't one to shy away from being rude when someone irked me, but I couldn't seem to get the word *no* out of my mouth. I had a visual of me fighting him and losing terribly. He leaned into me, and his nostrils flared. He stiffened but recovered quickly.

"You are new to this?"

If he meant vampires, demons, and shifter wolfdogs, then I was as new as a baby giraffe on wobbly legs. "Yes," I answered, despite all my warning bells being activated at once. People turned to us as we navigated a path through the thick dance floor. They moved as if sensing something toxic and not wanting to touch it. They did, however, touch me. I was groped, pulled a few times, and could've sworn someone licked my hand. The deeper we walked inside, the darker it became until we came upon a wall of black. Paris passed through the wall first, and I almost slipped out of his grasp, but he seemed to sense my hesitation and tightened his grip on me, pulling me hard. My clothes fluttered under a breeze, and I caught the smell of my onions in my pocket.

Onions. Shit, I had to get back to Mom. She was going to murder me.

After the pressing darkness lifted, I blinked a few times to clear my head. We'd stepped into a separate room with its own bar. I guessed a few dozen people were scattered about. Some were lounging on sofas, others under dark shadows doing something I did not want to guess. Pedro sat inside a cage bolted to the corner. The one unswollen eye met mine. There didn't seem to be anything behind those eyes. I'd seen the same look on Dad the few days after Mom left him. He'd been dead inside. I swallowed the lump in my throat.

"What do you think about my pet?" Paris asked. "I acquired it recently."

Pedro was the enemy. That's what Dad had said. The enemy of the Nine. But all I saw was the man that made my mom laugh when he'd almost burned the deck by grilling bacon. The man who had taken Alex and me fishing on a boat for the first time. I had cried when Alex caught something and Pedro had explained how it would be a disrespect not to use what we killed for sustenance, shelter, or protection. I didn't see evil in him. Not like I had with Xcian. Seeing him there felt so *wrong*. "What did he do to deserve to be caged?"

Paris snorted. "*It* breathes." Paris walked toward the bar. "Come. Let's drink."

No. I meant to say it, but my legs followed him anyway. "I should go." Panic settled quite nicely inside my chest, giving me some mental clarity to get out of this place. I turned to take the entrance we'd just come through, but I faced nothing but a brick wall. *No. can't be.* I pressed my hands along the wall trying to feel my way to an opening. *No way. I wasn't insane.*

Paris started to laugh, then, like a chorus, they all started to laugh. I took in the room like a caged animal would, first, searching for exits. The only window in the place faced the club I'd just walked from. I couldn't see any other doors. Second, came weapons. A shit load of glass, alcohol and fire. Each table had a votive candle. I heard the air conditioning system, which meant air circulation so we wouldn't be inhaling the smoke from the torches along the wall. The whole place looked like a firetrap and no one seemed to care.

Paris stopped laughing and the whole place silenced. "Come," he said. "Drink with me."

Although I approached the bar, I had no intention of taking any food or drink from Paris. "What are you?" I asked.

He arched his brow with that smirk on his lips. "Humans do enjoy a good label. Don't they?" He trailed his tongue across his teeth as his fangs grew.

Vampire. My blood seemed to swell inside of me. "I take it you're not a priest."

Paris threw back his head and laughed. A sound like shrieking brakes. Then he licked his lips again, his eyes lowering to my throat. Hunger speared his expression. At that moment, I realized there were worse things than Xcian. Worse things than the malice.

"Sire," a male, wearing combat gear and knives strapped to his chest, said. "Maddox has arrived."

"Good," he said. The evil spilling from his voice made me shiver. "Let's get this started." He took my elbow. "Come. Do as I say, and you just might survive this."

The threat I needed to hear. The label I'd somehow managed to walk intentionally into—victim. I hated the feeling. He pushed me to sit on the sofa behind a table littered with more drinks, and he sat next to me. He settled himself comfortably as if getting ready to receive a lap dance, and waved his hand. Then he leaned into me, and I felt his cold body too close. "Don't beat yourself up. I marked you the first night we met. You were always going to come back to me." The smile on his face looked like madness.

A door appeared between two torches and in walked the ugliest man on the planet. He wasn't tall but built like a house. Literally. Thick head, neck, shoulders, all the way to his feet. I'm sure this guy would have to walk sideways to get through any normal doorway. And his eyes were black too. Not like Paris black but like demon black.

The man wore a crisp gray suit and shoes that had to be more expensive than my college tuition. He wore a signet ring on his plump pink finger and a gold watch on his left wrist. He was followed by six others not as thick as him, but all wearing black with knives and a few guns on hips. A woman with a hood over her head and her hands tied in front of her had been pushed onto her knees in front of us. I gasped. The man savagely ripped away the hood and tossed it aside. The woman had dark hair in a braid, whisps poked every which way. She blinked a few times, trying to ground herself in her surroundings. Beautiful in an elegant sort of way, her eyes landed on me. A familiar recognition flashed through her expression except, I didn't know her.

"I bring you the princess. I want the traitor returned," the man's equally thick voice said. He sounded as if he had a mouth full of teeth. I didn't try to look closer.

The woman dragged her eyes to Paris. "I should've known a rat was behind this treachery. Does your father even know what you're doing?"

The demon-man slapped her, and I had to suppress the urge to jump to her side and get slapped too because I wasn't a warrior. A fighter. I chained Xcian when he was asleep. Almost shot him by accident. I promised myself I'd never hold a gun ever again. I wasn't brave. She snarled at her jailer. I didn't even see tears in her eyes.

"I'd be nice to me considering what I have planned for you tonight." Paris made a show of palming his dick.

I felt sick. Panic rose.

"I am mated to Xcian, the Sword of the Nine. He will kill you."

I stiffened at the mention of Xcian's name. And when Paris draped an arm over my shoulder, my heart sank. He leaned in and inhaled me deeply. "Really? Because this one carries his scent and favor. Don't you, *pet*?" He glided his long nails across my jaw.

The woman's eyes nearly popped out of her head. *Serena*. The woman had to be Serena, who Xcian would have babies with. "Xcian will kill you if you harm us," I managed to croak out.

An evil gleam passed Paris's eyes. "I don't see your precious savior anywhere. Do you?"

Maddox growled. "I don't give a shit about Xcian's harem. Give me what belongs to me."

At the word harem, Serena met my eyes. Xcian had lied. He *had* mated her.

"I have another proposition for you, Maddox," Paris said, playing with the tips of my hair. "I happen to have leverage for you to obtain something you might need."

Serena scowled and pressed her lips together. I knew she wanted to send another warning to Paris but didn't want to get slapped again.

"What games are you playing, Paris?"

"One of the trinity. A Guardian. One you can make

a pet of."

This time, both Maddox and Serena looked at me. Maddox dragged his eyes back to Paris. "Word has it the boy is in transition. Might not survive it."

"Ah, but if he does, you'll need a tool to make him yours." Paris slid his fingers under my chin. I pulled away sharply, earning a scratch under my chin for my efforts. Blood welled in the wound. Paris leaned in before I could pull away and licked it. "Ah, yes. This one is ripe."

I was sure Paris could hear the drumming beat of my heart. Possibly even smell my fear too. My hands shook and I shoved them into my pockets, feeling the onions. I should've gone home right away. Tempting fate had been a mistake. Calling Hawke now would be too late, though I found my phone in the pocket too. And my pocketknife.

"He is the younger Diaz, and his brother would move Heaven and Earth to save him."

I felt my throat sour. Alex. Oh, gods, no. I wouldn't let myself be used against my brother the way they used me against my father. The demon's eyes changed to glee. Pedro trapped in chains forgotten. The hunger in his eyes when he took me in made me want to hide.

"I'll give him to you for the girl. And I keep the traitor. My people like amusing themselves."

No. Please. No. I projected to the demon. I knew it was moot when a smile broke his face and made insanity that much harder to resist.

"Deal."

That one word changed my whole life. That one word started a chain reaction that left me cold and raw.

That one word made me realize that these fuckers had no clue what it meant to be human. What it meant to protect family. I didn't stab Paris because I knew I'd kill him. I stabbed him because I wanted him to kill me, not use me to get to Alex. But as soon as the knife dug cleanly into his carotid and the blood started to squirt out like a water gun on my face, the thought of dying via vampire didn't sound appealing. At all. Too late.

The scene went from me puncturing his carotid in slow motion, to fast-forward speed and fangs. He grabbed me by the throat and slammed me on top of the table. Glasses and bottles crashed around me. People around us just waited and watched. Everyone shocked into stillness. Blood still squirting out of the side of his neck. I caught Serena moving. I wished she'd at least use the distraction to escape and maybe take Pedro with her.

I couldn't worry about that right now. I had a pissed-off, fangs exposed, bleeding vampire looking to rip my throat out with his teeth. I did the only thing I could. His mouth opened and he jerked forward to bite me when I shoved the onion into his mouth. Then a scream tore through the sealed room like a banshee. Paris' scream. Something that sent his league of vampires scoring to kill.

Covering my ears, I dropped under the table in time to see Serena break free. She had armed herself with two long daggers she pulled from Maddox and launched herself at the house of a man while gunshots and chaos exploded around us. The two groups started fighting each other. Vampires versus demons, and Serena and I in the middle. Something ignited and fire started to sweep through the room. I lost sight of Paris as the table I'd been cowering under overturned. Crawling frantically away, glass dug into my palms and knees. Limbs fell around me. Jumping to my feet, I caught sight of Serena using the two blades to cut threats down. She was a goddess. The whole thing was disgusting but fascinating at the same time. Something slammed against my chest, and I startled back as a severed head bounced away. I tripped over something and fell hard on my ass.

A body.

Not just any body.

Paris.

His eyes were glazed over and milky, his skin ashen and hollowed out like a husk. He still had onion layers clinging to his fangs. The ooze spilling from the wound on his neck had turned black. Like tar.

Tar.

Like the beer on tap I had ordered.

My stomach revolted and I dry heaved. Thankfully, I hadn't eaten anything in hours. Back to crawling as black smoke started to consume everything, I bumped into the cage and Pedro just sitting, watching everything. The smoke thickened, making it hard to breathe. My eyes watered. I couldn't leave him to burn. Quickly returning to Paris, I patted him down until I found a key ring. This had to be it. It had to be.

"Okay," I said, not looking at Pedro. With the screams, raging fire, and flashes of gunshots around us, I didn't think he'd hear me anyway, but I always talked when I was nervous. And I was more than nervous. The heat at my back warned me to get the hell out. "I'm going to get you out of here." My voice cracked. Another key attempt, another fail. "I don't know what happened, why you're in here." I lifted my eyes to his round, dark ones. They looked eerily like shark eyes. Flat. With nothing behind them. No awareness. No care. Nothing. With trembling hands, I inserted another key. Nothing. "But I'm not leaving you behind." Finally, the lock opened with the final key.

"What are you doing!" Serena in all her bloodied glory, with daggers in hand ready to strike Pedro, stopped me.

"No!" I jumped in front of her.

"Sebastian, get away from it. You have no idea what you're doing."

I shook my head, ignoring the fact that she knew my name. "What has he done wrong!"

"He's a *malice*."

"And what are *you*?" I snapped back.

Her eyes softened and she lowered her hands. Just then, Maddox came charging forward. The big mountain of a man hellbent on destroying Serena.

I shoved her away and the demon slammed into me hard enough to break something. To break everything. My body flew into the concrete block at my back, and then a zip of pain exploded throughout my body. I tried to get to my feet, but I couldn't manage it.

This is where I die.

All for onions.

The last thought before my body gave out.

Chapter Eighteen

Xcian

I paced the floor, scuffing the shit with my shitkickers and leaving a trail of blood in my wake. Blood of my enemies. Blood of the sonsofbitches who thought they could hurt what belonged to *me*. Sebastian's painful screams felt like a pick chiseling into my brain. The strength of it vibrated through my whole body, forcing me to clench my fists instead of swinging them.

Zane guarded the door leading into the bedroom where Sebastian's screams continued to echo. Again and again. I launched myself at the door, but Zane caught me. "Release me! I'm going to kill that fucker."

"He's healing him, Xcian," Zane said. "Don't force me to chain you."

I shoved my brother back, feeling the ripple of power just under my skin. Hawke and Noah moved closer, flanking me, forcing my hackles to rise.

Zane lifted his hands. "It's okay," he said to my brothers, who were going to eat shit in five seconds. "Just move back. No threats here, Xcian. *Xcian*, look at me."

I realized I was panting. I'd shifted. My fangs extended, claws, horns, and all. We'd arrived late to the club. The fire had consumed the place. Pedro had been carrying a wounded Sebastian out with Serena close behind him when we finally arrived. The malice had saved Sebastian because I hadn't been there. The thought made my demons push against the barrier, imprisoning them. Soon, they'd break free.

"No one is going to subdue you, brother. We're here to ensure Sebastian lives."

The thought of Sebastian *not* living sent me into a rage. I crashed a fist into the drywall, then another, then the dinner table went through the front window. I heard Noah say, *"Not the TV."* Yeah, that followed the dining table. My heart bled chaos and rage. I needed to burn the whole world to the ground.

I cupped my head and roared. Shards of glass rained around me. The chandelier, the windows, who the fuck knew. I didn't care. "Make him stop screaming!"

Then the screaming did stop. The silence turned into the most terrible thing in the world. *No. No. He can't be dead.* I rammed into my brother, slammed him against the wall just as he shifted. Before I could release the full extent of my demons, Hawke and Noah clamped a collar around my neck, and I ground my teeth as pain lifted from the small of my back, up my spine, until it felt as if my head was going to pop.

Then I passed the fuck out.

I woke up with a start, unable to move, chained to the bed, my energy depleted. I reveled in the silence for a heartbeat before I remembered Sebastian's screams. Then the silence that followed. My eyes peeled open, and I felt my brother close. "Let me out. Where is he? How is he?"

Zane sat on the chair beside the bed, and I stopped

moving. My brother had been a hot mess ever since he met his bonded mate. Love would do that to you. Rip your soul out of your body in torturous slivers until there was nothing left of you. But this was something worse. He ran his hand through his hair, down his face. Pale as hell. "I'm going to have to get Eric over here. Sebastian doesn't have long in this world."

Though it had been my demons who had latched onto the kid, they were restrained now that I'd been shackled, so I didn't know why I still felt the need to burn the world to ashes. I couldn't even find words.

"The healer tried everything but he's human." Zane said the word with clear distaste and got to his feet and started to pace. "Weak. All of them are so fucking weak."

"What about a human hospital? They can fix him," I finally said.

Zane cupped his chin. "He sustained a head injury and his pupils are blown, Sebastian."

Panic surfaced and I fought with the chains. "Get me out of here. Now." I had to go to him. To do something. I'd done nothing to save him. I'd ignored him for five days, hadn't reached out to him, and knew his security detail had been pulled. "We did this. We left him alone with no protection. Get me out of these chains or I swear to all the gods in the universe, I will lose it." Not that I could lose it with the chains draining my power.

"There's a way," Zane said, eyes wide and haunting. "If he's bonded, he can regenerate using his mate's life force."

I stopped struggling. True. Eric was no longer human, having bonded with Zane. They shared each other's souls, life, blood and magic. "He's brain-dead, Zane," I found myself saying the words with monumental effort. "He won't be able to agree to it."

"It could be one way." I had to give it to my brother for keeping a straight face as he knocked me out.

"Like Finn with you? That's the life you want me to lead? Tortured for all eternity." By the time I said those words, I was grinding my teeth. "Bonding isn't just for the fuck of it. There has to be something *there*. Trust, love, shit I'd never felt before. You know this. I don't *love* him."

"You have a connection with him and that rage out there for him was visceral."

"My demons, Zane. You know what I am."

"If it could be done. If there's a chance, will you do it?"

"It can't be done!"

"Will you!"

"Yes. Fucking bastard. Yes." The words tumbled out of my mouth and I wanted to take them back. No. Fuck no. I didn't want to bond with Sebastian. And something writhing in my gut told me it wouldn't be a natural binding. "How? We don't have the flames."

"The manacles do the same thing. They keep the demons from surfacing."

"And how do we bypass the fact that he's unconscious?"

"He's alive. The healer is keeping him alive just enough so you can go in and get him out."

"Get him out. Like a…" The realization of what Zane intended to do hit me like a freight train. "Fuck, Zane. Are you shitting me?"

"Noah can find him in his dreams."

"You mean nightmare."

"Doesn't matter."

"Then why doesn't Noah bond with him?" The thought made me grind my molars.

"Because Sebastian doesn't know *Noah*. He knows *you*. All you have to do is follow Noah, get Sebastian to the aether, and—" At that moment, Finnegan drifted out of the shadows. His arms out as if he were finishing up a grand performance.

"And I'll do the rest."

****

I agreed to it. I fucking agreed to do this. I clung to the sink, feeling the magic on my cuffs melt away all the excess power I would've had surrounding me. It wasn't my demons that wanted to save Sebastian. Or at least it wasn't *only* my demons that wanted to save Sebastian. I hung my head. The air stirred behind me.

Serena had been one of us since she'd been born as a matriarch. Her family compensated handsomely. In layman's terms—she'd been sold to us to act as a breeder for Zane. I knew the sting of being sold out. My mother had sold me out to to the gods, and Genesis had sold me out for power.

My reaction to Sebastian, to all of this shit, made no sense. And the weight of Serena's stare felt like a ton of bricks against my chest.

"I'm sorry," she said. "Sebastian saved my life. I didn't know you and he were something. Are something. Paris mentioned scenting you on him."

"I kidnapped him, held him for a few days for Zane. That's all." *Liar.* "And how the hell did you end up with Paris?"

"Maddox caught me at the border."

"You could've been killed, or worse."

"I could protect myself."

"Obviously not."

Hawke appeared at the doorway and glared at us. My state of undress didn't help matters any. Naked, with Serena, the love of his life, though he was too stupid to do anything about it. Well, now he'd have to. Lest let Galen lead the Nine. "Zane says to hurry. We don't have much time."

We had all the time in the world. But not Sebastian. The thought of him dying made me incoherent. I tried to stir something inside of me that would explain my connection to the kid, and came up empty. I'd be bonding with Sebastian. Like Finn, I would suffer.

Nothing changes in your life, Xcian. You've been suffering since the day you were born. You were meant to suffer. At least, unlike Finn with Zane, Sebastian was human and would die. Wouldn't be reincarnated, so my suffering would last one human lifetime.

Serena tossed me a pair of joggers I slipped on before meeting everyone in the bedroom where they had Sebastian. The temperature in the room was below freezing. Our breath hung in the air. It took a moment for my body temperature to adjust, but it did quickly. We weren't human. Cold and hot didn't affect us as such, but Sebastian lay in the bed paler than anyone I'd ever seen. Blood matted the pillow behind his head, which had swelled like a balloon. Covered only by a thin sheet, his naked body looked frail. Dying. The first sting of tears welled behind my eyes and pain pressed into my chest.

Yeah, there were feelings there. I just hoped it was enough to save him. Though he'd hate me later, at least he'd be alive. I cleared my throat. "How is this going to work?"

Zane led my attention to Noah spread out on the floor next to the bed. "Hey, bro." He waved, the magic cuff glinting in the fading light.

"You are all wearing cuffs," Zane started. I realized Sebastian wore similar cuffs. "It will link the three of you. Follow Noah, get Sebastian out of whatever headspace he's trapped in, and into the aether. Finn will meet you there."

I turned to Finn under shadow. I didn't trust him, but it was too late to doubt now. I turned to Zane, my sight blurry. My fear unmasked. It lifted from the depth of my soul, reminding me of the day we'd been separated. I'd looked to him for guidance. For instruction. For something because when Genesis called to Lucifer for me, I'd all but shit my pants. It had been Zane who saved me that day eons ago. Zane who took my place in Hell.

My brother.

He cupped my face. We were almost eye to eye. Then he leaned his forehead against mine. The same thing we did that day when we'd both been teens, living our first round of life. "You can do this. I know you can. Just follow your heart."

I snorted. "I don't think I have one that works." Fuck. My brain took that moment to come offline. "I'm broken, Zane. I'm fucked up inside. What if I make it worse? What if he comes back tainted because of me? Maybe he's at peace now. Maybe…" I couldn't say it. *Maybe it'd be better if he leaves this world instead of joining mine.*

"I know you, Xcian. You are the Sword of the Nine. Protector. You are not broken. And if the fates deem to take him still, so be it. At least we *tried*."

Try shit and see where the pieces fall. Zane's motto in life.

I nodded.

As everyone else left the room, I slipped into the bed beside Sebastian, smelling the iron of blood, the sulfur of demon fire, and another scent underlying it all. The wildflowers that reminded me of home. *His* scent. I took his cold hand in mine and closed my eyes.

Chapter Nineteen

Sebastian

I couldn't feel my body, but I screamed anyway. I tasted iron in the back of my throat from so much screaming. And then I chased a dark light as it zipped to a finite point, and then burst open into a raging fire.

I screamed again.

"Seba, run!"

Familiar surroundings. A circle. Flames. Alejandro dying just out of reach.

I couldn't run. My feet were cemented to the ground. It swallowed me and, for a second, I was in a numbing darkness. The darkness didn't last. It pulsed. Faded in and out. Dreamlike visions swam in front of me, but they didn't feel like dreams.

Alex stood in Mom's hotel room, his expression of dread as Doofus lunged for him and they both fell over the railing and into a twenty-story drop. Screams. So many screams erupted around me. Alex dead. Dead. Dad. Dad there. Standing among the enemy, morphing into something with jagged claws and sharp teeth. I took a step away from him, but he became all that I could see. All that I could feel. Trapped.

Then the floor dropped out from under me, and I couldn't breathe. I clawed at the noose around my neck. Darkness, a tangible thing, pressed its weight into my chest, spilled into my mouth, filled my vision, and took my breath.

Killing me.

The pressure snapped. I fell onto solid arms. The noose yanked away. Painful breaths followed, then another and another. Spots danced in front of my eyes like jellyfish.

"I got you," he said. "I got you. You're safe." Familiar words that sang in my head. I blinked the haze and silver, blue eyes appeared along with silver hair, and a pale complexion.

"Xcian," I whispered through the pain in my throat, and hugged him. He kissed the top of my head and I felt safe. Always safe with him. Protected. Alejandro protected me from bullies. Protected me from Dad sometimes. Thinking about my brother made tears burn through my eyes. "Alejandro," I managed to croak out. "I can't leave him. He needs me."

Xcian's expression turned tense as if he were about to snap any minute. "We'll get him out. I promise. But we have to move." He lifted me into his arms as if I weighed nothing. I circled my arms around his neck, and buried my face into his neck, inhaling him. He smelled of sulfur and iron.

The surrounding air turned thick. A presence that pushed against my skin. Then I heard it. Alejandro screaming. I pushed off of Xcian, forcing him to drop me to my feet. I stumbled and he held me tight. "What is it?" he asked.

"Alejandro. I hear him. It's this way." I started to move on still shaky legs, but Xcian grabbed my hand.

"No, it's this way."

I turned to the way he pointed and saw nothing but

a wall of blackness. A dead silence. I shook my head. "No, Xcian. Alejandro is over here. Don't you hear him?"

At that moment, Alejandro screamed. A gut-wrenching terrible scream, and Xcian lifted his eyes in that direction. He'd heard it. "No. I don't hear it," he said, glaring at me.

"You lie!" I struggled to get out of his vice grip, but it only made him hold me tighter. "Let me go. I have to get to him!" Time was running out. I felt the pulse of it against my body, my head. An explosion of pain consumed me, and the dark shifted, forcing me to my knees.

"Hurry. There's no time!" Someone yelled. Alejandro. Maybe. Pain burst into my head, pushing against my skull. I was dying. I didn't know how I knew, but I knew.

Xcian cursed and lifted me in his arms again. I tried to fight. But my limbs just wouldn't work. "Alejandro, Xcian, please, don't leave my brother."

The vibration of his body against mine soothed me. "We'll get him back. I need you to trust me."

I trusted him. I did. Maybe. I wasn't sure.

We passed a dark wall and entered an enclosure of some kind. A cave. It smelled of dust and mint. A pallet covered in pelts sat under open skies. I leaned my cheek against Xcian's chest. The steady vibration lulled me into a haze. Then Xcian lay me down on the pallet. Stars twinkled in the night sky beyond. He stretched out next to me, never letting me go. A chill lifted the hairs on my skin. Naked. We were naked. How did we get naked?

Our bodies pressed together. Me tucked under his

chin. His arms cradling me so that we were flushed together from head to toe. Legs intertwined. I felt prickles of hair on my skin. His long, thick cock against my stomach. Every touchpoint sparked heat into my body, erasing the tingling and shooting something magical inside of me. I closed my eyes and felt the stirring inside my mind. Unable to give words as an explanation, I could only feel. The drumming of his heart as if he were everywhere. A light fragrance of fresh blooms tickled my nose. A contrast to the smell of the cavern. An image of fall leaves and wildflowers on stretches of prairie land roads. All Xcian. I'd scented it before. When we were together, his lips on my body, his mouth on my cock. The thought, his scent, knowing that we were naked, in bed, fused together, made me half-hard. I wanted Xcian in any way he'd have me.

I pulled a little bit away, breaking some of our connection to look up at his face. Finding feeling in my limbs, I trailed my fingers down his exquisite face. "You're so beautiful," I whispered.

That seemed to be something he was waiting for. The space between his brow crinkled as if he decided something, and he slammed his mouth against mine. Our kisses always chaotic and frantic. Until it slowed and deepened. This one stayed on the heated, chaotic side.

Chapter Twenty

Xcian

"What is this," I snarled.

"This is your happy place. Bonding takes place in your Eden construct," Finn said with a smirk on his face I wanted to punch.

"This?" I gestured to the cave where I'd been with Genesis. Where she took me in as a boy, where I grew up training. Where we had eventually fallen in love. Or at least I thought we had. Being here. My happy place. "This is a lie."

Finn shrugged. "This is your construct. Not mine. If it's a lie, then this is the place you chose to show your bonding mate."

I growled and took a step closer, though I couldn't do anything with Sebastian's limp body in my arms. "This better work to save him or I will make sure you live forever."

That made Finn drop his smile. "This will save him if you complete the bonding. Fuck him and get it over with." Finn disappeared.

Fucker. Bonding of soul and body always required a joining of some kind. All of it subliminal if it were real. It could be saving someone from death. It could be sharing an emotional experience. Trusting implicitly. Something had to spark the joining process. Sex usually did the trick. Especially since this was all a lie.

No going back now, especially with Sebastian dying. Dying! I laid Sebastian on the pallet, feeling his life draining away, the fates calling him home.

Naked, I almost considered doing nothing and holding him as he faded away. Letting him go. But then he looked at me, trailed his fingers down my face, called me beautiful, and I lost it. The world needed Sebastian Diaz in it. And I kissed him. I ravaged him completely. Took him in a way no other person had ever taken him before. I had fucked him senseless, and he had opened up to me. Pliant and submissive in every way. He trusted me.

And it had all been a lie.

I opened my eyes and squinted against the bright sun entering through the slivers of the window drapes. A beam splashed against Sebastian in my arms. The numbness wore off quickly, and the weight of him in my arms in this position made me wince. I heard someone shuffling in the room.

Zane came into my line of sight, looking like death. He nodded. "It worked," he whispered in the room. That should've been a happy proclamation. We saved his bonded mate's son. Eric would be forever grateful if he ever found out. Which he could never find out because that would mean telling him what I did.

Right. I made Sebastian a target. Not only for my demons, but for everyone out there looking to hurt me. To my defense, Eric did that too. When he mated Zane.

"The healer wants to examine him," Zane said.

Right. Meant I had to let him go. "I'm not letting him go. He can examine him around me."

Zane sighed. Fuck it. He's the one that fucked me

over. I wasn't going to suffer any more than I had to with this shit. Zane didn't argue.

The healer was a long, willowy man with salt and pepper hair, leathery skin that made him look ancient, like prehistoric, and unnaturally long fingers, their tips blackened. The result of using magic. Magic drew from a person's life spark. Draining them until they literally shed their skin. That transition either killed them, turned them mad, or made them young again. And the cycle continued.

Hatcher looked on the verge of shedding, using the last of his magic on Sebastian. And he didn't seem afraid of it. Made me wonder how many times he'd already shed. It gets easier with time. The young ones were the ones to usually die. The man ignored me completely as he looked over Sebastian's head wound. Since I had Sebastian on his side, he had easy access. Then he trailed a finger from Sebastian's neck, along every ridge of his spine, to the crack of his ass. I growled, feeling my demons stirring within. It was then I realized, I didn't have my cuffs. "You may want to watch where you touch my mate," I growled out.

My mate.

Fuck. My bonded mate. The need to protect Sebastian from everyone surged from parts of me that had never been touched. Keeping him locked up in a bedroom that I only had access to was damn tempting. I couldn't help but feel Zane made a mistake. Hawke or Noah would've been a better mate. Their demons weren't visceral, controlling assholes I had let out from time to time to have fun. To ease my own pain.

The healer lifted black eyes to me, and I felt a slight tug at my core. A tether forcing my eyes back to

Sebastian who parted his lips and inhaled. Content. Sexed out. Relaxed. And when I moved my knee an inch where it had been close to his flaccid cock, I felt the sticky residue of what we had done. What I had done. A lie. Like a wet dream, but still a damn lie. I swallowed the guilt and panicked. Unsure where I ended and he started. I started to move when the healer stopped me.

"You must remain together so that he can heal."

"Like this?" I asked, sickened to my stomach.

"Yes. Touch is important. It'll only be a few days at best."

"Days! What if I have to piss?"

He arched a brow, calling my stupidity. "I know what you did, and you should know a forced binding is...unnatural. It goes against the fates, and they are fickle bitches. You're going to want to try to fake normalcy. At least until the bond can be broken."

"Wait, what? It can be broken?" On instinct, I hugged Sebastian closer. *Fuck that, no. He's mine.* "How is that possible?"

"It's not a true bond. Finnegan explained your restraint when you led the boy to your Eden." Fucking Finn. I wanted to tear his head off his shoulders. The healer went on. "It worked to an extent, but the lie makes the bond weak. It may be enough to heal the boy, but we cannot let the bond dissolve on its own. It'll—"

"Make me go mad. I know. The reason forced bonds are something not done."

"The power of the aether will sustain you. *That* Finnegan was correct in assuming. The reason you and the boy still live."

Again, with *the boy*. Every time he said *the boy*, I hugged Sebastian tighter. "How long before you can break the bond?"

"A few months at best."

A few months. *No. Yes. Fuck.* "Yeah, okay."

The man nodded and left.

I heard Zane thank the healer at the door and he walked inside. A newly bonded mate could be volatile. I was livid. "I need you to clear the cabin. Everyone the fuck out," I whispered harshly, feeling Sebastian's blood begin to circulate, his heart a steady drum against my skin. Alive.

"Xcian."

I bristled at the way my brother said my name. I knew the apology was coming and I couldn't stand it. "Zane, so help me, if you don't get everyone, especially that fucking wraith of yours, out of my scented range, I will tear them to shreds with my teeth."

He sighed. "Yeah, okay. A few days. Call me with updates. At least."

I didn't agree to shit, and he left anyway.

The following twenty-four hours were brutal. I couldn't move away from Sebastian. Every time my bladder got full, and I had to relieve myself, unwrapping myself from his cool body hurt. Like every cell in my body took up arms and were stabbing me with their trillions of swords just under my skin. The first time I rolled out of his arms had been monumental. I'd been dripping with sweat despite the cool temperature in the room. They had lowered it to keep Sebastian in stasis, but now that he was healing, I raised the temperature, got more blankets, and slipped beside him again. I needed to change the sheets. The stench of blood on him was too overpowering. But that would have to wait.

Later...

I drifted into sleep.

And woke up on the edge of a nightmare. Not mine. Sebastian's nightmare about his brother. I felt the cry, the pain, the fear all at once. Morning had broken through, and Sebastian had kicked out of the blankets. Sweltering with heat. Dying for being human. Too tired to do anything else, I held him. Ran my hand up and down his body, touching him wherever I could. Saying nonsense, soothing words to him. Promising him that everything would be okay. That we'll get Alejandro. That this was all a dream. He settled.

The next morning, I got out of bed, ate breakfast, moved Sebastian to another clean room, and stripped the bed. I hauled everything outside, the sheets, the pillow, mattress, and added his clothes too, and lit everything on fire. Then I lifted all the windows and let the place air out.

Serena called me. Thank fuck. I was about to burst at the seams. "How is he?"

"Alive, but not good. He's still feverish. Having nightmares. I don't know what to do."

"Call the doc, Xcian. She works with human physiology. He's human. She might be able to help."

I ran my hand through my hair. "Yeah, good. I'll do that. How's everything at home?"

"Good. Eric is pissed at Zane because Zane won't tell him what's going on with Sebastian, and Layla moved into the mansion, so Zane is about to go nuclear. He's taking it out on Pedro, who hasn't said a word except that he wants to speak with Sebastian."

Fuck. I could imagine. If Zane felt half the way I did about Sebastian, I felt sorry for Pedro until I remembered that he was malice. Our enemy. "If it wasn't for Pedro, Sebastian would be with Maddox now."

I shut my eyes, imagining everything that could've happened because I had left him to defend himself alone. I knew the moment Sebastian woke up he was going to fight me tooth and nail. I had managed to keep things in check, somewhat. Now...now I was afraid he'd hate me. Run. Leave me mad. "Serena, I don't know if I can let him go once he wakes up," I heard myself say. "He's going to want to bolt unless I do something." A stretch of silence followed my words.

"Don't imprint memories on him, Xcian. His mind is fragile right now."

"What else can I do? The healer says months, months! I'm going crazy right now thinking about him waking up and leaving."

She sighed. "Common goals. Make him need you for something."

"We don't have anything in common."

"At the club, Paris was willing to exchange Sebastian for Maddox because of Alejandro. Sebastian must realize that he's in danger."

"He thinks his brother is trapped. The root of his nightmares is him trying to get his brother out from some sort of hell."

"Then use that. Let him investigate it all. Keep him busy with you. Before you know it, Hatcher will be ready to break the bond."

The thought made me flinch; my chest hurt. I rubbed it. "Yeah. That might work."

"In the meantime, call the doc."

At lunch time, I called Dr. Roberts. She arrived an hour later.

"You did the right thing by calling me," she said. "The high body temperature is indicative that his body is fighting infection. It's not worrisome, since you are acting like his antibiotics and healing him. He still needs hydration." She ran a line into his vein and tethered him to an IV bag. "He also needs nutrients. I've left instructions. Just change the bag as needed. It shouldn't be for more than twelve hours at the rate he's healing." She threw back the sheet below his waist, revealing his cock. *My* cock. I almost pushed her back but used my body to stop her instead. "What the hell are you doing?"

She smirked. "I'm running a catheter. He will need to relieve himself."

I clenched my jaw. "No, no more intrusions. I'll clean him up."

"Mr. Crawford—"

"I said *no.*"

She got to her feet. "Very well."

"If he doesn't wake up in twelve hours, call me back."

I nodded and walked her out. Unable to do anything else, I sat on the bed beside him and made sure our bodies were touching. Skin to skin. That didn't help my sex drive, either. I was hard when I woke up, and harder still now. I couldn't help but think of taking Sebastian for real this time. Filling him with my seed. Lathering it around his skin so he'd absorb my scent. Be mine. I wanted to spread his ass cheeks open and taste him.

Fuck. My erection hurt. I clamped my hand around its girth and gave it one tug, wincing at the sensitivity. I'd never get Sebastian to want to stay with me. He'd wake up and escape. The thought made me squeeze harder, and I welcomed the bit of pain and dragged faster. Harder. Sebastian would have to learn his place beside me until the bond could be broken. He'd have to submit the way he did in our shared dream. I didn't care if it was a lie.

Pleasure racked through my body, and I hit the back of my head against the headboard, moaning loud. Alone, no one would hear me, anyway. I sucked in deep breaths thinking about how my mate would react to my intrusion against his hole. Fuck. The thought had me close. So close. I shut my eyes. I bent my knee, my foot flat on the mattress, my legs spread wide. I reached just under my balls with my left hand, circling my finger against my hole. Like Sebastian, I'd never had a man fuck me. I'd never inserted anything inside my body. Never had the desire to feel full with another man.

But him.

The thought of it sent me spurting, and I came in pulsing jets, coming on my stomach to at least keep the bed clean.

Fuck. Fuck. Fuck.

I calmed my breathing and heard…breathing. I opened my eyes to look at Sebastian. His chest rose and fell with every deep inhalation of breath, the sheet around his hips tented. He turned his head toward me, his hips moving. "Xcian, please," he whispered. Slowly, he dragged his hand to his erection, over the sheet. "Please. Don't stop. Please." The space between his brow folded, his lips dry. I couldn't deny him even if I tried. My demons wouldn't let me ignore his need; our bond wouldn't let me ignore his need.

Fuck!

I pulled down the sheet and exposed his long cock. Such a beautiful sight. His tip glazed with precum. I had no playbook for this shit. Calling Zane and asking him for advice seemed stupid. I should be able to pleasure my mate. He was mine. His body belonged to me and his pleasure and all that came with it.

Mine.

But it's a lie.

"Xcian, please." His eyes fluttered open, and locked on mine. That did it. I spread his legs, positioned myself between them, and gave his cock one long lick from base to tip, tasting him. I never tired of how he tasted on my tongue. His clean scent, mixed with my own heady one, made the memories of the fields spread wide open inside my mind. Peace. All I felt was peace. Then I delved and stretched my mouth and took Sebastian all the way down my throat. The sounds he made, the hissing, saying my name, and then finally moaning long and smooth as I licked him clean, felt like home.

I pulled away and let his limp cock out of my mouth and watched as he fell back into sleep. My body coiled tight. I leaned in and inhaled him. My heart bursting at the seams.

This isn't real.

Except it felt real.

One thing was real. I wasn't letting Sebastian run from me, ever again. I'd do anything to keep him at my side.

Anything.

Chapter Twenty-One

Sebastian

"Seba, run!"

The echo of my brother's screams climbed with me to the surface as I opened my eyes to a dark room. For a heartbeat, I floated in nothing before everything hit me all at once. The abrasion of the sheet at my back. The weight of a blanket on my body, and a pinch in my arm. I managed to roll my head and saw an IV stand tethered to me. The left side of my body felt warmer than the rest of me and I saw the reason why. Xcian lay curled at my side, asleep. Naked. His chest was against my shoulder, his head tilted into my temple. His hard abs against my arm, his hips and...oh, God, his erection poked into my hip, his leg over mine, and his hand over my heart. Every contact against my skin shot an electric current through me.

Dreaming. The only explanation for him naked beside me. I'd dreamt a lot about Xcian since I met him. But the most current ones, the one where he'd been with me trying to find Alejandro, felt real. Then he...then we...shit.

A dream.

I turned my head away and the movement had him lifting his lids and pressing deeper into me. His thumb rubbed my sensitive nub. "Sebastian?" his voice thick,

180

deep, and sultry went right to my cock.

I tried to talk, but my tongue felt too heavy, too dry. And I needed to take a piss. "I have to use the bathroom," I managed to croak out.

Xcian quickly got to his feet with no concern in the world that he was naked. As if that were a totally normal thing. Yeah, Xcian and I had sex. I'd seen him naked, and he'd seen me, but it'd been chaotic. Without thought, almost as if the act of being naked were secondary. We couldn't have sex with clothes on, right? But this was deliberate. And it felt right. I didn't even feel the need to cover myself as he carefully lifted the sheet off my body and unhooked the IV bag, lifting it to make it mobile.

"Can you stand?"

I needed to catch a breath first. Xcian taking care of me? As I lifted myself, he placed his large hand on my back to help me sit up, and I shivered against the heat of his touch. The world tilted as my inertia settled. My body was stiff, but I wasn't in pain. I touched the back of my head, feeling tender, but whole. Xcian watched me with a curious expression. I had lots of questions, but I really needed to pee. I lifted myself on my feet, and a flood of shivers ran through me, but then Xcian stood at my side. One hand holding the IV bag, the other around my waist, allowing me to lean on him. "Just go slow."

I did. Hated that he stayed in the bathroom as I relieved myself, then washed my hands, cupped some in my palm, and slurped water. "I'll get you some more."

I was just too damn thirsty and took another palmful before wiping my mouth and letting him take me back to bed. I sat down, already tired from my efforts, but I didn't get back under the sheet. "Do I still need this?" I pointed at the needle in my arm.

"No. I'll take it out." He hung the bag and grabbed a first aid kit. Then he knelt between my legs and my body...yeah, woke up. Him so close. He glanced at my half-hard cock and then my arm and carefully pulled out the needle, and left me with a purple bandage over the small prick.

"Really?" I asked, indicating the bandage.

"Purple is definitely your color."

I almost chuckled but realized Xcian made a joke. "Did you just try to be funny?" He looked away quickly but not before I caught a pepper of blush on his cheeks. "You did. No way. This is creepier than the monster you." I meant that as a joke, but his eyes turned colder. "Sorry. I didn't mean—"

"It's okay. You should rest. I'll go get you some water and make dinner."

Make dinner? Another creepy feeling fell like a stone into my gut. But at least he got dressed before he walked out of the room.

Stupid, Sebastian. Stupid. I wanted to thump myself on my forehead, but I couldn't manage it. Alone, I took in the bedroom. Small. Rustic. A window covered in a green drape I didn't recognize. I didn't recognize any of this. I got to my feet and walked to the window, pulling the drapes aside. Nothing but trees. A gravel road. Another prison. I turned and my bare foot hit something cold. A manacle without the chain.

What happened?

As if the question brought back the memories, I remembered the vampires. The demon. I remembered. I stumbled, hit the IV pole and it fell over, crashing against the dresser before it hit the floor.

I couldn't breathe.

The bedroom door flew open—

I opened the cage to let Pedro out. Serena in front of me.

—Xcian came rushing in. Holding me.

Maddox had charged for Serena. I pushed her out of the way. He slammed into me. And I...I...I died.

"How am I alive?" The words came out hoarse. Xcian held me and a sense of safety washed over me. I shook my head. "Xcian, please."

He flinched at my words but hadn't released me. "Get dressed and come eat. You're weak. I'll answer your questions after you eat."

He was right. I was too weak to do much of anything else, and I knew I'd need time to process what my mind kept throwing at me. The real and the not real. Was Xcian real? He led me to the bed and sat me down, then dressed me. Even helped me put my legs through the pant hole and lifted them over my hips as I clung to his shoulders. "Is everyone okay? Please. At least tell me my mom, my dad, Alejandro."

"Everyone is alive," he said.

"Serena?"

"She's alive. You saved her life. Thank you."

Right. Serena was his mate. I remembered that now and quickly lifted my hands from his shoulders and took a step back. The space between us felt too wide. I wanted to hold him, but Xcian had someone. He had lied to me about not mating her.

He just stood there, watching me, with no expression on his face that I could read. "Thanks, I'm okay." Lie. And he knew it. But didn't call me out on it.

He walked out of the bedroom, leaving the door open. I followed him out, needing my strength back so that I could find Alejandro and save him, even if it meant escaping Xcian again.

I kicked the cuff under the bed, unsure if it'd be of any use without the chain. When I walked out of the bedroom for dinner, I had expected something like soup. Ramen. The easiest shit to make. Not a juicy grilled steak, potatoes, and greens. My stomach rumbled, my mouth salivated. Hunger made me dizzy.

"Sit down," Xcian said, serving me a hefty portion of everything. "You lost a lot of blood. Need to bring up your iron."

"Did you cook this?"

"There's more to me than the monster inside," he grumbled, and quickly turned around so I wouldn't have to see his expression.

Yeah, I deserved that one. "I'm sorry. I didn't mean—"

"It's okay. Eat."

The order rumbled right through me, and I found myself picking up my fork and knife and digging in. I ate and drank lots of water. Xcian ate too, glancing at me as if he wanted to say something, but keeping his mouth shut. Once we finished, he cleared and washed the dishes.

"Go shower. Then we'll talk," he ordered, without looking at me as he busied himself with the dishes. I couldn't help watching him. The wide expanse of his shoulders, bare back, and long unkempt hair as if he hadn't bothered to brush it in days. And that round, tight ass.

I needed a shower. A cold one.

Chapter Twenty-Two

Xcian

Sebastian's arousal punched me in the gut, and I had to get away from him or throw him over the table and take him there on the spot. Watching his mouth move, his throat, the lust for his food, made me so damn hard I had to do something. I heard the shower running, and I wanted to get in with him. The urge so damn strong, I bit down to stop a growl.

Mine. Mine. He was fucking mine. I had a right to invade his privacy even if just to touch him. Feel his soft skin against mine. That would've been enough to tame the raging need inside of me. To breathe him in. Keep him close. The shit was driving me insane.

"You look like shit."

I spun and threw the knife I'd been holding at the fucker sitting on the counter. He anticipated the move and turned to shadow in time for the knife to go through him and slam into the wall behind him.

"Yeah, that's about right," Finnegan said, wearing his damn coy smile that practically reached his ears and made his eyes gleam. The first time I'd ever seen the wraith happy. "Let me guess. You want to restrain him. To keep him close. You want to maybe imprison him until he learns to love you back." He arched his brow. "Am I close?"

That's exactly what he'd done to Zane.

He hopped off the counter, his eyes bearing down on me. A toxic, menacing thing. "Fast forward two thousand years. Love turns to hate. Caresses turn to torture. Imagine that, and you know a fraction of what my father did to me."

"What did your father do to you?" All the stories I'd heard had been that Finn purposely bound himself to Zane. Sought out the shaman to perform the ritual. Lucifer hadn't been mentioned.

He seemed to realize he'd said too much and waved his hand as if spreading smoke. "Don't listen to me. I'm already insane. I'm here for the kid's status. I may have heard a thing or two about your condition. Your intent to play the hero and figure out what the hell is going on with Alejandro."

I knew damn well that Serena wouldn't have told Finn shit. The sentient being knew too damn much. At least he could never use it against us. His loyalty would always lie with Zane, and now Eric. The thought of me being in the same boat as Finn, watching Sebastian love someone else, made me sick. For a moment, the earth shook at the thought. Then I realized it was me, shaking with anger.

"You won't last a week if you don't keep it together."

He was right. I was tearing apart at the seams and my demons were waiting. Silent. Knowing they'd be free if I popped like a balloon. "What can I do?"

"Tell him sweet nothings. Seduce him like you have been doing. Humans thrive on that shit, and the kid is already enamored with you. He doesn't have to know it's a lie. And by the time he does, the bond is broken and you're free." He shrugged. "Or you can imprison him, break him until he goes insane and takes his own life, or kill your competition off. Whatever works."

Kill the competion. Finn had tried to kill Eric by convincing the human to hang himself. All of Zane's betrothed had met their end before their mating. Sebastian had been attacked at the house and on the road by the malice. Yet, Genesis who led the malice, wanted Eric and Zane together. Killing Sebastian would've put an end to their union.

Rage, deep and potent, exploded within me, and I grabbed Finn by the throat. My body shifted into my true form. I released a piece of my demon power and Finn couldn't shift to shadow. Like Genesis trapped in a web, he couldn't escape. His eyes widened, black. So damn black. "*You* sent the malice after Sebastian. *You* killed all of Zane's betrotheds."

Finn vibrated under my grasp and I had a fleeting thought that he could kill me where I stood. At that moment, I didn't care. "You touch him—"

"There's no need. Not anymore," Finn hissed out through his fangs. "Zane got his bonded mate. Killing him now would change nothing."

"I should send you back to your father in Hell," I growled out.

Unlike Genesis, Finnegan didn't fight. Just hung there, letting me snuff the life from his body. His eyes closed, and I released him. He dropped, gasping to the floor, and didn't wisp away like usual. I took a step back. The further I got from him, the better. There was no permanent solution to Finnegan. Every time we killed him, his father would send him back each time a little bit crazier than the last.

"Finn!"

I looked up in time to see Sebastian scurry into the kitchen and drop beside Finnegan, who was still seeking air to breathe. Except now, the fucker was exaggerating the shit and coughing, cupping his throat. My eyes landed where Sebastian held the wraith's arm, gently, the other around Finn's back as he helped him to his feet.

"What is wrong with you?" Sebastian spat at me. He looked younger than his nineteen years. Too young to be mine. Too young to be involved in any of this shit.

And too innocent and naïve.

He helped Finnegan sit at the table. "I'll get you some water," Sebastian said, and glared at me on his way to the sink, where he filled a glass of water. Finnegan smirked at me before looking like death when Sebastian returned to him and carefully set the glass on the table. "What's going on?" Sebastian looked to me and then at Finnegan. "Is it my brother?"

I threw Finnegan a look that said shut up. He didn't get it or ignored it. "Yeah, it is." He even sounded remorseful. The fucker.

I moved closer, taking a seat next to Sebastian. Only then was I able to breathe. I took a chance and placed my hand on top of his on the table, and he hadn't snatched it away. "Your brother's going to be fine," I added.

That made him curl his fingers into mine. Accept me. And suddenly my world cleared. I could breathe. Finn dragged his eyes from our joined hands to my face, and a small smirk lifted his mouth. Fucker. Finnegan had been going through this for close to a thousand years. I'd been at it for two days, and death seemed a kinder resolution. It was hard not to sympathize with the fucker. Except he killed innocents to keep Zane.

You'd do the same.

I would. I'd burn the world to keep Sebastian. What did that make me if not a monster?

"What can we do?" Sebastian asked, breaking me from my thoughts. The strain on his features made me lean further into him, healing him. His cheeks turned pinker, his lips rosy. Life filling him up. My life. *Me.*

"I think you should go see the shaman in Rosebery," Finn said. "She may provide you with answers."

Sebastian nodded, enthralled by the prospect of answers without deeper inspection of the question. "You mentioned something about a guardian," Sebastian said, making me clench my teeth. Fucking Finn. "What does that mean?"

I got to my feet and Sebastian looked up at me. "I think we can get better answers with the shaman. Thanks, Finn. You should go."

"Go?" Sebastian said. "No, wait."

"No," I said, my voice booming in the room. "He's leaving *now*."

Sebastian got to his feet. My power flowing through him made him stronger, and he didn't even shiver this time. "Would you stop ordering people around? Finn should stay."

"No. Finn is going back to the mansion to make sure Alejandro remains safe."

That wasn't a lie. I preferred Finn at the mansion with the brother. I didn't trust my mother or Genesis, and them working together made me all kinds of itchy.

"Why wouldn't he remain safe? I thought he was safe with Zane and my father."

I sighed. A pounding headache hit my temples. Thankfully, Finn spoke up. "He's right. I'll remain vigilant and make sure Alejandro remains safe. I'll contact you if anything changes while you go on your scavenger hunt." He smirked and poofed.

Sebastian turned his glare to me and poked me in the chest. "You made him leave. Why are you such a, a brute?"

"Why do you trust everyone but me?"

"You haven't told me anything."

"You haven't asked."

He opened and closed his mouth, then sat back down. "Fine. I have questions."

"I know you do," I grumbled, grabbed a couple of beers from the fridge, and set one down in front of him before I sat down to try to wrap my brain around what I was supposed to tell him.

Truth and lies. The biggest lie of all was that I'd never lie to him. Smack me in the head now.

"What happened? I remember onions."

I cocked my head. "Onions?"

He shook his head as if clearing his thoughts. "Doesn't matter. Who's Maddox, and why did he want Pedro back?"

Serena already told me most of this, and I had already prepared what to tell him. Half-truths to keep him close. "Maddox is a malice who works for Genesis. He's her second in command. She wants Pedro back because Pedro is a malice." *Get that through your head.* I didn't add. "He somehow managed to get your mother pregnant. Not something common and Genesis wants to poke and prod him to find out how."

"Pedro saved my life," Sebastian added. "Why would he do that if he's evil?"

"He probably has his own agenda we don't know about yet."

"But you don't really know."

Damn, this kid believed everyone to be unicorn and rainbows. "No," I gritted out. We wouldn't know until he talked.

"Why would Genesis want my brother?"

"I don't know."

Sebastian shot to his feet. "Liar. You're such a goddamn liar!"

I was up and on him before he could blink. "I'm not lying. Everything is legend and myth. There aren't any hard facts. For all I know, your brother is just in a damn coma. You're the one who wants to believe otherwise." I realized I trapped him again. And I should've moved, shouldn't have let my controlling, possessiveness out on him, but I couldn't. I needed more contact. I needed *more. Play nice. Give him what he wants to hear.* "But we can find out for sure. I can take you to see the shaman."

His whole body seemed to melt. "Really?"

I'd give him anything he asked for as long as he kept me close. Anything. "Yeah. But you were hurt, Sebastian. During the fight. You need to rest."

He planted his hand on my chest. The cool touch of his hands on my skin sent me rushing over the edge. He opened his mouth to say something, and I slammed my mouth against his. I couldn't help it. I needed to inhale him. To feel his lips on mine. To breathe him in. And I did. I kissed him hard. A desperate thing that pulled against every reason I had not to do this. He smelled of soap and us. The pulsing of his heart against my skin felt like heaven. If there was a heaven. Or at least, not hell. I sucked his bottom lip before releasing him of the kiss. His brown eyes blown. A good blown. His lips wet, and his tongue fluttered out and licked it. I cupped his neck, my thumb gently caressing the pulsing artery. Alive.

"Xcian, what are we doing? You're mated."

"I'm not."

"But Serena said—"

"I'm not *anymore*. I already talked to her, Sebastian. I want you." I kissed him just under his earlobe. He trembled against the touch. "I am yours," I whispered. "Only you." Not a lie. I belonged to Sebastian Diaz, heart and soul. At least until the bond could be broken. And the way Sebastian responded to me, I realized Finn was right. All I had to do was take what he offered. He'd give it freely if I didn't fuck it up, and I didn't want to fuck it up.

"Are you sure?" he asked, his voice trembling. "I'm not just a hole, Xcian. I can't do this if that's all you see me as."

"I don't. And Serena is in love with my brother, Hawke," I said. Not a lie. I could do this. I could give him truths among the lies. "What do you want me to do to you, Sebastian?" I knew what I wanted to do, but I wanted him to say it. I needed him to say it. I pressed my lips against his. The whole world seemed to narrow to this one moment in time. Everything at my peripherals blurred, except for what stood right in front of me.

"Make me come," he said into my mouth. "Xcian, I want you to make me come."

Fuck yes.

Chapter Twenty-Three

Sebastian

I was a horny, selfish asshole. "Make me come." I wanted his body, his mouth on me. I wanted to feel what only he could give me. This feeling of being complete. Whole. Unbroken. I wanted to be full of him and have him bring me down, bit by bit.

His kisses deepened. All teeth and tongue. He explored every inch of my mouth, and I tried to follow along. The heat of him pressed against me made me shiver. I wanted more. So much more. We were alone. We'd done this before. This wasn't new and yet it felt new, more potent than before. More than desperate need and desire. Xcian slowly released my lips and cupped my face, feeling my tears.

"Sebastian," he said. His voice filled with concern. "Did I hurt you? Are you okay? We don't have to. We can just lie down. I'm so sorry." His blabbering made me feel fuller, if that was even possible.

"Lying down would be good," I said.

He led me back to the bedroom and let me go. The loss of his touch made me feel hollowed out inside. Then he ran his hand through his hair, just the top. It still fell perfectly straight. "You should rest."

He wanted me to sleep. Alone. My brain must've shattered when Maddox threw me against the wall as if

I were a rag doll because I wanted more from Xcian. I wanted everything. I almost died. Died. And I'd been given a second chance. I wasn't going to ruin it. Not for something as petty as fear of the feelings inside me. Xcian may have been a monster. A killer. Who knows what else? But he protected me. And he was *mine*. He'd admitted as much.

Standing in front of him, I lifted my sweatshirt over my head and dropped it on the floor. Then I lowered my joggers and stepped out of them. Xcian's pale eyes glowed, even in the waning sun. His eyes slowly took me all in, and I didn't hide myself this time. His eyes stayed on my cock longer than the rest of me and it took notice. Hard and weeping.

I narrowed the gap between us, and his eyes lifted to meet mine. God, he was beautiful. With or without clothes. I trailed my fingers to his temple and loved the way he leaned into my touch. I could've sworn I heard him purr. "You're so beautiful, Xcian."

His whole body stiffened as if I said something wrong. Not a muscle moved, not even his eyes on mine. I couldn't even tell if he was breathing. "You don't know what I've done, Sebastian. What I still have to do."

The pain in his voice made me want to hold him tighter. "I want to finish what we started." I kissed him softly on his lips. Then softer again. Then I pulled his bottom lip, flicking my tongue against them. Taking control made me feel bold. And Xcian didn't push me away. He wanted me too. A plaything. A pet. It didn't matter. For now, this was all that mattered. Us. His lips on mine, my hands on his body, exploring every inch of him. Slow and soft.

I pulled away and untied the lace of his joggers, the crotch already tented. He took over and lowered them as I watched. Standing totally naked, his cock bobbed between us.

Nervously, I wrapped my arms around his neck, a flutter of fear threatening me to call the whole thing off. Not fear of him, but fear that I'd screw this whole thing up. Fear that I'll make a fool of myself and not do things right.

His fingers dug into my hips. "Sebastian, what are you doing?"

I started to sway. "Dance with me."

The corner of his lips cocked in a half smile. "There's no music."

"I know. But you've heard of music before, right?" He started to sway with me. The way his naked body vibrated against mine, he probably was restraining the urge to throw me on the bed and fuck me silly. Like he had in my dream. The impossible wet dream that still lingered in my memory. I didn't want it fast and hard. I wanted it slow. I wanted to cherish him.

Tonight, I needed Xcian.

A blush peppered his cheeks. Something I'm sure he only saved for me. So damn adorable. "See, is this so hard?"

The radiant smile that followed almost broke me. "No, smartass. I've just never danced naked with anyone." He lifted his chin in thought. "Nope. Never. And never for me is a long damn time."

My cheeks blushed too, and I hugged him tighter. My head on his shoulder. My body slowly awakened to every contact our bodies made. Like an electrical current bringing me back to life. "Are you doing something to me with your superpowers?"

He stiffened under my touch. "No, why would you say that?"

I shrugged. The motion had me rubbing on his skin. "I feel different."

He slipped my hair behind my ear. "This is nice. Being here. With you."

We continued to sway. The movement soothing in its own way. "You know, I've never been with anyone before. Will you let me, uh…" I couldn't even say it. Kill me now.

He cupped my chin and forced me to look at him. "I told you. I am yours to do what you want. I didn't lie about that either."

The husky sound of his voice made my cock stir again. I thought about the dream. I wanted to do that to him. Make it good for him. *Just say it, Sebastian.* "I want to touch you. Everywhere. I want to finish what we started the night we kissed."

"You mean the night you chained me to the bed."

A smile cracked through the tension. "Do you want to be chained this time? I promise I won't try to escape, or shoot you."

Xcian swallowed, and my eyes trailed the column of his throat.

I realized I looked away when he lifted my chin again. Then he kissed me. A soft, warm kiss on my lips that felt like heaven. It erased every stupid thing I just said. Slow and soft. Then we were moving toward the bed. He spun around so he dropped on the bed first, and scooted back while I stood there, watching him. Then he spread his knees open, his long cock stiff and angry. "Do what you want, Sebastian."

I almost lost my train of thought, and quickly headed to the bathroom. Lube. I needed lube. I could do this. Sure. I wasn't a total idiot. I knew how men got off. I'd seen movies, and I'd caught Alejandro watching some porn website of gay guys getting off. Yeah, I sneaked a peek. My hands shook as I searched and found nothing. Then I came out and Xcian had a smirk on his face and something in his hand.

A lube bottle.

"Uh, I don't have a condom."

"I'm not human, Sebastian. I don't carry human disease."

Right. Yeah. He wasn't human. Oh, God. He wasn't human. What the hell was I doing? It had been so much easier when he'd taken control. I wanted him to take control again. It'd make things easier. I wouldn't have to think. Xcian didn't move from his position on the bed. Watching me. Waiting.

"We don't have to do anything but lie down together," he said finally.

I climbed on the bed, over him. He winced slightly as my body brushed over his sensitive cock, but I took his pain with a kiss. I could've simply kissed him forever, except my lower body had other plans. Xcian opened his legs so I fit between them. "Move lower," he breathed, and I did until our cocks slotted together, and I started to grind against him. The muscles in my arms started to shake as I tried to hold myself up so as not to crush him. Not that I could crush him. His fingers dug into my ass. Pretty sure they left a mark on me. I wanted him to mark me completely. To take control. To make me his. I started to pull away, but he grabbed me and held me against him.

"Uh, huh, you started this. You are going to finish this."

"Maybe I changed my mind and I want you to fuck me, Xcian." Did I? Did I want him inside me?

He growled, his mouth doing all sorts of things to my lips and tongue. Pinned against him. "I want you, Sebastian. I need you inside me."

The desperation in his voice made me want to pleasure him, made me want to give him the stars and moon. I wanted to be everything he needed. I answered him by taking the lube and squeezing a generous amount on my fingers. Then I rimmed his hole. He closed his eyes and leaned back, spreading himself more open. "Look at me, Xcian," I said. He quickly opened his eyes. They were so beautiful. "I want you to look at me."

He did. His pupils blown, his lips parted as I dipped a finger inside. He felt so warm and so damn tight. How was I going to put my cock in him without hurting him?

"You won't hurt me, Sebastian."

"Uh, do you have a prostate?"

He chuckled, and I felt so stupid. "Yes. My body is human, for the most part." I brushed against that sensitive spot, and yeah. He had a prostate. He moaned loud, precum dripping from the tip of his cock. He bit his swollen lip. "Fuck me, now. Please."

Damn. Did he just say please?

"Sebastian, please."

I inserted another finger when he growled, cupped my hips, and spun me over. I yelped as my back hit the bed and he was sucking me. The warmth and wetness of his mouth on me, pulling, licking. Fuck. I could do nothing but squirm and beg and moan. He took me close to the edge, then pulled off with a wet pop. I ground in frustration until he squeezed the cool lube on my sensitive cock. I inhaled sharply as he climbed over my erection. My heart stuttered, feeling the rim of his tight hole at my tip. "Ex," I said. That's as far as I got when he slid down my shaft. His hole swallowed my member in one long glide. The tightness of it made me hiss, and then he moved. Fucking himself on my shaft. Sweat beaded his brow. His expression one of pure bliss, then he crushed himself over me and ravaged my mouth. Not slow. Chaotic. All him. His cock pressed between us.

"Ex, I'm not going to last."

"Fuck," he said, "Neither am I."

He must've found that spot because he moved faster, the friction turning me into a weeping mess until I exploded, almost painfully, then so good. My cock pulsed inside his hot body. I watched as he arched his back, his lips parted, and he came. Jets of his fluid spurted on my stomach, and he didn't hesitate to spread the liquid against my skin, marking me, scenting me. He glossed my lips with his wet fingers right before kissing me again, long and hard. The taste of us heady and potent. Real.

The euphoria, the pheromones, something rattled my brain because when he finally collapsed on me and quickly fell to the side, sliding out of my body, I said the words I shouldn't have said. But I was too tired to care. Too tired to think. An echo of the words followed me down to sleep.

"I love you."

Chapter Twenty-Four

Xcian

"I love you."

The three words humans used to try to define their existence with another person. It wasn't the first time I heard the three words over the centuries. The reason I decided to be a one-and-done lover had been after so many hard breakups that started with *I love yous*. Humans didn't know the meaning of the word, and for Sebastian to use it on the edge of passion pissed me off. Then he knocked out. Like, yeah. I love you, but I'm too tired to figure this shit out. When my world was falling apart. I had bound myself to him. Soul and body. It should've been because I loved him, the way Zane loved Eric. Not to save his life.

I rolled out of bed, feeling his semen leak out of my ass, and down my thighs. Proof of what I'd allowed him to do to me. I should've just fucked him and got it over with. Not give him control over me.

I jumped in the shower and put the shit to scalding, just north of blistering.

I washed ruthlessly until my skin and ass were raw. It worked though, hadn't it? I had Sebastian where I wanted him. At my hip. The demons content. The magic that linked us silent. Everything as it should be. All I had to do was play the bullshit card and take him to the shaman. Let him hear for himself that Alejandro would either survive his transition or die.

I got out of the bathroom with a towel around my hips heading for the door. Sebastian didn't need me to heal him anymore, and I needed to get clothes. I also needed a car if we were going to make the trip. So why was my body moving toward the bed? Why did I pull my towel out and clean Sebastian of the mess I'd left on him? Still sticky. Already dry. When the hell had I climbed beside him content when I touched him? My demons so damn quiet inside me.

I let out a relieved breath and figured I'd think about it tomorrow. Right now, I just wanted to hold my mate and sleep.

The following morning, I woke up to a racket outside, and alone. The bed empty. Sebastian gone. I jumped to my feet and threw the bedroom door wide open, stepping out. The first glare of sunlight forced me to squint and see nothing but shadows for a second before my eyes adjusted and came face to face with Eric.

I dropped my hands to my sides. "What the fuck are you doing here?" Sebastian jumped in front of me. On instinct, I wrapped my arms around his waist and pulled him closer to me. That's when I realized I was totally naked.

"Uh, maybe you should go back to the room and get dressed."

Eric dropped a bag at my feet. "Serena sends you clothes. You remember, Serena? You're *mate*. The person you're supposed to *bond* with."

I opened my mouth to tell him off when Sebastian turned and put a hand on my chest. "Let me talk to my dad, Xcian. Just go get dressed so we can leave."

Already dressed in tight black jeans, a T-shirt and boots that were clearly his own clothes, Sebastian was sending me to my room. This had not played out the way I thought it would in my head. I scanned the cabin just to be sure we were safe, felt Zane just outside, then slipped back into the bedroom and changed into my clothes. I wasn't a heavy sleeper. I was usually a light sleeper. So how the hell had Sebastian gotten out of bed without me feeling him? I'd been dead to the world. Anything could've happened while I slept. Shit. I finished dressing a little fast and a lot pissed before I walked back outside. Zane glared at me as he made coffee in the kitchen. Eric and Sebastian continued arguing. I picked up something about responsibility and rules. I took Zane's offer of coffee and sipped it.

"A little warning would've been nice, asshole."

Zane rolled his eyes. "I tried calling you. It'd be nice if you pick up your fucking phone." I didn't even know where I left my phone. "He looks good." Zane led my eyes to Sebastian. He and Eric looked so much alike, it was hard to pick them apart. Except for Eric's obvious age and salt and pepper hair. The man wouldn't age anymore. Forever forty-something or some shit. While Sebastian would continue to age, die. The ceramic cup burst in my hand. Coffee splattered all over my clean shirt, pants, and floor.

Suddenly, Sebastian was there. In front of me. Safe and sound. "Ohmygod, Ex, what happened? You're bleeding."

He took my hand and led me to the sink where he ran the water over my bleeding hand. Zane shook his head and glared at me. Eric finally stopped arguing and watched us. Their stares bearing down on us should've bothered me, but I could only look at Sebastian's delicate features, smooth neck, the pulse of his carotid. Alive. He was alive and he did look good. And taking care of me. Talking. Asking me something I didn't have an answer to.

"Ex?"

My wound healed almost instantly, and I blinked away the rest of the world. Only Sebastian mattered in my world. "What?"

"We need to get you cleaned up." He shoved me out of the kitchen. "We'll be right back," he called over his shoulder.

"Sebastian," Eric admonished. "Don't—"

But whatever came after *don't* was cut off by the door slamming behind us. Then Sebastian slipped his fingers under my wet T-shirt and pulled it over my head. I helped, though I didn't know what the rush was, until he slammed me with a kiss. Something visceral and needy. I cupped the back of his head and plunged my tongue into his mouth. He released me of my wet pants, and slid his hand into my boxers, cupped my aching cock. Fuck. The shit hot against his cool hands. Sebastian ran a touch colder than me. I bit his lip and moaned into his mouth. "Don't start something you can't finish," I growled.

He pushed me into the bathroom. Somehow, we managed to turn on the shower, undress, and slip into the tub while kissing. Touching. Every point of contact felt divine. The fact that I didn't start this made me even bolder. I would satisfy my mate. *Mine*. I took hold of both our cocks and slid them up and down in my fist. Sebastian dug his fingers into my shoulder, arched his back, and moaned. Fuck. I leaned into him and bit his throat and sucked, leaving a bruise for sure. Marking him as mine. The contact drove him over the edge, and he came. The sound and scent of it had me chasing after his release, and I pulsed into my fist. Shuddering, I hugged him. He fit perfectly tucked under my chin. "You're mine, Sebastian. Tell me, you're mine."

"I'm yours," he breathed out. "Only yours."

I shut my eyes against the throbbing in my head. I wanted to believe that so damn much, but it wasn't real. It wasn't real and I wanted to roar. There was something wrong with me and I couldn't wait the couple of months to get this shit cut off. I wasn't strong enough to live like this.

Finally, my heartbeat slowed, and a knock brought us back to reality. Sebastian gave me a clumsy kiss on the lip. "I'll meet you outside. Let me deal with my dad, okay?"

I had no clue what the hell he meant by that, but I nodded anyway.

He quickly got out of the tub. I heard him fumbling to dry and dress, and then I was alone. I planted my palm against the cool tile in front of me and leaned into the shower spray. Whatever the fuck this was, wasn't normal. Zane had not felt half of this shit. So why? Why the fuck?

I slammed my fist against the tile and split it. Blood swelled to the surface of my knuckles where I'd punctured the skin only to heal as I watched. It took seconds when it should've taken longer for the skin to meld.

What was happening to me?

Chapter Twenty-Five

Sebastian

I couldn't stop the smile on my face. The ridiculous wide smile and the blush that heated my face as I walked out of the bedroom, newly sexed and washed. I felt so damn good. The sun shone brighter. The scents around me stronger. And my dad...angrier.

That didn't stop me from feeling great. Dad glared at Zane. Zane didn't even ruin my mood. Both of them watched me from the kitchen. "Well, thanks for the clothes." Hint. Leave now.

Dad crossed his hands over his chest. "We're not leaving."

Zane seemed resigned to his fate, though the guy could physically force my dad to do anything he wanted. I never got over the kidnapping thing, and blamed Zane for all of it.

"Dad, it's none of your business."

Dad glared at me. I'd only seen that glare ever directed at Alejandro. "Don't you dare speak to me like that, young man. I am still your father."

Anger surged inside of me. "Are you? Are you still my father? Are you still even human?"

Zane moved, made to reprimand me probably, but my dad lifted his hand and Zane stopped. The way my dad controlled the inhuman monster surprised me.

"What do *you* think?" Dad asked.

I should've known he would throw it back at me. That had always been his parenting style. Alejandro was sent to the principal's office for fighting and thought it unfair, and dad would ask, well, what do you think should happen? Or what would you do in his place? No, he hadn't changed at all. "I don't know what to think anymore." My anger deflated as my dad approached me and drew me into a tight hug.

"I'm still your father and I love you, Seba." I melted into his hug. "I only want what's best for you."

"I know," I said into his neck. "But I need you to trust me."

"I do," he said, pulling me away. "But I don't trust *him*."

Dad didn't bother to hide the disdain for Xcian, who strutted into the room like a god. Hair gleaming wet and tied into a bun at the back of his head, wearing black combat pants, a black long-sleeve shirt that stretched his broad chest, and black boots. He looked ready for war as he glared at my dad. The thought of Xcian hurting my dad made me pause. Thankfully, Zane took Dad into his arms. A possessive *don't touch him* warning to Xcian who ignored us all and walked outside.

"I don't trust him," Dad whispered to me.

"He won't hurt you," Zane said, and planted Dad a kiss on his neck. An act so intimate, so endearing, it reminded me that Zane would protect Dad from any threats. Including his own family. Though the thought that he'd hurt me or Alejandro or even Mom if he deemed *us* a threat did cross my mind. They weren't human. And I didn't trust any of them.

Not even Xcian. Which hurt my soul.

Xcian came back inside, the light of the morning sun behind him. "We need to head out. We got about a seven-hour drive ahead of us."

"Where are we going?" Dad asked.

Xcian dragged his glare to me before answering. I gave him a small shrug. "Tijuana. We're going to pay a visit to the werewolves." With that, he walked back into the bedroom, his boots thumping on the floor.

Dad walked outside. Zane sighed and ran his hand through his hair. If he expected sympathy from me, he wasn't getting it. The guy looked like shit. "Maybe next time don't kidnap someone to get what you want. Nothing ever turns well by force and violence. Remember that."

Zane clenched his jaw, the muscles bulging on his cheek. Xcian stood near the bedroom, bag in hand, watching us. I gave him a smile he didn't return before he too walked out, following Eric.

I deflated. This was going to be a road trip from hell. Or to Hell. Or whatever. I walked out with Zane behind me. Dad opened the back door for me. "Get in."

Great. I slid into the back, behind the driver's side, while Dad slid in beside me. Xcian drove while Zane sat beside him. During the ride, I told Dad everything. I told him about what Finn said about being a guardian. About the nightmare that felt real with Alejandro trapped someplace between our world. I told him everything I knew up to that point and he listened, silently, throwing glares at the back of Zane's head every now and again.

"How much do you trust the Crawfords, Dad?" I asked. I didn't care that two of them were sitting in front of us. "They were all complicit in my kidnapping, if you haven't forgotten. And this god of creation, Genesis, wants Alejandro and is willing to use me, *us*, to get him. And your husband has told you *nothing*?"

"Sebastian, perhaps we shouldn't discuss this in the car?" Xcian said in a tone that should've had me obeying. I felt like I wanted to obey. Needed to obey him. I shook it off and kept going.

"Why? It's the safest place. You two can't turn into monsters, and my dad has to listen to me!" Because they were all trapped inside a damn car.

"Did you know this?" my dad threw out to Zane.

"It's a possibility but impossible to prove, Eric. There's nothing that can be done but make him comfortable."

Dad blanched. Thankfully, Zane couldn't see him. "He's being tortured. Or did you forget that part," Dad snapped. "I had a right to know."

"No. You don't have a right to know. You still don't know the dangers of our world, and my job is to protect you."

"From my sons!"

"Yes! From every threat, and I will not apologize for it."

The silence that followed felt weighted with so much regret. I held my dad's hand as they shook slightly. Dad had no idea the mess we were all in, trying to catch up with thousands of years of monster history and evolution.

"Pull over," Zane ordered.

Xcian stopped the car on the curb. We'd already driven a few hours and the roads were deserted, wherever the hell we were. Zane got out and opened

Dad's door. I thought my dad would argue, but he didn't. He followed Zane away from us as I got out just to breathe. The inside of the car too damn cramped with Xcian inside it. Then Xcian got out. We leaned on the car and watched them from afar. I couldn't hear what they were saying, but they were arguing. A good one.

"Do you like causing strife between them?" Xcian asked.

"He deserves to know the truth."

"The truth? Or your truth."

"What's the difference? My truth is *the* truth."

"It's a truth from your perspective. There's a larger play here that you are not privy to."

I crossed my arms across my chest feeling guilty for forcing drama on my dad. "Then make me *privy*."

"It is not your place to know."

"If it's about my family, then yes. It is my place to know. And I thought you wanted to help me?" His eyes met mine. A cold, hard expression in them. The similar one he wore all the time sex wasn't involved. "You know what. Forget it." I slipped into the car and slammed the door shut. Just because.

My truth? As if there were different versions of the truth. Dad needed to know what type of family he married into. He couldn't trust any of them. They were all working on different agendas. I didn't care. I needed to find my brother.

Xcian got into the driver's side, turned on the car, and locked the doors. "What are you doing?"

He didn't answer and skidded onto the road, leaving Zane and Dad behind. I turned to look at them through the rearview window. Dad looked pissed. I couldn't see Zane from this far, but he didn't even bother to move. I giggled. "You are so *wrong*."

"They were getting on my fucking nerves."

"Will they be okay?"

"Zane'll call Aris to send a car. They'll be fine. Maybe even kiss and make-up."

That made me bristle inside. "My dad deserves better."

Xcian didn't say anything much after that. We stopped a few times to eat and put gas, but we weren't heading to Tijuana. A few hours later, we were driving into a hot desert and tall buildings.

"I hate to break it to you, but this isn't Tijuana."

"I know. I lied. The shaman isn't in Tijuana."

The Vegas strip exactly as I imagined it. Filled with bright lights and lots of people. Traffic included. We drove into a gated parking lot leading into one of the taller hotels. Maybe I felt a little intimidated by the place. Still wearing just a T-shirt and jeans. Despite Xcian wearing dark like he owned it, he still looked really good. He'd belong anywhere.

A tall gangly man approached us as we got off the elevator. Xcian was still holding my hand.

"Mr. Crawford. Didn't realize you'll be in this weekend."

"Neither did I," Xcian responded, all growly grouchy. The guy met my eyes and I smiled. He looked at me suspiciously. Didn't smile back. "Oswald, this is my guest," Xcian said without looking at me. Oswald looked at me again and I smiled again. "We're going to be meeting with Amelia. Can you ring us when she arrives?"

"Of course, sir. Do you have any luggage?"

"No," was all he said. After he got the keycard, he

practically dragged me to the elevators again and we headed to the top floor.

"Wow, you come here often, huh?"

"I own the hotel."

I almost swallowed my tongue. "Okay, so that clarifies something for me." We stepped into the private elevator.

"And what's that."

"I always knew demons ran this city."

Xcian laughed. I didn't mean it as a joke.

Chapter Twenty-Six

Xcian

Demons didn't run the city. They enslaved it. My own demons woke up as soon as we hit the strip, tasting the sex in the air, savoring it, and making me dizzy with need. Humans filled all types of addictions in this city. Gambling, sex, booze, drugs, you name it. Those lucky enough didn't actually live here. Those unlucky traded their souls to the demons that offered them anything they wanted, for a price.

I pulled off my shirt and my skin prickled from the cool air inside the penthouse. I watched Sebastian give the place a wide-eyed sweep. Seven thousand square feet of space. Tall ceilings, glittering crystal, floor-to-ceiling windows overlooking the strip. It lost its appeal the first time I stepped inside it. Back when it was newly built.

"Wow, I knew you had money. All evil men with planes and access to remote getaways and a dozen safe houses they used to lock and torture people must have money. But this, wow."

"I'm going to shower. Join me," I ordered. I didn't wait for his response. Dropping the rest of my clothes in the bedroom, I walked naked to the ensuite bathroom, complete with benches and sprays that massaged as well as soothed. Bristling that he'd made me wait, then walked inside fully dressed as if I hadn't given him specific orders, I growled.

"Maybe—"

That's all the convo he got out when I pulled him under the shower and pressed his body against the tiles. He gasped, and I shut him up with my mouth. I needed this if I was going to survive the shaman, and dammit, my mate was going to give it to me. I absorbed his emotions as if they were my own.

"Xcian," he said, breathless, giving me his neck as I planted open-mouthed kisses on the mark I'd left him earlier. "Take off my clothes."

"No. This is good."

"Is it enough?"

No. It wasn't. I didn't say anything though. I shouldn't continue taking pieces of him when I knew I'd be hurting him in the end. It was wrong. Sebastian deserved better. Not lies. Not monsters. Not me. But I'd take whatever he gave me. Frustrated that I didn't do as he asked, he pulled off his tee and peeled out of his pants. Then he shoved me back, forcing me to sit on the bench. Before I could open my mouth, he'd dropped to his knees. All rational thought left me when he licked me from balls to tip. I almost blew my load just by looking at him there. "You don't have to."

"I know. I want to. I just don't know what I'm doing, so be patient."

I almost snorted. "Have you met me?"

He gripped the base of my length and licked my tip. My eyes practically rolled into my head. "I have." He gave tentative licks from the base to the tip as if I were a popsicle, then he nuzzled it, his nose on my balls before taking one into his mouth, then the other, all the while his cool hand pumped me slowly, milking me until a pearl of cum pooled at my tip.

I slid my hand into his hair wanting to pitch my hips forward and fuck his beautiful mouth when he took me all in. I braced myself and rocked my hips. The heat of his mouth, the carefulness and attention he gave me, felt better than the hard blowjobs and anything I'd experienced in the past. Sebastian didn't just blow me. He explored, touched, caressed. He slowly, so slowly, brought me to the brink until I exploded inside his mouth. He swallowed everything I had and smiled. His face red with blush. An innocence I wanted to tap into.

"I want you to mark me," he said. "I want to be yours. I want everyone to know that I belong to you. Is that a thing?"

I still couldn't breathe right. I dragged him onto my lap, and he straddled me as I cupped the back of his head and ate his mouth. Sucked hard, bit him until I knew it stung. I wanted to leave imprints of myself on him. Fuck. I'd hurt him. I growled. "I don't want to hurt you, Sebastian. I want to be what you want."

He cupped my face so I had to look at him. Those damn expressive eyes held more than he could ever know. "I want you."

"You still don't know me."

"Then show me who you are."

"You saw," I whispered.

He climbed off of me and shut the water. Without a word, he stepped out of the shower and handed me a towel. I followed his lead, unsure of what else to do. In the bedroom, he dropped the towel and turned to me, having to lift his head a little to look me in the eyes.

"Show me."

"Sebastian, you don't know what you're asking for."

"Maybe. Maybe it won't matter."

"That I'm a monster."

A slow smile lifted the corners of his beautiful mouth. "As long as you're *my* monster."

This kid would be the end of me.

I drew upon the power of the gods and shifted. My muscles expanded, my bones lengthened making me taller. At least seven feet tall. My skin turned a pale shade of ice blue like the clear morning skies. Fangs extended, and two horns grew out of my forehead. The shift made me stronger, clear-headed, and immortal. The magic of the gods consumed me. I'd never let anyone touch me while shifted. With my senses heightened, the energy I absorbed was twice as potent. I didn't want to share that with anyone.

Until now.

Sebastian hadn't run away. Tears streamed down his cheeks, and it took everything I had not to brush them away. He took a step forward, and I took a step back, hitting the dresser at my back.

"I'm not going to hurt you," he said, in a tone that made me purr in contentment. My chest rumbled like a damn submissive. I wasn't submissive. I was a dominant warrior. I growled and shook my head.

Sebastian smiled. "Stop being so stubborn and let me touch you."

Talking in this form wasn't impossible, but harder since it was all grunts and growls. My mouth was too full of sharp teeth meant to tear into flesh and bones. My fingernail claws to strip my enemies into shreds. I pulled some of it back. Some of the visceral reaction to his nearness too. His hand trailed over my pounding heart. "You have a strong heart," he said. Never leaving my eyes, which were glowing white. Then his knuckles brushed against my stomach, and I clenched. My cock hung thick and long. He grazed my pubes, and lower, fingertips sliding against my long shaft and back up. His arousal smelled ten times as potent, making all the cells in my body pay attention. "This won't fit inside me," he said.

The thought of being inside Sebastian had my cock throbbing. I shook my head. "No. Not as a virgin."

"But you can get off, like this."

"Yes," I growled.

"You won't hurt me."

"Never."

"Then do it. Tell me what you want me to do for you."

He continued to stroke my massive member. I pulled back my fangs, my claws, and turned us around so I sat on the bed, then I cupped his hips and led him onto my lap. At least this way, we were at eye level. He cupped my face, and I closed my eyes as his fingers brushed against my sensitive horns. My cock acted like a prod between his legs. He ground into me and I bit my lip, drawing blood. He leaned forward and licked it. And I lost it. Fucking lost it. I dropped him face-first on the bed and crushed him with my weight. He didn't fight me. No. He pushed up his ass permitting me to do what I wanted to do to him. My erection slid between his cheeks.

"Try, Ex," he breathed out. "I want you to try."

Fuck. Sonofabitch.

"No," I growled out. I didn't want to hurt him. I

never wanted to hurt him. But I would. When he found out this feeling was a lie, formed from the bond to save his life. I couldn't. But I could pleasure him without penetration.

"Spread your cheeks for me."

I heard the pounding of his heart. Felt the pulse of his lifeblood between us. We were one, and I tasted his emotions, searching for fear. The delicious tart flavor of lust was all I found. He wanted this. Wanted me. He spread his cheeks and I gave him a good lick. He yelped and released himself.

"Sorry, I wasn't expecting that." Then he opened up again. His pucker so beautiful and tight. I licked again and heard him moan. The sound of it fueling my own need. I speared him with my tongue, sending him close to the brink, making me painfully hard. Like this, I couldn't tell where I ended and he began. On the giving and receiving end of pleasure, my senses took it all in. My demons sated by it.

"Fuck me, Xcian. Please."

Fuck. "No," I growled again. "I don't want to hurt you."

"Please. Please, I want it."

Fuck!

I tore the side drawer for the lube and slathered my two fingers, retracting my claws, and shifting back to human so as not to hurt him. I rimmed his hole. All sanity gone. On instinct, he clenched.

"Just relax."

He breathed and I inserted my finger. So hot, and so fucking tight. So damn sensitive. I inserted another, stretching him, making sure I sensed any real pain, any indication for me to stop.

"Keep going, please, Xcian."

Shit. That's all I needed. I stuck in another finger and felt the sensitive nub. Sebastian cried out my name. A sound that drew all my needs and wants to the surface. And I needed and wanted *him*. I lubed my cock and cupped his hips, lifting him on his knees and breaching his hole. Then I entered him slowly. The slide gave. His asshole so damn tight and hot. The whimpers he let out, all of it had me over the edge. I couldn't name the surge of emotions rushing through me. But it felt right.

Mine.

Then I started to shift back into my god form. Slowly, feeling his ass tightening around my thicker cock. I was lost to all the sensations flooding me. Lost to him. And I didn't want to be found.

Chapter Twenty-Seven

Sebastian

My asshole was stretched to the limit as Xcian shifted back to his monster form. I'd never felt so damn full, so damn stretched. There was pain and pleasure all rolled up into one, at least until he moved and grazed my prostate. Lights flashed before my eyes, and I let out an ugly sound that should've been desire and lust but sounded like death. I didn't care. I wanted more. I needed him to move. To take me. So I pushed back, feeling the cool slide deeper.

"More, Xcian. Please. Please."

Driving his impossibly long and thick monster cock inside of me, I felt his claws extend and dig into my hips, not slicing skin but close. So fucking close. And I wanted it. I didn't care. Nothing hurt at the moment, only pleasure. I heard him growl, something inhuman. And then I turned my head to the side and saw us reflected in the closet mirror and oh, gods. Xcian had gone full monster mode. His skin glazed blue and glowed. Fucking glowed as if he'd been tattooed with glyphs that were igniting. And I saw his massive blue cock pound into me where our bodies joined. I couldn't see his face. I wanted to see his face.

"Xcian," I said. "Turn me over. I want to look at you."

I didn't think he would. Such a stupid thing to ask for. But I needed to see him when he came inside of me. I just needed to. He pulled out and I winced but felt suddenly hollow inside. As if he'd been meant to fill in the space inside of me. I turned over and he held my legs open, added more lube on his cock, and drove back in. The glide easier this time since I was already open. And there, he hit that sensitive spot and I struggled not to come. My dick weeping between us. I wasn't going to last. I bit my lip hard, tasting blood, and keeping my eyes open. His were glowing as I suspected. His horns grew, too, longer. His skin thickened like scales. But his cock remained velvety smooth inside of me. No pain. Fuck. I needed to come.

His lips parted and I cried out as my release pulsed with jets of cum between us. I'd gone boneless under him as he pounded into me, seeking his own release. And then he roared. My body couldn't contain the amount of semen he jetted inside of me. It ran down my ass as he continued to chase the pleasure for a few long moments. Lathering it over my skin again until he crumbled into my chest, using his forearms to keep himself from crushing me. But he crushed me anyway. Then, I watched as he shifted right in front of me. His horns retracted, his skin turned his usual human pale color, and his body condensed until he turned back to his human size, breathing hard against my cheek. The most beautiful thing I'd ever seen.

"Fuck, Sebastian. You're going to be the death of me."

"Uh, hello. You fucked me silly and are crushing me. I think it's the other way around."

He slid off me, taking his cock with him. His

breathing ragged. I didn't move. Letting my body adjust to the emptiness, the lack of.

"Did I hurt you?" he asked, glazing his finger against my now sensitive hole. I winced.

"A little." I wasn't going to lie. Now that the pleasure was gone, yeah, I felt as if I rode a mule. Not that I ever road a mule before.

He drew me into his arms, not caring about the sticky mess on my skin. Both of our fluids on me. The scent of what we were—joined. The thought made me want to wear it always. I instantly felt better. Not just after sex better, but my body seemed to be adjusting and the pain dissipated. He always ran hot and every part of us that touched blazed. "I think you're doing some healing mojo on me," I said. "Because I'm feeling a lot better."

He kissed my forehead. "I'm just awesome that way."

I chuckled. "Are you going for banter?"

He shrugged. "It's a new thing for me."

"What is?"

"This. Cuddling. Fucking in my shifted skin. Feeling…" He stopped.

"Feeling what?"

"Completely sated."

Not sure why, but that stung. I remembered my stupid I love you to him. That had been after sex, but it hadn't been a lie. I knew I loved Xcian the moment he saved my life the second time.

I loved him. I couldn't explain the feeling any better than that.

And I was a sex toy for him. So stupid to think I could be anything more. I hugged him anyway because although it wasn't real for him, it was real for me. And I wanted to know more, everything about him. "Xcian?"

"Sebastian," he purred.

"Tell me something about yourself. How old are you? How does all this work, you and your brothers?"

"Well, I'm old. A thousand, give or take, like Zane."

The mention of Zane made me bristle.

"You don't like him very much, do you."

"No." Xcian pulled me tighter against his chest. I wanted to look at him but I ran my fingers slowly up and down his ripped chest and abs instead.

"Zane is not as evil as you think."

"Right, because what person would force someone into marriage by kidnapping his son."

"Okay, maybe, he overreacted, but it was to keep Eric safe."

"Just Eric." The implication was clear. Zane would protect Eric even from himself.

"Zane protected me from Lucifer."

I gasped and lifted myself up on my elbow to look at him. "*The* Lucifer."

Xcian chuckled and ran his fingers along my cheek, slipping my stray hairs away from my face. "He goes by many names, but prefers Lucifer. We all have to train with one of the gods."

I lowered myself again, listening to his heart as I listened to his story. His voice taking on a sadder tone.

"Zane was meant to go to Genesis as eldest and I had been gifted to Lucifer, but.." his voice trailed as he took in a breath. "I was just a little older than Aris and so afraid. All the stories about Hell were of darkness and pain. I tried to run away but Zane found me. Father would've killed me had he known, but Zane protected me. He took my place and suffered in Hell. Lucifer and Finnegan did things to him. Things that changed him. And it's all my fault."

The next question stuck in my throat because I knew something more had happened between Xcian and Genesis, and I couldn't let it go. "What did *she* do to you?"

He stiffened under me. A slight pause of his fingers twirling the tips of my hair. I didn't think he would answer, but he did. "I was sixteen when I was sent to her. She knew I wasn't Zane and had been livid. It didn't help that she and Lucifer have hated each other for eons. She refused to teach me anything I needed to learn to ascend. To prepare me to receive my Anunnaki powers. At least for the first few years."

I felt the soft tug at my scalp as he started to play with my hair again. His eyes focused on the ceiling above us. I stirred closer, every inch of my body touching the side of his, wanting to give him more of me.

"She finally realized Lucifer wasn't giving Zane up and started paying attention to me. She played with my affections and I fell in love with her. The goddess of creation, who wouldn't?" he chuckled but it was sad. "Anyways, she was looking to replace the human realm with an army of her own. She figured out how to use humans as vessels for her own souls and just needed a spark of power. My power. She bled me, kept me alive enough to keep pumping my blood, until my ascension when she could no longer contain me."

"How long?"

"Eight years, Sebastian," he said. "I spent eight

years with her and it felt like an eternity. And to know that I helped her create the malice. Because of me, they exist." He choked on his words.

I lifted myself on my elbow to look at him and cupped his face. Sad eyes met mine. "It wasn't your fault," I said, putting as much force as I could into my words. "You were a kid. You couldn't have known."

"I can't help but to think how things would've been different had Zane gone to her instead. Maybe he would've been able to fight her, stop her."

"Or maybe, she would've gotten a stronger blood source for her army. Or maybe, she would've killed him. Or maybe… There are so many maybes. You can't live with regret because of maybes. It had been Zane's decision to protect you. You said so yourself. Your brother." A wedge in my throat stopped me from saying more.

He cupped my cheek. "You think of Alejandro."

"He always protected me. I think he's still protecting me, even now. I hear him and he's telling me to run, but I can't just run. I have to save him, Xcian. I have to."

Darkness passed through his eyes, dimming their glow. Then he placed a soft, careful kiss on my lips. A kiss that made me believe that Xcian wouldn't abandon me. A kiss that sang with truth and bloomed in my heart.

He pulled away and ran his thumb gently over my lips. "We'll figure it out. I promise."

I nodded and rested my head on his shoulder. The scent of him all over me, inside me. "Um, maybe we should get cleaned up."

"No. I want you to carry my scent."

I snorted. "I'm not going to walk around with sticky semen on my body, Ex. Not even for you."

His chuckle lifted my heart. "Just leave it for a little while longer. Your body will absorb it."

The thought of being scented by Xcian, letting every nightside creature know that I belonged to him, made me preen. I didn't move as he drifted into a deep sleep. I listened to his even breathing, feeling the pounding beat of his heart against mine. Not quite in sync. My stomach growled, reminding me of the exertion that now led to a hunger of a different kind. I untangled myself from him easily enough and rather than showering, like I probably should have, I used a towel to lightly remove the stickiness, but not all of it. With nothing to eat in the place, I got dressed and headed for the lobby.

Oswald caught sight of me and jumped into action as if he'd been zapped by something. The guy looked like a live wire. "Were you looking for something?"

"Food?"

"Perhaps, room service."

Duh, I didn't think of that. I should go back to the room and wait until Xcian woke up.

"Or perhaps, you're searching for something more?" a second voice said. This one from a very curvy woman dressed in a very revealing blue dress. Long auburn tresses fell in perfect spirals around her face. Bright blue eyes held a hint of malicious mirth, and blood red lips lifted one corner as if she knew something I didn't.

"Ms. Rosebery, how nice to see you," Oswald said stiffly.

When Finn had mentioned the shaman, I thought of

a little old lady. Maybe a cane, facial hair. Not this beautiful woman in front of me. Xcian's type. Jealousy rimmed my heart. A cruel emotion. I got rid of it, thinking about how I needed to save my brother. "Well?" she said. "I know a delicious place we can explore." The way she said delicious hinted at not the edible delicious things

"Uh, maybe we should wait for Xcian?" My head felt fuzzy. Even more so when she took my arm and drew me closer to her. She smelled of berries. Surely, a beautiful woman who smelled of berries couldn't be some evil sorceress witch wanting to kill me, right?

"We'll call him in the car. Come. I'm sure you're *famished*."

I was. Famished. And dizzy. And although I wasn't into going with strangers who were creepy shamans, I suddenly found myself nodding like an idiot. I wanted to go with her. I *needed* to go with her like I needed to breathe. "Yeah, uh, sure. And we can talk."

Her smile never wavered, but her eyes darkened, and her nostrils flared as if she were smelling me. Smelling Xcian on me. Shit. I still had his semen on my skin, in my ass.

"Yes. We can talk." She looked at Oswald still beside us. "I'm taking Mr…"

"Diaz," I answered.

"Diaz to the Chateau."

The guy shifted on his feet. "Mr. Diaz, perhaps you should remain here. We have the best gourmet foods *here*."

A tingle swept through my left side and I realized that the woman had linked our arms. "Oh, don't fret, Oswald. Just let Mr. Crawford know I am entertaining his guest until he arrives."

Oswald didn't look too happy, but the woman didn't care. And I didn't either, and let her lead me to a fancy sports car just waiting for us. I didn't even remember getting inside. But we were speeding along. The dark settled around us.

"So how do you know Mr. Crawford?" I asked.

"Mr. Crawford has used my services in the past. Quite a lot actually."

"And what services are those?"

"You'll see. No sense in spoiling the surprise. How are you acquainted with Mr. Crawford?"

"Oh, my dad married his brother, so I guess that makes him my uncle." Eww…the thought of it made me sick, then made me giggle. "We're not related-related."

"And what brings you to the city of sin? You look too…young."

"And human," I blurted. "Are you human?" My tongue felt light. I wanted to tell this woman everything. We turned into a dark road and things shifted under shadows a little bit. Then a sign appeared in neon lights. The Chateau.

"You know about the nightside?"

"I'm trying to get my brother out of Hell. Finnegan said you might be able to help us."

"Finnegan? Lucifer's offspring sent you to me?"

"Yes."

"Why would you want to save him?"

"He's my brother."

"And?"

"He's my best friend. I love him more than anything. It's what humans do. They protect those they love."

"And your brother would protect you too?"

I shrugged. "Yeah. He's done it in the past."

"Good. That's good to know." She drove the car into a parking spot under a massive warehouse.

"What is this place?"

She smiled. "This is where you might find your brother, Sebastian. This is Hell."

Chapter Twenty-Eight

Xcian

Someone should murder the inventor of the telephone. Grumbling, I rolled out of bed and plucked the thing off the cradle. "Someone better be fucking dying."

"I hope not, sir," Oswald said. Sniveling more than usual.

"What is it?"

"Sir, your guest has found himself enthralled by Amelia."

I turned and planted my hand beside me just to be sure Sebastian somehow turned invisible but was still in my bed. Empty. I clutched the phone too damn tight. "The Chateau?"

"Yes, sir."

"How long ago?"

"Seven minutes, sir. I've been trying to—" I hung up the phone and tossed it. Leaning forward and staring at the carpeting, trying to calm down. The thoughts rattling around in my head did nothing to soothe my soul. Sebastian had used me. Sexed me up to force me to pass out and left me. He'd done the same shit at the cabin when he chained me. Same principle. Fucking used me. I should let him experience the consequences of being with the shaman. I rubbed my chest just above my pounding heart, letting my mind settle. The other explanation of why my mate had left with the shaman was that she had compelled him. She was baiting me, and fuck if I wouldn't rise to the occasion.

And let's not forget my need to have my *mate* at my side.

Fuck! I grabbed the phone and launched it at the wall. Then I started to dress. Five minutes after the call, I was riding my motorcycle through the streets toward ghost town where the shaman had taken up residence in an old, abandoned warehouse she'd used as her palace. Fucking shamans and their mystic magic. I missed the days shamans were loyal to packs and performed healing rituals, wore robes, and carried staffs. This new age shamans were all about peeling the fun out of humans. Turning them into rats in a maze and watching them come undone for the sport of it.

Humans were treated like shit and they couldn't even defend themselves because they didn't know the real dangers that lurked in the nightside. Sebastian was right about that. Their truths were skewed because they weren't privy to the *real* truth. They were at war with a threat they didn't even know existed. And while the Nine were meant to protect them, the threats now extended beyond demons, beyond the malice. We couldn't protect them from everything looking to use them as chew toys. But fuck if I couldn't protect what was mine.

And Sebastian Diaz was mine. Amelia knew it and took him anyway, declaring war. I called Aris. "Yeah," he said. "State your emergency."

"I'm headed to the Chateau."

"You mean the soul-sucking Chateau that belongs

to one crazed bitch shaman? That one?"

I growled.

"Just making sure. What's the scene?"

"She took Sebastian. I'm a mile out. Not waiting. Just giving you a heads up in case clean-up is needed afterward."

"Fuck, Ex. That's not how this works."

"She has what's mine."

"And his life is not worth *more* than yours. Especially not now."

I stopped the bike. "Mother announced it?"

"After you bonded, yes. Serena is gone. Hawk is furious. We have no more matriarch or patriarch. No one to birth the Nine, and I think mother wants Alejandro dead. Doofus suspects it and won't leave his sight."

Shit. "Why didn't you tell me this sooner?"

"Well, you were on your honeymoon," he said dryly. "And I'm assuming that's why you didn't pick up when I *did* call."

I hated phones.

"I can't wait. Send whoever is available. I'll try not to make a mess before backup arrives."

"Oh, and don't forget to try *not* to die." Aris hung up.

I shoved the phone in my pocket and walked inside. Mystic magic and illusions forced by drugs tasted acidic on my tongue. That was the extent of the shaman's capability. Smokes and mirrors. The grand hall was nothing but an old rutted-out warehouse. Speakers surrounding the place screeched out music. The lights weren't even real. A makeshift wood plank held up by crates made up the bar, and I didn't even want to imagine what was in those drinks. People, humans in varying degrees of undress, frolicked, fucked, and licked each other.

I wasn't immune to the aphrodisiac in the air, but my god powers allowed me to push it out of my system before it impaired me. So when I finally reached the shaman's hall, I was lucid. Though the moment my eyes landed on the stage, I wish I'd allowed some of the drug into my system because now Amelia knew exactly what Sebastian meant to me. And she smiled.

"Come, sit." She patted the arm of the chair beside her. "Let's enjoy the view."

She led my attention to Sebastian on stage with a slew of women and men all on display, performing an orgy. Sebastian wore a fishnet top and black lace panties, revealing his long legs. The thin fabric barely covered his erection, and the straps of the panties curved under his ass cheeks, making his ass readily accessible. He was high. And the only reason I remained human and hadn't shredded the whole place was because she'd secured him inside a cage. Alone. I sat.

"The tether between you and your mate is strong. I'm jealous. I never thought you'd be pulled off the market, and by a male. A beautiful one too. He'd be a welcomed addition to my scene here." She handed me a drink I didn't touch. Unlike my mate, I knew not to take offerings from strangers.

"Don't tempt me, Amelia. If you know how strong my bond is, then you know I will rip this place to shreds if you so much as touch him."

Sebastian looked good. I wanted to climb inside the cage with him, lock us in, and fuck him until he called out my name again. He gripped the bars and jutted his hips between them, offering himself to me. Another asshole reached for him, and I clamped down on his wrist, grinding bone. "Touch him and die."

The guy moved back.

I hadn't realized I'd moved from my chair to the cage, intent on locking us both inside. The thrumming of magic infused in the cage's design—a warning. A magic similar to the cuffs that drained my power.

The bitch.

I'd deal with her after I got my mate out of this hellhole.

Unlocked, I pushed open the cage door. "Get out," I ordered.

Sebastian shrunk away from me. "I can't." His eyes lifted over my shoulder to the bar. I turned, saw nothing, and returned to look at him. Pupils blown. Sebastian was beyond fucked up. "She has my dad on a noose. He'll push him if I go with you," he whispered.

"Sebastian, look at me."

His eyes slid to mine. I reached in, making sure I didn't pass the threshold fully into the cage. "Come to me. *Now*." I infused my words with influence. I should've known it wouldn't work. He shook his head. The gods hated me. I should've been able to control my mate. Even Zane could influence Eric, but me? Nooo... I was sure Amelia was getting a kick out of this. "Sebastian, we have to go get your brother. I'm going alone if you don't get out." The words a lie. He lowered his hands and took a couple of steps forward.

Close enough, I clamped my hand around his wrist and pulled. The magic surrounded me for a second before I had him in my arms. Safe.

Then pain exploded through me.

I shoved Sebastian away from my body and he hit the cage door, slamming it shut on his way to the floor. His eyes were two round disks looking at the tip of a sword sticking out of my chest. The blade had punched through my sternum, out about ten inches. It would've killed Sebastian too. That thought sent me falling over the edge. Whoever meant to end me, missed my heart by millimeters. Then he made the mistake of pulling out the sword.

I spun to face the coward that would try to kill me from behind. The gaping wound in my chest bled freely. Didn't matter. I shifted into my god form. The man didn't have a chance. A tool sent by the bitch still smirking at me from her throne. I'd get to her soon enough. First, I needed the blood of my enemy. The man, a human, took a step back, the sword forgotten in his inexperienced hands as I ripped him from shoulder to pelvis like a piece of paper and threw the two pieces aside.

Sebastian looked on, frozen on the floor. Safe.

Moloch pounded against my flesh, and pulsed in my veins. The demon cries of content filled my vocals. I gave them voice. I gave them power.

The demons inside me loved the chase.

And I let them free.

Chapter Twenty-Nine

Sebastian

I'd never thought I'd be happy to see a nightmare, but when Noah appeared out of nowhere and did something to calm Xcian down, I thanked whatever god had made him.

And now, we sped through traffic with half of Xcian leaning on my chest, as I cradled him. "He's dying!" I cried.

As soon as the warehouse had emptied, no more people to rip apart, Xcian had crumbled to the ground and shifted back to human in a series of convulsions. His monster side and human side were warring with each other. Noah had to clamp a cuff to his wrist to get him to stop. But it hadn't made it any better. His eyes were glazed over, unseeing. His breathing rough and phlegmy. The pores on his skin bled. He was tearing apart at the seams.

I planted kisses on Xcian's bloodied face. "Don't die," I cried. "Please. Don't die. I'll be better. I promise. I love you. I love you. Please don't die."

"ETA thirteen minutes. Get the chamber ready," Noah said to someone on the phone.

I didn't even know how long we'd been driving, but we made it back to the city. Dawn approached fast. Noah sped through the streets and finally into a gated community, and then up to another gate leading to a huge mansion. The SUV stopped with a jolt and the door was torn open. I stumbled out, ignored, shoved aside, as three people pulled Xcian out and carried him onto a gurney. I started to follow when Noah grabbed my arm.

"I'm not leaving him!" I managed to extricate myself from his tight grip, leaving a bruise for sure, and sprinted after Xcian. We entered through the garage, into a side entrance leading through a narrow tunnel into what had to be an underground section of the house. Noah grabbed my arm, stopping me in my tracks as the three pushed Xcian through a steel door.

"It's hermetically sealed. You can't go in."

I was about to argue when he dragged me to a separate room with floor-to-ceiling windows looking into the room where the three men prepared Xcian with a breathing apparatus and carefully lowered him into a pool of water, then sealed him inside.

"I don't understand. What's happening?"

"He's released his demons. If we don't stop him from being overstimulated, he will pop like a balloon. This will help. I hope," he added.

"He could die?"

"Yes."

"Did he know that before he shifted?"

"Yes."

"Why?" I shook my head. "Why would he do this to himself?"

"To protect *you*." The blame was clear in his voice. "Stay here. I'll get Zane."

I couldn't unsee all the blood. I couldn't unhear all the screams. Unlike at Alex's place, these people hadn't turned to ash. They hadn't crumbled into dust. They had been human.

Because of me. He did it because of me.

The men left, and I was alone in the room. I couldn't see him inside the chamber. They'd turned off the lights, but I felt him still. A connection that flowed like the tide. Pushing stronger against me and then pulling away as if he were fighting to reach me. I placed my hand on the glass surface and tried to extend my strength toward him. Nothing made sense. Except the tingling that lifted from somewhere deep within me, to the edge of my skin. I felt him. "Don't die on me," I whispered. "I love you."

The door behind me opened and Zane walked into the room. Only he wasn't alone. A woman with pale hair and silver eyes walked in with him and a man that looked the splitting image of Zane, only hardened and older. The woman looked at me, nostrils flaring. She hated me instantly. I didn't care.

Zane took me in and he too gave me that same shameful look. I hated him. "Where's my father?" I asked. My voice shook, and I despised sounding like that ten-year-old boy who needed his dad. I was the nineteen-year-old scared boy who needed his dad.

"He's with your brother."

Right. Alex needed him more than I did right now.

The woman walked to the window and looked into the chamber as if she could see Xcian beyond. Then she turned to Zane with even more anger than she showed me. "What have you done?"

"Xcian agreed to bind with the boy to save his life."

"A forced binding?"

"It was only going to be temporary. Hatcher will be returning in a month to reverse it."

The woman sneered. "Your brother will be dead in a month, and for this." She glared at me. "You risk your brother's life for a *human?*" Her glower couldn't get any deeper. "Or is it because he is your mate's son."

"My bound mate," Zane hissed out. "Yes, I didn't want Eric to feel the loss of two children."

Two? I couldn't keep shut. "What are you talking about? Is Alex alive?"

The woman sneered my way.

"Yes. Alex is still alive. Sebastian, this is my mother, Aurora Crawford, and my father, Alastair."

I'd forgotten the father was even in the room. "What are you talking about? What forced binding?"

Zane seemed to look to both his parents for guidance, then turned to me. "After your excursion with Paris and the demons, you sustained a mortal injury. You were dying. Xcian agreed to bind with you to share his power, to heal you."

"But the binding is unnatural," the mother hissed out. "It's killing him."

"A lie," I said, feeling my heart break into pieces. "His feelings for me are a lie?"

Zane cocked his head and I realized he probably hadn't known about Xcian and me. But there was no Xcian and me.

The woman laughed. "The only feelings Xcian has is honor bound to his brother who forced him into this *lie.*" She walked closer to Zane, who, despite towering over the woman and being more intimidating, seemed to cower. "You will fix this. Now."

He nodded.

Then she turned her silver eyes at me. "And this, this human, will be remanded to the cells until we figure out what happened."

"Mother," Zane said, finally speaking up. "The boy is of no consequence. He isn't a danger to anyone. I'll keep an eye out—"

"No," Alastair spoke up. "Your mother is right. You are tainted by the human. And now you've tainted your brother. Galen will decide his fate."

I swallowed. The way Zane's eyes widened didn't bode well for me under Galen's scrutiny. Zane nodded, agreeing.

The parents both walked out.

"Zane, what's going on? Who's Galen?"

Zane's nostrils flared as he dragged his gaze from my head to my toes. I was still wearing the panties and net shirt. My feet bare. He pulled off his knit sweater and threw it at me. "Put that on and cover yourself. Just do as you're told." Clear disdain laced his words. He hated me. I was the nuisance he'd prefer to get rid of. He didn't care about me breathing. He'd forced Xcian into it so my dad wouldn't suffer the pains of losing me.

I quickly put on the sweater, which fell to my thighs as two men walked in. "Take him to a cell," Zane ordered.

Darkness quickly enveloped my eyes and I realized a bag had been secured over my head. I panicked. "You can't do this!" I tried to fight.

"Don't fight, Sebastian. It'll be worse for you if you fight."

"You bastard." I fought.

It got me nowhere. I was gagged, bagged, and hauled out of the room. It wasn't until we reached the elevators that they started hitting me. First my face, then my ribs. Cold hands cupped my hips.

"Little cocksucker wants some cock?" a male voice said.

No. No.

"Don't fucking touch him. Xcian will scent you on him."

The guy snorted. "Xcian doesn't give a shit about this male."

True. All of it true. But the guy seemed tempered by the threat and didn't hurt me again. We walked through a narrow tunnel underground. I smelled the moss and my bare feet against concrete. It seemed as if we were walking forever when I was finally shoved, and the bag ruthlessly pulled out of my head. With my hands free, I lowered my gag. The cell slammed shut and I still tried to wrench it open.

"You can't do this! Kidnapping is against the law!" I could've sworn one of them chuckled. "Xcian will come for me!" I cried, tears running down my face. "He'll come," I whispered, but the truth said something different. Xcian's feelings for me weren't real. Our time in the cabin, after I woke up from my injuries, hadn't been real. Vegas hadn't been real.

It'd been real to me. All of it.

The only sound now was me sniffing my snot, and then the cold making my teeth chatter. I curled into a ball, hugging myself. I didn't want to think of all the nasty around me. The shaman had been right. She told me not to trust the Crawfords. She told me they wanted to ruin this realm. To bring about a cleansing. She told me that if Alejandro could be saved, that he would lead a new guardian race and the Nine would become extinct, and who wanted to be extinct?

I didn't want to see Xcian extinct. I didn't want my father to suffer the loss of Zane either. But I didn't know who to trust anymore.

I almost fell asleep when I heard a whisper. Then my name. "Who's there?" If I started talking to ghosts, I was going to lose it.

"It's Pedro," the voice came back.

"Pedro." I got to my feet and clutched the bars. Not that I could see anything or get free. It just helped to ground me. "You're alive."

"Barely. How's your mother? The baby?"

I wiped my face. "She's good. They're good. They're here now. In the mansion."

He hissed. "Then she's in danger. So are you and Alejandro."

"Pedro, why did Doo—Leander attack you?"

"Are you sure it was me and not Alejandro it meant to attack?"

I opened and closed my mouth trying to remember that day.

"Sebastian, Aurora Crawford is a dangerous woman. You must see that now."

She was. A horrible woman. And Zane too. "Yeah. But what can we do?"

"Escape. I'm sure word will get around that you are down here, and your father will get you out. You must come back for me. Trust no one but Serena. She will help you."

"Pedro, I'm not—I mean, I'm not strong or brave. I don't know what I'm doing anymore. I just want my brother back. He'll know what to do."

"And we can get to him, Seba."

"How?"

"I can contact Genesis."

"Genesis wants me so that she can have someone to control Alejandro."

"She wants Alejandro safe. That's what matters right now. I promise you. If you let me out, I'll make sure she helps him. But you're the only one that can help me get to her."

Pedro was right. Alejandro waking up was what mattered. I'd figure everything else later. I nodded, though he couldn't see me. "Okay. Okay, I'll do it."

"Don't let them change your mind, Seba. They'll try. To keep him. They already brainwashed your father into believing things."

I hated this.

"I know it's hard to know who to trust, *mijo*." The term of endearment stung. "Just keep thinking about saving Alejandro. Make that your mission. Be driven by that one outcome, and everything will be set clearer."

He sounded as if he spoke from experience.

And I had no choice. I couldn't trust Zane, my dad, Xcian. I couldn't trust anyone. I needed Alex.

"Okay," I said. "I'll do it."

Chapter Thirty

Sebastian

I stood in shackles surrounded by the Crawford family with Xcian chained to the bed.

That morning, or night, I couldn't tell how long I'd been down in the cells, I'd woken up to a man staring at me with intense dark eyes. Galen. The only brother I hadn't met. I sat up, driven to crawl as far away from him as the cell would allow. He'd said nothing to me for a long time before finally retreating.

Leaving me breathing meant I'd passed whatever judgment he'd made. Then I was hauled to a large bedroom inside the house. Xcian lying on the bed, and he'd healed enough that he was lucid. A thin sheet covered his hips.

I wore the same dirty knit sweater, no shoes, and I desperately needed a shower. There weren't any windows in the basement, so I gauged the time by the dinners I'd had to eat. Half of which I gave to Pedro since they hadn't even fed him at all.

Xcian's silver eyes burrowed into mine, and I felt a surge of pain rumble through me. A scream only he and I shared, despite his family in the room. Xcian was holding himself together by fraying threads.

"Why the fuck is my mate in chains?" he growled out.

"He tried to escape when we let him out," Zane said. True. I'd also refused a shower and clothes for this divorce, too.

"I'm here to sever our fake binding, *babe*," I hissed out like a disgruntled employee getting fired for no reason. The fact that he did it to save my life, that he risked his own life for me, thrown out the window because he still broke my heart. I wasn't sure if that was better than death. "Didn't think you'd care what I looked like."

His silver eyes slowly dragged to Zane's. "It's killing you. It was wrong. We're ending it now."

Finnegan emerged out of nowhere and stopped in the middle of the room. He turned to me and gave me a lazy once over. I heard Xcian tug at his chains.

"Finnegan, you fucker," Xcian growled.

The guy laughed. Beautifully mastered from his gorgeous deep black hair to his square chin. Like me, his features were a mixture of roundness and sharp features. Despite his asinine attitude, his eyes softened. As if he knew the existing pains all too well. Then a cold wall rose around his emotions and he sneered my way. "You are nothing, *human*. You will always be a pawn in this game. It's better if you realize that now."

And to think that I had believed Finnegan when he told me about my brother. When Xcian had hurt him. "Fuck you," I said dryly. I was done with this. *Done*. "Do this so I can get away from here."

"You're not going anywhere," Xcian hissed out.

Finnegan smirked. "The Crawfords are a fickle bunch. He'll forget you as soon as the tether is severed."

"Good," I said. Though it hurt. More than I wanted

to believe it hurt.

Finnegan shoved me toward Xcian, who growled but hadn't moved. I wasn't sure if he could move in those chains. "Hold hands. I need a connection."

I took Xcian's chained hand in mine. The warm touch sent a flitter of awareness through me. Mine. Xcian was mine. But no, that was a lie. I felt him let out a sigh as if he needed that connection too, then the screams inside my head faded.

Finn lowered his head, his chin on his chest, and he started to glow a shade of black. All Xcian's brothers stood around him and the air particles around them shimmered too as if Finn were drawing from all their power. My eyes landed on the one named Leander. The shifter. Doofus. The one I had come to love. That had been a lie too. He seemed to realize it because he lowered his eyes from mine.

And then a sharp sting coursed through my fingers, into my skull, branching out along my spine, and I heard something snap.

The light went out, and darkness pressed in around me. A swell writhed over my skin, making me burn and then cool. The light returned. Everyone was looking at us. Finn lifted his head. The black swallowed the whites of his eyes. "It's done."

I pulled out of Xcian's hand. He didn't fight. He breathed like a caged feral animal. "Get him out," he ordered.

Hands were on me. I couldn't tell who dragged me out. Tears pricked my eyes, and I didn't look at anyone while being shoved out of the room. Once the door slammed behind me, I fell on all fours, heaving.

"Come on," the guard said. A different one who

didn't force me to my feet. He actually sounded as if he could be kind.

My stomach clenched, and I felt like spewing. Then Serena was crouched next to me. "Here, drink some water."

She held a bottle of water in her hand. "I'm sorry," I cried. "I never meant for any of this. He should've let me die."

I heard her sigh, then her hands on my arm. "Come on."

I used her for support and drank the offered water. My heart wanted me back in that room demanding to ask him if it had all been lies. But my rational mind told me to get over it. I'd fallen for the monster. "Don't listen to Finnegan. He told me the same thing when I was betrothed to Zane."

We started walking. She still held my arm. "It's true. All of it. One big fat lie."

She sighed. "I had time to acclimate to the way of this world. There's a larger fight we don't see. Horrible things out there seeking to destroy the human realm."

I knew the evil she spoke about. I'd seen them first-hand. Including the Crawfords. "Are you sure they're not the evil in this world?"

She didn't respond. The guard glared at me.

We reached the dungeons and walked along the corridor to my cell, the guard a safe distance behind us. "Will you help me escape?"

"Sebastian, it's more dangerous for you out there."

"Are you sure about that?" Once in front of my cell, I turned to her. "We're just a pawn in their game, Serena. You to breed them, and I to control my brother. Let's get out of here."

She took a step back, and the guard made it clear he'd hurt me if I didn't get inside. I got inside and watched as he slammed the cell shut. "Trust Zane, Sebastian. He doesn't wish you harm."

"What did he do to my father?" I asked. "My father would never allow this."

"Zane has sent him somewhere."

"You don't even know, do you. You trust blindly, Serena. Just like my dad."

She didn't say anything, and they both walked away.

"Is it done?" Pedro asked.

"Yeah. I'm a single man." I wiped away the tears that never seemed to end.

"Good. Then it is time."

It was time to sleep because my body took that moment to crash. I fell on the pallet I'd created with the old blankets that'd been left behind. I didn't care that they smelled like mold and other shit. I was too tired to care.

My days consisted of sleep. I refused to eat, drink, or move. It could've been hours or days before I heard the thumping. Like drums during a war. Then gunshots. They sounded like muffled pops from the dungeon but were unmistakable.

"Sebastian," Pedro said. "Get ready."

"Ready? Ready for what?"

He didn't have to answer though because I heard the buzzer that opened my cell door and then Hawke and Serena appeared at my cell. "We have to get out," Serena said. "The mansion's been compromised."

Hawke wore a grim expression, blood peppered his clothes, and he held an assault rifle across his chest.

"Now," he ordered.

I got to my feet, dizzy. "What about Xcian?"

"He's awake and can protect himself."

I looked at Serena. "Mom? Alex?"

I lifted my eyes and saw my mom. I rushed to her and hugged her. She felt frail and the baby bump was more prominent between us. "I can't believe they kept you down here."

"Layla," Pedro reached out for her, and she instinctively moved away. Her face went pale.

"Pedro?"

"No time. We have to leave," Hawke said, shoving me.

I hated being shoved. "We can't just leave him."

"You're right." Hawke lifted the gun to shoot Pedro when Mom got in the way.

"No!" mom screamed. "Please."

"Get out of the way, Layla. You know he's not one of us." Hawke didn't lower the gun.

A loud gunshot echoed in the chamber. My heart leapt to my throat. Hawke shot my mom. The only thought racing through my mind as chaos erupted around us. I dove for the panel and released Pedro. He'd saved me once. He could save Mom now because I sure as hell couldn't.

I just wanted out of this dungeon, to protect my family. Then Mom screamed.

I looked down the hallway just in time to see Pedro holding Serena in front of him, a shank against her throat. A body lay on the floor. The shooting had been between Hawke and the body on the floor. Not Hawke shooting my mom. In the tight space, Hawke couldn't even bring up his weapon.

"Pedro," I snapped. "What are you doing?"

"Saving us," he said back, then to Hawke. "Get in the cell or she dies."

"You won't last, *malice*," he spat out,

"I'm not doing this for me," Pedro responded.

Hawke took a step inside the cell. He barely made it inside when Pedro slit Serena's throat and shoved her hard into Hawke's arms. Pedro slammed the cell door shut and picked up Hawke's discarded rifle. His eyes slid to me, standing next to the panel that could open the cell. I could let Hawke out. Give him Pedro like he wanted.

"Do it," Pedro said. He'd lowered the gun so that it faced the floor. "Do it and they will kill your mother, our baby, and Alejandro before they gut you. Is that what you want?"

Make a choice, Seba.

Hawke roared. An inhuman sound full of grief and hatred.

Something I'd never wanted to hear again.

Mom was sobbing. Pedro had the bloodied shank made of an iron nail in his hand. An iron nail. Humans were so weak that one iron nail could kill us.

"Move," Pedro ordered. "You want to stay behind, fine. I'm taking your mother to a safe place."

"Pedro, you killed her. She was my friend," Mom said.

Pedro drew Mom into a hug. "Lies, Layla. They are not friends. I'll protect you and our little girl."

Mom gave me such a dreadful look I had no clue what to make of it. I couldn't leave her to Pedro, and I didn't trust Zane or Xcian and now Hawke would kill me for what I'd done.

Serena. Dead. Because of me.

If Xcian thought I should've been beaten for a fake ID, he was going to kill me for this. I was the enemy now. Dead. Either way. I walked out behind Pedro and Mom. Chaos surrounded us, and we were able to escape through the same underground tunnel to the garage. From there, Pedro stole one of their SUVs and we drove out. From a distance, you couldn't tell that a war was going on inside that house.

"The area is warded so that humans don't see what's going on."

"You're not human." Mom's voice sounded so small.

He paused and glanced at Mom sitting next to him. "No. I'm not."

"You didn't have to kill her," I said.

Mom sobbed.

"I did have to kill her." Seeing him frazzled, shaken, and completely nuts, I saw the hints of non-human in him. It was the eyes. The pupils too large. The sallow skin. "They would've killed your mother and our daughter."

"You cannot have known," Mom said, sobbing. "Serena was...she was my friend."

Pedro growled. "Serena would've done the same to you had she known."

"Known what?"

"That your mother carries her replacement. That our daughter is the matriarch. The last of her kind because Aurora Crawford wiped them all out." He ran his hand down his face. "Aurora, Genesis, they will all want what's in your belly because she is the last, the only one left. Our daughter. And I won't let them have her. I love you, Layla." Mom couldn't get far enough away from him. "It's something I'm not supposed to feel, but I do. I love you and I will do anything to keep you and my daughter safe."

I clamped my mouth shut and stared out the window unable to think, to reason with any of this. Serena. Oh, God, Serena. If I had anything in my stomach, I would've thrown it up. But I didn't. Because Zane had kept me in a cell. I cried instead. Surprised that I had tears to spare.

"We need to get to Genesis. You said—you said we can get to Alejandro." Pedro didn't say anything, and I knew. I knew he lied to me too. I'd fallen right into his trap. "Was anything true?"

"All of it was true, *mijo*," he said. "All of it but being able to get to Alex. He'll wake up on his own. We can't do anything for him. He'll wake up when he's ready."

My truth had been a lie. Xcian had been right about that. I'd made everything worse.

I recognized the place as soon as Pedro pulled up into the alley. "What are we doing here?"

"Just get out and don't run. You do and your mother dies. *Entiendes?*"

He got out of the truck, grabbed my mother by the arm, and took her out. For a moment, I heard Alejandro scream. *"Run, Seba!"* Was this what he was trying to warn me about? Had he been in my nightmares trying to save me?

It didn't matter. I couldn't run.

Pedro opened the door and hauled me out with his free hand. Mom clutched against me, shivering. I wrapped my arm around her. "Just do what he says. I think he'll protect you," I told her.

"What about you?"

I didn't know, but I had to lie. "I'll be okay. Trust me."

She snorted. "You were supposed to just go out for onions."

I chuckled too. That fell flat when we entered the church, took the gated entrance underground, and came up to a large hall. Pedro said something to two large vampires who looked at me and my mom.

"Follow," he said.

We followed him deeper into the hall. Lit only with candles, shadows danced on the walls. The room was furnished with a few sofas, chairs, and tables. My eyes quickly found a skeletal version of Paris. His eyes sunken, inhuman. Loose skin, against an emaciated bony frame. My heart jolted inside my chest. My mind screamed for Xcian, though I knew he'd never hear it. He'd never save me. Not anymore. I was alone.

Mom dug her head into my shoulder. A man hung from the rafters in front of Paris. Dead. I recognized him as the bartender Gideon, the one who had greeted me at the club.

"Traitors get their comeuppance," Paris said. "We can't have people we don't trust in our midst now, can we?"

I swallowed the lump in my throat.

"I came through. I need safe passage to the sanctuary," Pedro said.

Paris looked at Pedro. His eyeballs looked too big inside his caved head. "You are a conundrum, malice. Why do you care so much about this one?" He lifted his chin to Mom, who shuddered.

"That's none of your business. And not part of the deal." Pedro shoved me forward. "You can have him, as agreed upon."

Mom squealed and reached for me, but Pedro hauled her back into his chest. "I'll be fine, Mom, really. Pedro is going to protect you." My voice trembled and I hoped she didn't notice. I needed her safe. Alive. I glared at Pedro. "If anything happens to her, Alex will rip the spine from your body when he wakes up."

Pedro smiled. Yeah, that was inhuman too. But he nodded in agreement. Then he lifted his eyes to Paris. "The sanctuary."

I had no clue what that could be, but Paris snapped his fingers and three vampires appeared beside him. Big, burly dudes. "Give them safe passage."

They nodded, and Pedro started to follow them with Mom in tow. She fought him, got free and ran to me. I caught her in a hug. "I'm so sorry. I did this. I brought him into our lives."

There was enough blame to go around. "No, Mom. You're human, remember that. Stay alive. Promise me. You'll stay alive." She nodded against my shoulder when Pedro carefully took her hand.

"Come on, Layla," he said, kindly. "I'll protect you."

She wiped her nose and let him lead her outside.

Paris purred and patted the space beside him. "I'll be gentle if you don't fight me. I promise." His inhuman voice sent a prickly sensation coursing through me.

"Alejandro will find me," I quavered, and stepped back as Paris got to his feet. How he could move, stand, being nothing but bones, defied all logic. Everyone around us just watched.

"*If* your brother survives his transition."

"Xcian."

"Is not bound to you. Means you can be claimed, fair and square. And I claim you."

"I don't agree to it. I don't give consent." I took another step back.

"I don't need your consent." He lunged.

And I screamed.

Chapter Thirty-One

Xcian

The pulsing light exploded into shards. Pain followed. Then an electrical hum I'd come to find comfort in throughout the centuries surged through me. The power of the Nine ran through my veins, and the demons I'd locked inside of the aether of my making.

Normalcy.

The binding severed.

I felt free. No longer compelled to burn heaven and earth to find my mate. Though the feeling lingered, like a burn slowly healing. I'd woken up to the house in chaos. The malice had breached our wards with Genesis at the helm. The only reason we had escaped was because Zane had already sent Eric and Alejandro to the vault ahead of us.

Eric paced in the living room while Aris had arranged a small command center of a couple of laptops and communication units. Galen had arrived just as the fight had started, and Hawke was still missing with Layla, Sebastian, and Serena.

"They should've contacted us," Eric said. "Why haven't they contacted us?"

Aris lifted his eyes to Eric cautiously, then to mine in silent communication. He found something. Unlike Zane, I didn't care about Eric's sensibilities. We needed answers. Now.

"What is it?"

"I was able to link into the security camera feeds. I have visual, but no audio of the cells."

Eric stopped pacing and looked at Aris. "Cells? What cells?"

"We had a dungeon in the mansion where we kept threats," Noah answered dryly. "Put it on screen one."

Aris did and the television on the wall came to life. I knew Zane had kept Sebastian in the prison under the mansion, but seeing it tore into me hard. And it wasn't me who hissed out this time. It was Eric. Eyes glued to the television, watching his son on a dirty pallet, wearing nothing but a dirty knit sweater, curled on the floor shivering. I clamped my hands into tight fists just as Zane walked into the room.

My brother looked at the screen and disconnected the call he'd been on. Then he locked eyes with Eric.

"Why the fuck is my mate in a cell?"

"He's not your mate, and he was deemed a threat."

Eric made a noise. "A threat? My son. My innocent son who you kidnapped!" Something seemed to finally fall into place for Eric. His eyes gleamed, and his lip trembled. "I have to get out of here." He started for the door but Noah blocked his path.

"Move," Eric ordered.

"Eric," Zane said in a voice I'd never heard from him. One of pain and guilt.

"I am not going to be your prisoner anymore."

Zane flinched.

"I'll go with him," Galen said. "Nothing will get past me."

Zane looked ready to snap his own jaw, grinding

his teeth so hard. "Fine. Ten minutes, then bring him back."

Eric glared but didn't argue, and they left.

For a fraction of a second, Zane's expression fell to something horrible, then hardened. "Play it," he ordered Aris.

The scene that unfolded before us made me want to hurl something. The whole room thickened with the need to kill Pedro. I could do nothing but watch as Hawke and Serena let out Sebastian. An argument ensued with Pedro, and Sebastian released the malice. Pedro got Serena, used her as a shield to get Hawke inside the cell, then killed her before shoving her inside.

The only thing I could see was Hawke cradling Serena, sobbing, and I was glad we had no audio. Aris fast-forwarded the feed to show when Maddox arrived with backup. They collared Hawke who hadn't fought back, and took him out, leaving Serena on the cold hard ground of the cell. Zane broke the silence that followed.

"Anything about Mother or Father?" Zane asked.

Aris shook his head.

"She's in on it," I hissed out. "Mother with Genesis orchestrated this."

"You don't know that," Zane defended.

"How could you not know this!"

Zane dropped on the sofa and leaned forward, his hands in his hair. For a moment, he said nothing. Then Zane lifted his eyes. "Play it from the angle of the crypt. Did Sebastian and Layla go willingly?"

The convo about our mother over, apparently.

"Zane, you can't possibly think that Sebastian meant for this to happen," Leander said.

"Look with your eyes. Haven't we been fucked

enough times to know better than to trust *humans*?" The feral expression he wore drew shivers down my spine. "Play it again, Aris."

There was no denying that Sebastian went willingly. He had the option of opening the cell door to let Hawke out, but he hadn't. Whatever Pedro told him had been convincing enough to have Sebastian serving up his soul to the devil.

"Why?" Zane asked me. "You knew the boy best. You were bonded. Why would Sebastian betray us?"

"You locked him in a fucking cell! Why would he trust us?"

"Mother—"

"Betrayed us! She was working with Genesis to ensure that Galen ended up with Serena, and you couldn't even stand up to her!" Anger was a raging fire underneath me. "We are the last of the Anunnaki, Zane." That realization cut through every one of my brothers listening in. "We have just this one life left."

Zane perused the room at each one of us. Zack, Leander, and Aris were still very much human. All of us were living our last lives. Hawke missing. Possibly captured. Serena dead.

Zane slammed a fist through the wall. Then he planted his palms between the hole and leaned forward, dropping his head. "Why did Sebastian believe he could save his brother?"

"Finn mentioned it to him," I answered.

"Finn," Zane whispered.

The male appeared sitting cross-legged on Aris's desk. "You called?"

I had to give it to Aris. The kid didn't even flinch.

Zane slowly turned around. The predator in him

rose to the surface though he knew he couldn't kill Finnegan. The wraith, his sin. "What did you do?"

"Me?" he asked, pointing at himself in shock. Then he hopped down and walked to the other end of the living room. Far from Zane, who hadn't moved. The wraith wasn't stupid. Zane could cause him pain.

I wondered if that appeased the wraith. I had been unlucky to experience a fake bonding for less than four days and had lost my mind. Finnegan had been tethered to Zane for more than a thousand years. Pain had to be all he knew.

"I did nothing."

"You planted the seed in Sebastian that he could save his brother." Finnegan lifted his eyes to me. He had played *me*. Serena had suggested the same thing, but I had been the one to agree to lead Sebastian on about saving his brother just to keep him close.

"It wasn't Finn," I said. "That falls on me."

Finn snapped his mouth shut, then shrugged as if he didn't give a shit. The front door opened, and Eric walked inside with Galen trailing behind. Eric stopped when he saw Finn, then his eyes slid to Zane, then back.

Finn smirked. The fucker knew exactly what he was doing. He may not have done the deed, but his kind planted ideas. They were the voices in your head giving you all the reasons why this was the way to go. Right up until it slammed you in the face. Zane would never be happy while Finn lived.

Alejandro, the god killer, his only hope.

"Did you find him?" Eric asked. "Did you find Sebastian and Layla?"

The mention of Layla had Zane bristling. Eric's ex-wife would always be an important person in Eric's life.

She had been the love of his life and the mother of his boys for a human lifetime. Until Genesis decided to change fate.

"Genesis," I said.

Finn sneered. The goddess of creation had loads of enemies. Even my own demons bristled at her name.

"She has been testing fate for years. She set Pedro on Layla." I looked at Aris who lowered his eyes. "Pedro was malice when he met her."

"Impossible," Galen said. "Malice cannot conceive."

Finn lifted a finger. "Actually, that's not entirely correct." He crossed his arms across his broad chest and leaned against the wall. "A malice and a Nephilim can conceive."

"Layla is Nephilim?"

"She is my cousin twice removed from my mother's side." He chuckled. No one else did. "Sorry." He cleared his throat. "Yes. And she carries the last matriarch now that Serena is dead."

"What are you saying?" We had all forgotten about Eric in the room. "Layla meeting Pedro had been a set-up? Zane and I..." He glanced at Zane who wore an unreadable expression while Eric was coming to a conclusion that would lead him to nothing good. "Genesis set this all up? This isn't real."

"She set you two up because she needed Layla." Finnegan winked at Eric. "Sorry, bud, but there's really nothing special about you."

Zane growled and I pushed him back. "Why didn't you tell us this before?"

Finnegan shrugged. "No one ever asks me anything."

I had to breathe to calm down. "Where is Layla now?"

"Pedro's taken asylum at the sanctuary. No one can touch him now."

"No," I looked at Eric. "But we might be able to get to Layla."

"Assuming she's not working with Pedro," Zane hissed back.

"She's not," Eric defended. "I know my wife. She wouldn't work against me." *Unlike Zane.* The underlying words were perfectly clear. "Take me to her. Please."

Finn looked at Zane and smirked. *Wife.* Not ex-wife. Everyone caught that. "Ah," he said in an exhale. "How the tables have turned." Then he perked up and turned to me. "Road trip."

An hour later, we were at the sanctuary. Unable to pass the barrier, we stopped just outside the small community. A series of small cabins hidden within the mountains.

"She'll never let us through," Galen said.

The *she* in question being Soteria, goddess of protection. And she took her job seriously.

"I can go through," Eric said.

"No," Zane said.

"I'm not asking you."

"Let's just try first without sending anyone. Yeah?" I added.

Soteria met us outside the boundaries. Not a surprise. She must've sensed the six pissed-off gods wrapped in demon power in her vicinity.

"I haven't seen you all for centuries," she said. "That was a good thing."

Soteria looked like any other human female. Jeans, a Metallica T-shirt, boots. Her dark hair was tied in a ponytail. There was nothing extraordinarily beautiful about her, which was how she preferred it. I'd seen her in the field of battle. She loved to be underestimated.

"You are harboring a killer who needs to be tried," Galen said.

Soteria cocked her head. "Most of the people here are criminals running from something they deem to be unjust. What else is new?"

Zane fisted his hand as Eric approached her. "Please, ma'am. Pedro, this malice, has my ex-wife and son hostage here."

"There is no one here that does not want to be, I assure you. The sanctuary does not allow for it."

"Please, we'd like to just speak with her. To be sure."

"Layla Ortega, the Nephilim?"

Eric visibly shook. "Yes."

"Stay here."

She vanished, and a few long minutes later, Layla walked out of the clearing. Pedro stood behind her, and a collective growl swept through us. Pedro said something to her, then released her hand. Before Zane could reach for Eric, he breached the wall of magic and ran toward Layla. She ran toward him and they hugged. Eric cupped her face and kissed her forehead. Zane couldn't take anymore and headed for the car, where he watched from afar.

"It's my fault," she sobbed. "I brought him into our lives, Eric. I'm sorry. So sorry."

"It's not your fault, Layla."

Another hug. Then a barely there whisper as if Eric

wasn't surrounded by gods without super hearing. "Come with us. We'll protect you."

She shook her head. "No. I don't trust them." She turned to Pedro, and I sensed her fear. Then she turned to Eric. "Stay with me," she said. "He can't hurt you here either."

Zane pushed off the car, hands fisted. Eric didn't even look his way.

"I can't, Layla. I have to do what I can for Alejandro."

She cupped his face. "I know. I know. I'm sorry. You're such a good father. I know you'll do what's right for our sons." Then she pulled away. "What about Sebastian? Did you find him?"

My blood started to pound in my ears.

"I thought he was with you?"

"No. Pedro left him with some awful people. A thing. Paris. At a church. You have to find him, Eric."

The mention of Paris made my blood boil.

The thought of Sebastian under Paris' spell, tainted, infected, made me seethe.

My brothers stepped closer to me. Our mutually linked need to protect flowed through all of us, but especially when it meant protecting a bonded mate.

We didn't have to speak our intent.

We all felt it.

Chapter Thirty-Two

Sebastian

Pain.

A burning that dug into muscle and bone.

Screaming. *My* screams.

Then nothing.

A blankness so white I thought I'd been cooled in a snow globe. Snow. I missed Chicago snow. Alejandro and I used to build snowmen and forts. Throwing snowballs until we were too cold to move, and then Dad would call us in for hot chocolate. The image appeared in front of me, and I felt my brother beside me.

"Real or not real?" I asked.

"Real. Though I always burned my tongue with the hot chocolate. Dad made it too hot."

I chuckled. "You're never satisfied with whatever he does."

"And you give him too much slack."

I turned to my brother. Darkness rimmed his eyes. "How long have you been here?"

His eyes darkened as he looked out into the distance. "I don't remember what Dad looks like," he said, softly. "Did Mom have the baby?"

I swallowed audibly. "I wanted to get you out, but everyone says you have to wake up," I croaked out, tears burning tracks on my cheeks. "I need you, Alex. I can't—" I tried to reach for him, but my arm crinkled like paper. Alex stumbled back, eyes on me. "Alex!" My body felt stretched to the limit, my bones popping free. "I need you to wake up!" I screamed and screamed and screamed until the world around me folded in on itself. I thrashed, I clawed, but I couldn't get the massive weight off me.

And then the tearing of flesh at my neck. The sucking sound as Paris sucked my lifeblood. I prayed for darkness. Prayed to be returned to Alex, but he wasn't real. This was my reality now.

My hell.

I slipped. My body went boneless. Fire spread under my skin, and I clamped down hard to keep from screaming. He liked when I screamed. He liked listening to me talk when my voice turned hoarse from so much screaming. I sounded like a sex worker with a smoking problem now. I almost giggled at that. But I felt more like spewing. My stomach writhed. My head dizzy. The worst part happened when he pulled out. The slip of his teeth out of my flesh. And then he licked me, and I felt like scratching off my skin. Everywhere. As my flesh seamed itself.

I shuddered as the cold draped over me. I should've been used to the smell of death and the cold. Burrowing into him didn't work. Paris was a slab of dead meat. How long had I been here? How many feedings was this? My brain struggled to remember. I had marked it somewhere. Where? Right. My forearm. Paris had given me my blade back and he watched as I slit my arm. Blood pooled to the surface. He didn't lick it away. Didn't want to heal it. I had fifty-six lines on my arm. Fifty-six times he'd bled me. Every hour. And no one's come to save me.

Paris knew the right amount of blood to take not to kill me. Though I wished he'd just get it over with. I planned on doing it myself once I got enough nerve. Once he regained his extremities. I wouldn't survive what he planned for me.

He gave me a gentle kiss on my cheek and nuzzled his cold cheek against mine. "No one is coming for you, pet. And if they do, I will raze this place to the ground." Then he kissed me again. His lips hard and cold against my skin.

Gideon still hung in the rafters. Rotting.

Serena still dead.

Mom still with Pedro.

Alejandro still in his own hell.

Me in mine.

I got it now. Zane and his brothers fought the evil in the night. The Parisess and Amelias. They fought the Genesises and Lucifers so that humans didn't have to. Gideon was a warrior who deserved a better ending. Serena deserved better for her part in protecting people like me. The nobodies of the world. Humans. We were a delicate species that needed protecting. We couldn't come up against people like Paris and his minions. The shaman and her hallucinations. And even the demons Zane and Xcian had trapped inside of them.

You needed to become a monster to destroy monsters.

I got it now.

Too late. I could only pray that my mother would survive, and my sister would be protected. Despite Pedro being a psycho murderer, I think he would protect them. There was nothing for me in this world.

Paris eyed me with his now human eyes. My blood doing its job to make him whole again. He licked his lips and handed me a wine glass. One filled with his blood. "You can take my lifeblood and join us."

I turned my face. "I'll die human." The words I said every time he fed from me. Fifty-six times. Though with little emotion now. At least he couldn't force me to drink it. Apparently, the rules dictated that one had to go into the dark side willingly or it wouldn't work. Another rule concerning Paris' lineage was their deadly allergic reaction to onions. I would've laughed had Paris not chopped the head off the vampire who had spoken to me about it.

Paris was not the forgiving type.

He brushed his lips on the shell of my ear and grabbed my hand hard, putting it on his still limp cock. "When this fills, you will be begging for me to turn you."

I pulled my hand away sharply. "Fuck you," I said with little inflection.

"We will, soon."

Not if I died from blood loss, I thought. We were interrupted by two of his goons. They came and went since I'd been here. Most of them were tall, angular, and mean-looking. Paris had a type. He didn't want anyone prettier than him in his sandbox.

"Genesis is here," he said, fangs making his speech distorted. "And she's brought company."

I felt Paris' anger. My blood in his veins tethered us in a way I still didn't understand. "Get the soldiers ready," he ordered. Then he shoved me to the floor at his feet between his legs and secured a collar around my neck. The cool iron stung my sensitive skin where he had just bitten me. Then he pulled the chain. A reminder to behave like the subservient dog he expected.

I heard the footsteps of a dozen or so people approaching and Paris' displeased hiss. I instantly dropped my head. My dirty hair fell like a sheet against my face until Paris pulled on the chain, forcing me to meet the newcomers in the eye. Genesis, no longer wrapped in shadows, looked like a fashion model wearing a white business suit and stilettos. The white contrasted with her black hair, eyes, and blood-red lips. I chuckled. An ugly sound that I couldn't help making. "I thought you were dead," I said, my voice ruined.

I felt a slight tug from my master, followed by a gentle touch on my head, and I fought not to wince. "You'll have to tell me that story one day, my pet."

For some awful inexplicable reason, I felt content at making him happy that I almost purred. Purred! I cleared my throat instead.

"It takes more than a fledgling to kill me, slave," she hissed out. She didn't look all that pretty when she was angry. Then she dragged those murderous eyes to Paris. "Your father is not pleased."

I almost turned to look at Paris. Serena had mentioned a father too. That meant there was someone above him in the food chain. Paris' fingers continued to tap my head as if thinking of his options. "Father has left me in charge, *demon*. This is my lair. Do not believe for a second that I won't have you and your abominations exsanguinated. They are still good for one thing, so I've heard." The vampires seemed to work as one unit, and dozens stood surrounding the group with

Genesis. Color me impressed by Paris' army. "I have never tried malice," Paris went on, unconcerned that the air thickened with violence. "I prefer those with a much more powerful bloodline." He twirled his fingers in my hair. "He's delicious. If you've come for him, you should make your way back out. I'm not done with him."

"Perhaps, we can come to an agreement. I do not need him whole."

My heart thudded loud in my ears. Paris' touch now like fire along my skin. "What do you have that I want?"

"Serena is dead," she said coolly. "I know the identity of the last matriarch. You wish to father a child. She'll be the only option you have."

I sucked in a breath. *No. No.*

Paris tapped his fingers against my head when I wanted to break them. Me for my sister. Me for my dad. Me for my brother. I'd always be bait. I launched to my feet and lunged for her. I wasn't sure what I expected. Paris pulled the chain. Pain clamped around my throat. And I fell back on my bare ass.

Genesis laughed. Laughed!

Paris got to his feet and pulled hard. I had no choice but to return to him. He fisted my hair, forcing me to my knees. Tears streamed down my face. I tried to free myself but couldn't do anything but be on the receiving end of pain.

"You haven't tamed him as you should," she said, delighted. "He has spirit, I'll give him that. But he's worthless on his own. I mean, look at him."

I lowered my eyes as more tears wet my face. Paris sat again and put me back into his control as his dog.

This time, the chain had no give and it choked me. Soon, I'd pass out from lack of oxygen. Something he did sometimes as a form of power play. I felt my lids heavy, the drum of my pulse in my ears, almost passing out when it suddenly went lax. I inhaled sharply, the burn forcing my eyes to water. I looked up at the new addition to crazy and my heart couldn't seem to catch a break. I recognized them. Six men wearing black gear, carrying weapons. My eyes landed on pale cold eyes on a face of which I memorized every detail, every rigid line, every contour.

Xcian. And he looked ready to murder someone.

Paris gently guided my head to his lap as I continued to gasp until the dizziness went away. Then I just wanted to pass out again.

"The boy belongs to us," Zane said.

Shame, unbridled, coursed through me. Still wearing nothing but the lace underwear, collared, and used as a bloodbag, there was nothing left in me to fight. Zane's demand that I belonged to them made me bristle. The lie of the binding hurt too damn much. I hated Zane. Wanted to blame him for everything. If he hadn't kidnapped me to force my dad to mate him, if he hadn't kept me in a cell, if he'd been kinder to me, maybe I would've trusted him. Just as the thought left my frame of mind, his eyes turned to me, locked with mine, and something passed between them. Regret maybe?

Paris pulled my chain, breaking whatever connection we had. I had no choice but to submit to the vampire. I lowered my cheek on his lap and closed my eyes, lulled by his touch against my hair. Xcian had liked playing with my hair. Paris liked it too. I decided to chop it off if I survived.

I heard Genesis laugh. A seductive laugh. "Heir and Sword. Here to make a bargain? Perhaps you'd like to relinquish him to me in favor of your brother. Maddox is surely enjoying him, even as we speak."

"You are playing a very dangerous game, demon," Zane said. "Are you prepared to go to war over it?"

"Yes," she hissed back.

Hawke. I could still hear his cries as Serena lay dying in his arms. Serena dead because of me. I was sure Zane only wanted me back to torture me. The consequences of my actions. Maybe that's why they waited so long to come get me. Xcian said I deserved to get beaten for a fake ID. I could only imagine what I deserved now. I snorted a giggle and felt Paris still his hand on top of my head.

"What do you find so funny, pet?"

I hated the word pet, but I knew he used it as a show of force. I lifted my head at his coaxing. Cold fingers under my chin, almost soothing. At least I didn't care that Paris' kindness was a lie. Unlike Xcian. "They will judge me."

"Would you like to remain with me?"

My chest hurt at the thought of Paris' growing strength and everything else. My eyes landed on Gideon hanging on the rafters still. Maybe I could find a way to end things before it got that far. Maybe my dad had been right and death is the only kindness we're ever given by the gods. Tears pricked my eyes making everything blur. Then Zane spoke. The sound of his voice oozing an emotion I'd never thought possible from him. His own shame and guilt.

"Sebastian, I'm so sorry. You're allowed to hate

me, but don't give up on those who love you."

I lifted my eyes to Xcian. I loved him. With all my human heart and soul, but it wasn't enough. He'd never love me back. It wasn't enough to push the guilt away. He'd risked himself to save me and I'd betrayed them. Betrayed them all.

Too tired to focus, I lowered my cheek onto Paris again without answering.

"This has been fun, but my pet needs to rest before I feed on him again. I'm sure you can find your own way out."

A slow tear slipped out of my eye and landed on the vampire. I felt him wince under me. It would've been interesting before. Now, I didn't care.

"Release him, Paris. And I'll let you live," Zane said.

Another set of booted feet entered the hall. This one drew out whatever heat I had left in my body. I'd never feel warm again. Paris wrapped his finger in my hair but stopped petting me.

"Genesis," a deep voice said.

"Lucifer," Genesis said.

That had me opening my eyes to see the Lucifer of my grandmother's nightmares.

"Finnegan, I should've known." Genesis scowled.

Finnegan shrugged. He did that a lot.

"He does have his uses," Lucifer said.

Finnegan winced a little bit.

"You are being disobedient, goddess of creation. You have your malice. I have my demons. It's the way of things."

"The Anunnaki are our common enemy. I am just leveling the playing field."

Lucifer looked at me with those glazed eyes. Depth of despair and cold. Darkness but for a small twinkling light glazed over me and I turned to Xcian again watching me closely. My heart pumped fast, driving out the cold and giving me strength.

"They have one of the trinity and the matriarch. And the boy is the key to both."

Lucifer dragged his eyes to Paris. "The boy is human. We are not allowed to get involved. This whole notion of free will, yada, yada, yada." He waved his hand in the air. "I'm sure you've heard of it."

Genesis looked like she wanted to murder Lucifer who turned to me. "So, human. Choose."

The word got stuck in my throat. Especially when Paris pulled on the chain harder this time. I had no choice but to sit on his lap. "The boy is mine," Paris hissed. "As by my power of not being a god."

A god? Xcian was a god? How had I missed that?

Lucifer smirked. "Yes, yes, but the boy chooses who will have the right to smite you, vampire," he hissed out the word as if it were worse than human.

With that little incentive, Paris pulled my hair back, forcing me to expose my neck while he dug a sharp claw into it. The collar kept him from piercing my carotid. "Leave, all of you. You weren't invited, and I may leave this human intact, after I'm done with him."

I felt his cock like a rod on my tailbone. A few more days and he'd be well enough to do everything he promised. "Just kill me," I whispered.

Cold lips pressed against the shell of my ear. "Not before I fulfill my promise to you and fuck you until you beg me to end you." Then he licked my neck with his cold, dead tongue.

Zane grabbed Xcian to pull him back. They were leaving. Leaving me with him. Panic surged through me. And a shitload of fear. "No!" I screamed. "I choose Xcian!"

Chapter Thirty-Three

Xcian

The magical cuff Zane forced me to wear kept me from launching myself at the vampire and tearing his head off his shoulders. And that Genesis had inserted herself in all this drama had Moloch practically clawing his way out through my skin. And I wanted to release him. The thought of tearing limbs, of hearing the screams of the damned, of feeling the blood on my fingers was too damn tempting. The last time I'd gone against Genesis, I almost ripped myself in half. And the last time I'd turned berserker, I'd almost popped like a balloon. My chances of surviving this should I release my demons were not good.

Ripping Paris' head might kill Sebastian too, and the fucker knew it. The reason he didn't see us as a threat. But I didn't have to kill him to make him pay.

Blood loss had Sebastian pliant. Bruises banded around his wrist, neck, and thighs. And he had long gashes on his forearms. Perfectly measured lines as if he'd done them himself, with care. And he only wore that lace underwear.

My mate.

My fucking mate.

I don't care what Zane believed. The binding hadn't been completely wiped free. The surge to release my demons to protect what was mine surfaced and my muscles thickened. My monster pressed for release. And when Paris whispered the threat into Sebastian's ear and licked him, it was Zane who held me back.

Until Sebastian cried out my name.

Those three words had my blood boiling to the tipping point.

"I choose Xcian!"

Me.

He'd chosen *me*.

I tore the cuff off and slammed into Paris, ignoring the sounds of chaos around me. Sebastian the only thing that mattered. My brothers—Sage and Basil—were with me in an instant, gathering Sebastian, moving him away from the fight I'd precipitated with Paris. The vampires swelled on me, but my brothers knew getting Sebastian out was all that mattered. Noah, Zane, and I shifted into our god forms as we tore the place apart of malice and vampire alike.

I lost Paris in the melee, then Sebastian started to scream. He dropped to the floor, flapping his arms and legs as if burning although nothing was on him. Basil and Sage searched out the hall when Basil caught Paris on the bar, being burned by a malice. He didn't even need to point. I teleported to the fucker and ripped the malice apart, swatting the flames off the vampire. As suspected, his bloodlink to Sebastian ran too deep. I shoved the vampire to Basil. "Get him out and lock him up."

I dropped down to Sebastian, tears trailing down his cheek. "I can't," he said. "I can't." I started to lift him when something slammed into me hard. I went skittering across the wood floor, losing grip of

Sebastian. Jumping to my feet, I faced Genesis.

And she had Sebastian limp in front of her. His skin had gone sallow and pale. His breathing strained. "This is what you replace me with? A human?"

As if he were nothing but a rag doll, she flung him over her shoulder. A cry stuck in my throat when a shadow rose out of the floor and solidified into the wraith who caught Sebastian and then carefully lowered him onto the floor, away from the fight. I owed Finnegan too damn much up to this point. I turned back to Genesis. The goddess of creation had designed the malice to her cruel specifications. A fuck you to the God that made humans in this realm. She used them as puppets. Nothing more. And she had used my blood, my spark, to create them. But my blood hadn't been as strong as Zane's, so her malice hadn't met her expectations of soulless beings under her control. They had gone against her by following Finn's orders to kill Sebastian. And Pedro had conceived a child.

"You are *nothing*. Even your malice have defied you. Where is Pedro?"

She snarled. "*My* malice? You fathered them!"

Though the chaos between the malice and the vampires still played to the chorus of gunfire and screams, I knew my brothers heard it all.

"Your blood was weak." She smirked. "At least you were good for a fuck."

Maybe my younger self would have cared. But she got nothing from me. I didn't even hate her. That would mean I felt something for her. She was a threat to this realm. And I was the sword, protector. My job was to put her down.

Zane moved in my peripherals, pulling out the

sword of light. Forged in the fires of Hell, dipped in Anunnaki blood, blessed by the gods, the sword of light was the catalyst to trap a demon. Zane tossed it to me. It sailed through the air. Genesis caught the movement and slammed a jolt of power into my chest, sending me sprawling to the floor. The sword pinged somewhere to my left. My brothers charged her, but Genesis was older than time. One of the four original guardians and too damn powerful. "You think you can best me?" she howled. Her human form crumbled away in dust leaving her in her god form. Freakishly tall, long limbs, sharp claws. Wings ripped out of her back, and her eyes were two green flames.

Lucifer sat on Paris' vacated throne watching it all with a grin on his face. All he needed was popcorn. The fucker wanted Zane back. Zane, the fucking martyr, would sacrifice himself even to Lucifer if things went bad.

Lucifer got to his feet, dark eyes glaring at Finn, who still wore that seductive smirk on his face as if he were going into some whorehouse to find pleasure.

Genesis' back was turned to him.

Big mistake.

Lucifer roared and released hellfire from his outstretched hand aimed at Finn who charged Genesis. But Finn was faster. Somehow, the fucker managed to grab the flame and slam it into Genesis. I lunged for the sword and drove it into her belly just as Finn slammed into her back, skewering her even deeper into my blade. Her expression morphed into something dark. The blade lit up bright. Energy coursing through it and into my arm, forcing me to clench my teeth against the surging power. My body unable to contain it. A scream tore through my mind. Her scream, trying to fight my hold over her. Then I saw Finn shake his head at me. He kicked me hard and I stumbled back, pulling the blade with me right before he turned to dark matter and melded inside of her. Two powerful entities colliding created a maelstrom of energy ready to burst at the seams.

Zane grabbed my arm. Noah, Galen, and the twins were already heading for the exit. "Move!"

The air rippled with dark power.

Lucifer disappeared.

I handed off the sword to Zane and picked up Sebastian from the floor as I ran out through the narrow tunnel just as a blast wave erupted behind me. Zane's power was the only thing keeping it contained to the underground section of the church. We ran up the steps as everything behind us caved in with a sickening screech. Once outside, we all turned to the church, waiting to see it crumble. It didn't. The church remained standing. Zane dropped onto his knees, shifting into his human form right before he passed out.

Zack arrived with the van. We put Zane and Sebastian inside before jumping in ourselves and hauling ass out of there.

Finn had saved us. He'd saved me. Genesis' power would've killed me. I almost wanted to believe that there was some sanity left in the wraith that gave him a snippet of morality. Maybe he truly cared for Zane and knew that Zane would've bargained with Lucifer if he saw no hope. Maybe he knew right from wrong. But in the end, that *fuck you* smirk he gave Lucifer just before he annihilated Genesis, was all the reasoning he needed. He didn't do it to save us. He did it to go against

Lucifer. For all Zane's bitching, Finn kept saving Zane from Lucifer's hell.

I didn't care why he did it, only that he had.

We reached a set of cabins along the lake. "You'll have to bring Eric. Zane is going to need him to wake up."

Galen nodded, and he and Noah carried my brother in a gurney while Basil and Sage took another vehicle with Paris. I couldn't kill the fucker until his tether with Sebastian waned.

I carried Sebastian to a separate cabin. He stirred when I got inside, his arms tighter around my neck as he took in my scent. That small gesture had me almost filling him with kisses. "It's okay," I said. "You're safe."

"He didn't rape me."

Sebastian's words drove a knife through my chest and ripped me into pieces. I cradled him closer to me as I walked to the bedroom and sat him down, clueless as to what to say. How to make this right again. One thing was certain, Sebastian was my chosen.

As I peeled his soiled clothes from his body, revealing the bruises but no puncture marks as those would've been healed by Paris, those words were all I could think about. As if being raped would've changed how I felt about him. And nothing had changed how I felt about Sebastian Diaz. The broken bond hadn't stopped me from going insane at the thought of what they did to him. Of not saving him in time.

"I love you," I blurted like a massive idiot. "It's not the same love as human love. It's not something we could control or choose. It happens and we can't make it unhappen. And sometimes, I feel as if I need to burn the world to keep you safe. Sometimes, I want to hold you and never let you go. Time in your presence moves too fast because I want to be near you forever. I want to share my flame with you, my soul, my burden, my life however long or short that may be." I knelt between his legs and took his hand. "You told me you loved me once and I burrowed it away in my heart because I didn't want to believe in human love. But I believe in yours. And if you still want me, the human and monster inside of me, I'd like to make you my mate. It doesn't have to be a binding ceremony. We could have a human wedding. Whatever, however, you'll have me. I am yours, Sebastian Diaz. From the moment I laid eyes on you." I closed my mouth and clenched my teeth just to keep from talking. I had so much more I wanted to say. All the words I'd never said before. "Please, say something. Even if it's to tell me to go to hell."

"I...I need to shower."

I knelt there, frozen in time, unsure of my world except for the pain behind my sternum making it impossible to breathe. I couldn't get away from him fast enough. I managed to make it to one of the other cabins when I released the anger surging through me. I needed to destroy everything with my fists. The pain didn't matter. I'd heal. My flesh would mend but not my heart.

Galen stopped me. Holding me tight. I didn't have enough strength to fight anymore. "Stop it," he hissed out. "Don't make this about you."

Those words stung. A lot.

"He needs your strength right now, so stop running."

I wanted to be as far away from Sebastian Diaz as I

could get. But the thought had me crumbling instead. This wasn't about me. I hadn't been the one tortured. I hadn't been the one hurt. Sebastian needed me and I wasn't going anywhere.

Time was all I had now.

Chapter Thirty-Four

Sebastian

"He didn't rape me."

Why had those words been the first out of my mouth? I stood in front of the mirror facing my broken body. Hating myself. Guilt and blame something toxic writhing inside of me. My hair.

With trembling hands, I searched through the cabinets until I found a pair of shears and proceeded to chop off my long hair. Paris had liked running his hand down my hair and I yearned for his touch. Xcian had done the same and I needed him too.

A loud sob escaped my throat, sounding obscene in the quiet space. A few seconds later, Xcian appeared in the doorway, looking at me. I couldn't read his expression. I didn't want to. Was he disgusted with me? Did he regret saying he loved me? It couldn't be real.

"It is real. I'm right *here*, Sebastian."

I hadn't realized I'd spoken out loud. He started to walk inside but stopped when I stepped back. Pain flitted in his expression. I caught it like a fleeting moment in time. "I can help you with that," he said, pointing to the shears.

Without a word, I handed it to him. He led my gaze to the toilet and I sat on the lid, keeping my eyes on the brown tile at my dirty feet as he slowly approached me.

Gently, he slid his fingers along my scalp, smoothing out the pieces of hair, and dropping the cut strips. Then he started to cut. "Leander sheds like crazy," he started, using a soothing voice. "My parents used to go nuts. I'd have to drag him outside to the backyard to shave him sometimes."

"He doesn't shed naturally?" My voice sounded husky.

"He does, but not as much as he should. And he prefers the wolf version of himself."

"I miss him." I did. "I guess it's different now that I know he's a shifter and your brother. Makes it kinda weird." I chuckled, but it hurt my throat.

"He blames himself for what happened with Alejandro."

I didn't have words for that. The silence stretched as he fixed my cut and ran his hand over my scalp. "I get it now," I said. "The reason why you kill the bad guys."

Warm fingers pressed under my chin, and he forced me to look at him. "That isn't something for you to decide. I carry that burden."

I nodded. Not much else I could say.

"Let's get in the shower so I can check you out. Check out your wounds, I mean. Your body." Xcian babbling was the most adorable thing in the world. "Wash you."

I bit back a smile. Couldn't help it. Xcian naked in front of me was the next best thing to him loving me. He waited for me in the shower patiently. I trusted him. Knew that he wouldn't hurt me.

"I'm just going to wash you, okay?"

I lowered my underwear, releasing my own half-hard cock, and liked the way he took me all in. Despite my body being used, broken, I felt wanted.

He guided me under the spray, my front flushed against his, our cocks slotted together. I wanted to grind against him, create that friction I so desperately wanted right now. I didn't.

"I'm going to touch you. Can I?" I'd never heard him so unsure of himself.

"Yes, please."

He lathered his hands and ran them down my long, hard shaft. I shuddered at his touch.

"Are you okay?" he asked.

"Yes."

He washed me as if I were a delicate flower. Something he treasured. Taking care of my wounds until he lifted my forearm where I had etched the fifty-six lines. "Fifty-six hours," I said.

A shudder escaped his lips, and he drew me into a hug, sobbing into my neck. I didn't say anything but held him as tight as I could. The water mixed with our tears. It took him a few minutes to compose himself. We dried off in silence, and I managed to dress when I heard my father beyond the bedroom door.

Xcian had enough time to lift his joggers when my dad flung the door open. Practically snarling at Xcian before launching himself at me, tears raining down his face as he hugged me.

I loved my dad. I'd always felt comfort in his hugs. But at that moment, I realized I didn't need him as much as I needed Xcian by my side. I realized as Zane walked in looking like all kinds of death, that my dad needed Zane too.

Zane met my eyes and gave me a slight nod.

Between him and Xcian, they looked like two stone warriors ready to give their lives to protect those they loved, but unwilling to show a lick of emotion. I wanted to bang a club over their heads and shout *wake up*!

Instead, when Eric released me of my hug, I approached my stepfather and hugged him. He stiffened, unsure what to do. "This is where you hug me back," I whispered.

And he did. Pressing his face into the crook of my neck. "I'm so fucking sorry, Sebastian," he said. His voice full of emotion.

"I know. Me too."

I slowly pulled away from him and whatever emotion he'd had vanished from his expression. He lifted his eyes to my dad, standing behind me. "We should give them a moment."

My dad took a firm stance, crossing his arms across his chest. "I'm not going anywhere with you. Ever."

Zane did release an emotion. Anger. I'd seen that plenty of times in Xcian. Before he could stick his foot in his mouth, I said, "How about you both give me a moment alone with my dad."

Xcian didn't even look at me when he walked out. Which hurt me to the bone. Zane stood still, like stone, before he finally spun out of the room and closed the door behind him. I heard Dad move to the bathroom even before I turned around. Fiddling in the bathroom before he came out.

"You should rest, Seba."

I knew this look on him. He was in full daddy mode. I let him tuck me in because I was so tired. He sat on the bed next to me and carefully took my wounded arm. The lashes I'd given myself to mark time. Maybe to mark my death. He traced a finger over the already healing flesh. "I did this. I brought him into our lives."

"Dad."

He looked up, and I felt as if someone had stabbed my heart. "How can I love someone who does this to my son?"

I swallowed the lump building in my throat. "Zane didn't do this to me. Paris did. A vampire who took me."

"He kept you in a cell, Seba. I saw the video."

Tears were close again. Serena. Mom. "Is mom okay?"

"Yes. She's at a sanctuary. She prefers to stay with a killer than with us. What does that say about us?"

"Dad, Serena is dead because I let Pedro out. Because I believed in the goodness of people. But not all people are good. Zane, Xcian, and their brothers fight things...things you can't imagine that would rip this world to shreds if they could. They protect us." I squeezed his hand. "We're just trying to make sense through our own eyes, through our own truths, but don't you think we might be wrong too?" This had been what Xcian had tried to tell me when I'd been so adamant about getting Alejandro. I got it now. All of it. "Zane loves you. He'd do anything to protect you. He just doesn't know how yet, but he will."

"And how am I supposed to trust him?"

"Teach him. You have more power over him than you realize."

He chuckled and wiped his tears. "I should take him back to Maine."

"You should. Go on your crazy moose hunts with him. I'm sure he'd like *that*."

Dad started to laugh. Me too. The thought of Zane in the mountains trying to be silent for hours just to catch sight of a moose would be something I'd like to see. Dad inhaled. "You love him, don't you."

I didn't need to ask who. Xcian. "Yeah, very much."

Dad turned pink in his own thoughts. "They can be pretty intense."

I rolled my eyes feeling my cheeks heat up. "Oh, God, Dad, it's too late for the be safe speech. Alex already gave me one."

Alex.

The mention of him brought us back to the reality that he might die.

"Do you think he still suffers?" Dad asked.

"I don't know. But we can't do anything for him. Zane was right. He'll wake up." He had to.

Dad patted my hand and got to his feet. "Do you want me to call Xcian for you?"

"Please."

He kissed me on my forehead and walked out. Xcian walked in a few moments later. "Your father looked better."

"Yeah, I just had to clarify things for him."

Xcian sat where my dad vacated and took my hand in his. "Like what?"

"Like you and Zane are not so bad. That maybe we can make this work."

Xcian's silver eyes met mine. I wish I could read his mind. I got nothing. "Make this work. You mean us?"

"I love you," I said. "You love me. I want to help carry your burden."

"Sebastian. You don't realize what that means."

"It means we'll be stronger together. It means you'll be mine and I'll be yours and no one will ever take that away from us. Make me yours, Xcian."

It took a few long moments before he leaned into my space and softly kissed me. A kiss so gentle, my toes curled. "Yes," he said between kisses. "I accept you as my bonded mate." He kissed my throat where Paris had bled me, my wrists where he'd chained me, and he carefully peeled me out of my clothes and kissed every other part of my wounded body.

Chapter Thirty-Five

Xcian

I walked out of the room, leaving Sebastian resting. Zane and Eric were sitting on the sofa together watching something on the TV, Doofus lying on the floor. Aris and Zack were asleep on the sofa. They barely fit. Galen and Noah were debating something or other in the kitchen with the twins. Hawke still missing.

The Anunnkai had seen its last rebirth. We would be the last Nine.

"—don't put too much."

"—salt. I know."

Strike that. We were ten.

"I have an announcement," I called.

All eyes landed on me. Doofus lifted his head and whimpered softly. "Sebastian and I are getting mated. If you fuckers don't approve, keep the shit to yourself because I don't care."

Aris was the first to bust out laughing, then the rest followed. Basil and Sage threw rice. "For the newlyweds."

"Uh, I think that happens after the ceremony," Aris said. "And while they're both present."

Ten days later, under the full moon, I stood with my brothers around me. Zane helped me into the robe I would wear. He'd be the officiator of the ceremony since we didn't dare ask the Sentinel to return after Zane's mating went to shit. Zane had confined Aurora to the mansion, which had been cleaned and the wards repaired by Hatcher. Alastair's body was found in the pool. His head missing. We gave him a warrior's burial. And Paris was still rotting in the cells. Finn and Genesis hadn't made an appearance, which led us to believe that Lucifer probably had them both. It also made me realize the guilt I'd carried all my life.

"I'm sorry," I whispered.

Zane's hands stopped as if I hit the pause button on him. "Don't," he practically growled out. "You have nothing to be sorry for."

"The malice—"

He glared at me. Blue fire stirred in his eyes. "Weren't created by you."

"But everyone knows."

"We've always known, Xcian."

I couldn't breathe. A wedge stuck in my throat.

"Yes. We all felt the tether. Your blood is our blood. But the malice that she created using you have all been wiped out. What's left are remnants, diluted entities that are on the verge of extinction." He cocked a brow, warning me to deny it. I didn't.

"Would it be cheesy to say that I always considered you as both a brother and father to me?"

He snorted and went back to fixing my robe. "Yes. It would." But he smiled.

"Gods, did you ever think we'd be here? Mating the same bloodline?'"

"Well, I always knew I'd have Eric. You, well…" He shook his head.

I laughed and shoved him away. "Whatever. I have

a heart too."

"Yes, I always knew that, too."

I wanted to ask him what he thought about our fates. Had we not traded places, would our lives have been kinder? But I realized, it didn't matter. Our choices led us here, to this moment, and my heart felt so full, it couldn't be wrong. I loved Sebastian Aiden Diaz with all my soul. I belonged to him.

"Ready?" Zane asked.

I nodded.

We walked toward a bald spot behind the cabin where my brothers waited with my mate along with Eric. I inhaled watching Sebastian. He wore slacks, a button-down shirt, and my boots. The buzzcut made him look so damn young. His eyes landed on Leander, who decided to wear his human form for the ceremony. My heart about burst as Sebastian narrowed the gap between them. Leander visibly stiffened, but his eyes weren't filled with his usual panic. They were so damn sad. Sebastian drew him into a tight hug.

"I miss you," Sebastian whispered. No point, since we all had superhearing. "You saved me."

Leander's body went pliant against Sebastian. An act of submission. Maybe, hope. Sebastian waited for Leander to pull away first. He gave my brother a soft kiss on the forehead and turned to me.

Mine.

For whatever reason, the gods had given me my perfect other half.

We wouldn't be using the flame. Instead, he and I shared a cuff, and I took his hand and we stood together under the night sky.

Zane said the words that opened up the aether and

our world faded away. I opened my eyes to a field of wildflowers watching a young Zane and I playing in the distance. Sebastian appeared next to me.

"So this is your Eden," he said with a small smile.

"Zane has always been my home." I linked our hands and brought them up to my lips and kissed his knuckles. "Now I share it with you."

Sebastian inhaled.

The pull between us grew stronger. A magic beyond love, something more. "Do you feel it?"

"Yes."

We kissed. A kiss that wrapped me in warmth, safety, and home. I felt stronger because of it. Because of him. We sat against a large oak tree and continued to watch the two boys in play, his head on my shoulder, our hands intertwined. "I miss my brother."

"I know, baby. He's stronger than you think."

"You said you'd never lie."

"I'm not lying. If death had marked him, he would no longer be with us. He'll wake up." I planted a kiss on his temple.

"I love you, Xcian."

The words that meant more to me than anything in this world.

"I love you, too."

A word about the author...

Elle Arroyo grew up in Chicago where she writes paranormal romance.

Before she started writing, Elle got her undergraduate degree in Psychology with a minor in Criminal Justice. She then went on to work in foster care programs, mental health facilities, and youth organizations within the Latinx Community.

When not writing, Elle spends time with her family, binge watches anime, and reads anything with romance in it.

Elle continues to live in Chicago with her family. https://ellearroyo.com/